THE EDEN STORIES

THE REFORMATION OF MARS

Terry D. Toler

The Reformation of Mars

Published by: BeHoldings Publishing

Copyright @2019, BeHoldings, LLC
Terrytoler.com
All Rights Reserved

Cover and interior designs: BeHoldings Publishing
Editor: Jeanne Leach

For information, address support@terrytoler.com.

Our books can be purchased in bulk for promotional, educational, and business use. Please contact your bookseller or the BeHoldings Publishing Sales department at: sales@terrytoler.com

For booking information email: booking@terrytoler.com
First U.S. Edition: October, 2020
Printed in the United States of America

ISBN 978-1-7352243-1-2

OTHER BOOKS BY TERRY TOLER

Fiction

The Longest Day
The Reformation of Mars
The Great Wall of Ven-Us
Saturn: The Eden Experiment
The Late, Great Planet Jupiter
Save The Girls
The Ingenue
The Blue Rose
Saving Sara
Save The Queen
No Girl Left Behind
The Launch
Body Count
Mercury Protocols

Non-Fiction

How to Make More Than a Million Dollars
The Heart Attacked
Seven Years of Promise
Mission Possible
Marriage Made in Heaven
21 Days to Physical Healing
21 Days to Spiritual Fitness
21 Days to Divine Health
21 Days to a Great Marriage
21 Days to Financial Freedom
21 Days to Sharing Your Faith
21 Days to Mission Possible
7 Days to Emotional Freedom
Uncommon Finances
Uncommon Marriage
Uncommon Health
Suddenly Free
Feeling Free

For more information on these books and other resources
visit TerryToler.com.

BASED IN PART ON TRUE EVENTS.

The Reformation Of Mars

PART ONE

"What has been will be again, what has been done will be done again..."
Ecclesiastes 1:9

1

Boulder Bay, Mars, 1519, M.A. A.C. (March Annum After Christ)

Abigail "Abbey" Whyburgh wasn't a typical sixteen-year-old Martian girl. She knew how to read.

Women were forbidden to read on Mars. By decree of the Earl of Faxon, Henry I, 9th Century, head of the Universal Church of the Red Planet, women weren't allowed to attend school of any kind. One of about a thousand things women weren't permitted by law to do.

Abbey walked into the Pharsis University Press (PUP), the first publishing house of its kind on Mars. Henry V, the father of the current King of Mars, Henry X, and head of the Universal Church, had granted her father, Mainz Whyburgh, all rights to publish and print books ten years before. Henry X should have been the sixth but liked the sound of ten better.

Abbey could be arrested for even being in the building. Women weren't allowed to work. They weren't permitted to even enter business establishments. Her father ignored the laws and had constructed a back entrance several years before where she could enter unseen. He brought her to work with him almost every day. Mostly, she stayed in the basement out of sight of paying customers. There, she was taught every aspect of the business from typesetting to printing. She learned to read from typesetting the books.

Her older brother Eck was already hard at work on the printing presses.

"Hello, Abbey," Eck said with a smile. He could get in trouble if someone heard him call her by her shortened name outside of her home. Men were required to call women by the formal name given to them by the church. Women and girls could be called by their shortened name in private. Her parents often forgot and called her Abbey outside the home, risking the wrath of the church.

At least, back when they were still alive.

A quick hug and she said, "Do you have a lot of work for me today, Eck?"

"I want you to spend some time organizing the old books," he said, not mentioning her swollen lip which had become commonplace.

A storeroom in the back of the basement was full of books her dad had collected over the years. When their father died from the great plague the year before, Eck had taken over the business and was so overwhelmed with keeping up with the demand, no one had taken the time to go through them.

Eck lowered his voice almost to a whisper even though no one was in the building who could hear them. "Make sure there are no illegal books back there. We don't want to get shut down."

Fiction books, anything disparaging of the church, and any unauthorized religious materials were contraband that would be confiscated. Eck could even be charged with a crime if illegal books were found on the premises. PUP did so much printing for the church no one would likely ever bother them but better to be safe than sorry just in case. No reason to be arrested for something merely gathering dust.

The storeroom door was jammed, so it took Abbey several strong pushes with her shoulder to open it. Immediately, the smell of musty books rushed from the room. She cleared her throat several times to get the stench out of her nose and mouth. Gathering herself, she pushed away the cobwebs clinging to her hair and face as she entered the room and paused a few seconds to let her eyes adjust to the darkness.

Groping blindly for the light switch, she cut her hand slightly on a nail sticking from the wall. Because Mars was mostly a cold planet, God had made Martians with very thick skin to protect them from the cold. Exceedingly rare for something to break the skin and draw blood. The second time it had happened that day.

Abbey put her hand to her mouth and winced as she touched the bruise that had formed on her upper lip from where her stepfather Zwilling had viciously hit her that morning. She tried to put that out of her mind for the time being. For several hours, she was away from the horrid man. No reason to think about him anymore than she had to.

She started several piles. One for books to be discarded and thrown away; another for books whose binders could be salvaged; a third pile for books whose paper could be recycled; and a fourth for books she wanted to read. The spot she had designated for illegal books had nothing in it after two hours.

As she cleared the mound of books, she discovered a small group of books in the corner, conspicuous because they were the only ones in the room organized with any sense of purpose. Why did her dad separate those from the others? What made them special?

Abbey tried to finish the pile she had been working on, but curiosity got the best of her. Making her way around the piles, she grabbed a dusty chair, brushed it off, and sat down beside the group of about a dozen books neatly stacked in a small wooden bookcase.

The mystery deepened as she immediately noticed none of the books had a title on the outside. The front and back were blank. Hard cover, normal paper stock, grey in color, but not one word anywhere on the outside of the books.

That's strange.

She took a book from the end, blew the dust off the cover, and slowly opened to the first page.

What is this?

She read the first line of the first page aloud quietly to herself.

"In the beginning, God created the heavens and the mars. The mars was without form, and void; and darkness was on the face of the deep. And the Spirit of God was hovering over the face of the waters."

Is this what I think it is?

Bibles had been banned since the ninth century. The church had gone from house to house confiscating them and punishing those who were found with one. A commoner caught with a Bible was imprisoned and often put to death. Periodic raids hadn't turned up a copy in decades. If they still existed, they were well hidden.

The Universal Church of the Red Planet was the only recognized church on Mars. The king was the head of the church and the ruler over all the people. He was the only one who could interpret God's will for the people, and what he said was the rule of law. God's law and the king's law were synonymous, and the people had better abide by both.

A leader of the church, a Josser, read from the Bible at church and then interpreted it for the people. As far as Abbey knew, no common person had ever seen a Bible in centuries. Most likely, no woman alive today had ever seen one. Yet her dad had a dozen copies right here in this storage room. A surge of adrenaline pulsed through her veins.

Where did he get them?

Abbey carefully opened each book. All were exactly the same. Duplicate copies of the Old Testament and New Testament, before Christ and after Christ, written over several thousand years by dozens of authors. The last book had a folded piece of paper in it. She carefully unfolded it.

Obviously, her dad's handwriting.

To Eck and Abbey,

If you're reading this, I'm likely not with you anymore. I'm so sorry. If you've found these Bibles, then God has answered my prayers. I want you to know how much I love you. I've taken a great risk to print these Bibles and store them. I've been waiting for the right time. If I'm gone, you may be our last hope. We must get these Bibles in the hands of the people. They have to know what the church is teaching them is a lie. Read Genesis 3. You'll know what I mean.

Love you, Dad

Abbey turned to Genesis 3. Her mouth fell open as she read the entire chapter.

I have to go and tell Eck. He's not going to believe this.

* * *

God regretted that he had made human beings on Mars.

"Mars has been one of your greatest failures," Satan said mockingly. Standing before God, he was making the case that he should be allowed to destroy the planet.

"You should wipe them off the face of Mars," Satan continued. "Let me do it. I have a volcano ready to explode. Just say the word and I will kill them all."

"I need to give them more time," God said, ignoring Satan's scornful attitude.

"How much time do they need? Jesus died more than two days ago. The Dark Ages have gone on for more than a day." In heaven, a day was like a thousand years to God. A year on Mars was 687 days. Half of a year was called a *march*.

"Mars is the most backwards of all the planets you've created," Satan said without waiting for a response. "They haven't even developed cars or planes yet. A third of the despicable creatures died in the great plague and there was nothing they could do about it. They've been around for more than six days and haven't even developed medicines for the common cold." Satan roared in laughter as he said it.

"It's been some of my best work," Satan muttered under his breath.

God had created many planets with life. He placed a garden of Eden, an Adam and Eve, and a tree of the knowledge of good and evil on each planet. So far, all had eaten of the fruit from the tree and all had eventually destroyed themselves. Even though life on each planet always ended in destruction, most had made advancements in knowledge and improved their lives.

Each had experienced their own "Dark Ages," but all had come out of them at some point. Churches had thrived, and Christians had helped restrain evil. Jesus had come to the planets and died for all the people's sins. The elect, a group of righteous people, had always formed churches to advance the cause of Christ on the planets.

All but Mars.

Michael, the archangel, listened to the conversation and interjected.

"What if there are fifty righteous people on Mars? Would you destroy the righteous and the wicked at the same time?" he asked.

"If there are fifty righteous people on Mars, I will not destroy them," God said.

Satan drooped his shoulders and waved his arms in animated gestures, obviously disappointed.

"What if there are five less than that?" Michael asked, apparently not sure there were fifty on Mars. "What if there are only forty-five?"

"If there are only forty-five, I will not destroy them," God said with resolve.

Seizing the opportunity, Satan said, "There aren't forty-five righteous people. There are less than five."

"There are more than that," Michael said, angrily moving toward Satan. The argument became so heated, Michael drew his sword, and other angels came and stood behind him while a throng of demons formed behind Satan, all expecting a confrontation.

"There would be many more if you didn't oppress them with your godless church," Michael stated emphatically.

"They've had every opportunity to overthrow the church and they don't. The people are weak and spineless. I can devour them anytime I want," Satan retorted.

"Enough," God said strongly.

Everyone stopped speaking at his command.

"I am not going to destroy Mars. I have a plan. I have a person in mind. Someone I have chosen to bring my Word to the people."

Immediate silence pervaded the air as this new information was being processed by all the beings.

"Who have you chosen?" Satan asked, as panic and fear rose inside of him like a fire burning out of control. "Is it Abra? He's one of the five, but I have imprisoned him. He tried to overthrow the church with Calvin, but I killed Calvin. I'll kill Abra before I'll let him overthrow the church."

"Not Abra. Someone you would never expect," God said. "I will use the foolish things of the world to confound the wise. I will use the weakest person among them to overcome the strongest."

"I will kill this person!" Satan said emphatically. "Whoever it is, I will destroy him. I demand to know who it is."

"You'll see soon enough..." God said as he departed, his words echoing through heaven.

A young girl had found favor in the eyes of the Lord.

2

King Henry X was on his knees in his chapel for morning prayers.

"God, I thank you I'm not like the other men—swindlers, evildoers, adulterers, tax collectors," Henry said aloud.

"Your Excellency," Tomas Cornwallis, the Chief Minister (Josser) of the Universal Church and his trusted right-hand man interrupted his prayer. "I will be in your office ready to go over your day's schedule and other pressing matters."

The king also had the title of the Official Head of the Church of Mars which was the only recognized church on the planet. Henry could be called king or his excellency. Both were appropriate addresses and interchangeable.

Tomas bowed his head reverently and began backing out of the king's presence.

Henry struggled to his feet. He remembered the days when he was a mighty warrior and weighed a svelte one-hundred-ninety-five pounds of solid muscle, which had now turned to over three hundred pounds of less-than-solid blubber. Mars had a slighter gravitational pull than some planets, so most felt noticeably light even if over an ideal weight. Not so with Henry. The heavier weight and lack of activity had taken its toll on him. He let out a groan as his knees ached, and his back rebelled against the sudden movement.

I must find a more comfortable way to say my prayers.

Spring had come to Mars and was when he usually went off to war. "Wars are for the younger men," he had convinced himself. For the first time in years, he stayed home. While he enjoyed the one-sided fighting where victory was always assured, he enjoyed wine and women more. The only populated areas of Mars were around the equator. Ice caps dominated the north and south regions, so most towns and villages were formed in a region hundred miles north and south of the equator all around Mars. Consequently, Mars was not heavily populated, being the smallest of all planets except for Mercury. Nevertheless, there were pockets of resistance to the king's commands and war was seemingly endless.

He waddled into his office where Tomas waited patiently for him. Papers in hand, Tomas no doubt had several pressing issues to discuss. The king wanted to get the meeting over with as soon as possible so he could go back to bed.

These were the worst of times on Mars.

The best for the elite and friends of the king; the worst for the huddled masses struggling to survive the oppression of the church and the harsh physical conditions of life on Mars. Rebellions were springing up all over. The people were oppressed by the onerous taxes imposed by his father and added to by his decrees. Not taxes, really. "Religious Remissions" was what Henry I had decided to call them. Money paid in exchange for good works and special privileges from God for both the remitter and his family members.

Women, of course, did not participate. Their souls were condemned to hell, by declaration of his great, great grandfather Henry II and reinforced by biblical law by the Chief Ministers several times removed and each one since.

"What would you like to do about the queen?" Tomas asked.

"She would be the first on your list, wouldn't she Tomas?" Henry said with a chuckle.

Queen Katherine, Kathy when a peasant girl before she caught the king's eye with her beauty, had been imprisoned in the castle tower for more than two years. Her execution was scheduled one week from today.

"I hate women," the king said sternly, lifting the robe he was sitting on so he could get a more comfortable position in his padded chair behind a large regal desk notably free of any papers or clutter.

"You sure have enough of them around," Tomas said sarcastically. One of the few people who could joke with the king without losing his head.

The king had seven hundred wives and three hundred concubines.

"Can't live with 'em; can't live without 'em, as I always say," Henry said half laughing, half angrily.

"I have a new saying. Can't live with 'em; can't kill 'em." Henry roared as his strong, boisterous laugh bounced off the marble floor and ceiling.

"I guess I can kill him. I'm the king," he said with not a little glee.

He continued without giving Tomas an opportunity to respond. The king dominated the conversation as he usually did.

"Katherine defied me." His tone turned serious. "Her execution stands."

"She didn't really defy you. She just suggested you might want to eat less."

During a royal feast, the king was overindulging on food and wine, and Katherine had suggested he might consider stopping. Henry considered it an insult, a small offense, except others in the room had heard it. A small room in the tower with minimum food and drink had been her home ever since. He decided on beheading her a couple of weeks ago.

Tomas had been pushing for Katherine's exile rather than death. Henry knew Tomas was sneaking food to her, and she was probably repaying his kindness with her own personal favors in hopes it might save her life. The king didn't particularly care. Katherine would be dead soon, and Tomas was valuable to him. Queens were easier to come by than trusted advisors.

"That reminds me," Henry said, changing the subject. "I was on the roof of my palace last night and saw a woman bathing across the way. The most beautiful woman I've ever seen." Henry said the words with a lustful look in his eyes. "Send someone to find out who she is."

Tomas wrote something on his notepad.

"Do you think we need to do another search for Bibles?" Tomas asked. As Chief Minister, he was tasked with maintaining what was called "Scriptural Purity." The only knowledge the people were to have about God was what Tomas and his surrogates provided to them in his role as caretaker and protector of the king's gospel.

"I thought we got all of them." The king poured himself a glass of wine and took a big swig even though it was only nine in the morning. The first of many he would take throughout the day.

"We did. There've been no reports of any copies anywhere. The ones we confiscated years ago have all been burned."

"What about the printer? Whyburgh. His boy. Can we trust him?"

"He's never given us any reason not to."

"Make a note to make a surprise visit and search his place just in case. No one has ever made a printed copy. If they did, they could make so many we could never control it. We must keep an eye on the printers." He paused to think on it a moment then said, "If anyone anywhere is found with a Bible, they are to be made an example of in the square."

"Of course," Tomas said.

Henry downed another cup of wine, frustrated when he spilled a few drops on his robe.

"Clear my schedule today. I don't feel like meeting with anyone," he said with a yawn.

"I have a recommendation for his excellency to consider. What if we let women make religious remissions? We could raise considerable marches for the treasury." Tomas said it hesitantly. Marches were the currency of Mars also known as marrii.

"Never!" Henry knocked his cup off the table sending it flying across the room, immediately regretting the waste of good wine.

"Our financial coffers are dwindling," Tomas argued. "The people are struggling to put food on the table. The great plague has wiped out a third of our population over the last ten years. That's a third less people to pay into the coffers. We must replace the marches somehow. Many families would be enticed to pay marches for the women in their families if they thought it might redeem their souls."

"Women's souls can't be redeemed," Henry said. "God wouldn't allow it. No matter how many marches they give. My father made a mistake even allowing women to attend church. It's no place for a woman. Nothing good could ever come of it."

"What do you suggest we do to bring in more marches?" Tomas asked.

"Let's impose a new church law. Write these things down."

Tomas dropped his writing instrument at the sudden command. He scrambled to recover it.

Henry kept talking. "The punishment for breaking these laws are fines payable to the church. Number one. Women are not to look a man in the eye on the street unless spoken to."

Tomas interrupted. "We already have that law on the books."

Henry put his hand to his chin and rubbed it thinking.

"Do we enforce it?"

"Not really. If a man complains, the woman can be fined. But no one ever really complains. Her husband has to pay the fine. Women aren't allowed to work, so they don't have any marches. So, it just makes the men mad when it comes out of their pockets. They take it out on the women."

Henry rubbed his temples.

"I can't think about this right now. You think of something and bring me recommendations. That's your job anyway," Henry said gruffly.

"What about that man who was preaching against us over in the Borea Basin?"

A man spoke in the square, saying Adam ate the apple along with Eve. The church official teaching was that Eve ate the apple, but Adam refused, which was why God commanded men to dominate women. Women were the cause of all the world's problems.

"His name is Christopher. His father's name was Calvin. We executed Calvin last year. We can't find his son. He's disappeared," Tomas said.

"Find him. Any others like him?" Henry asked.

"There are a few. They're just in hiding. They don't dare to speak against us in public."

"Good. I don't have to tell you how important it is that no one knows what really happened in the Garden of Eden."

With that, Tomas was dismissed. As he was leaving the king shouted emphatically, "Don't forget to find out the name of the woman bathing last night across the street."

***

Abbey decided not to tell Eck about the Bibles. If he knew, he would be in grave danger. The handwritten note from their father was to both of them, and she would tell him eventually, but for now, she needed to keep the information to herself. A plan must be developed to hide the Bibles until Abbey could figure out what to do with the information.

I can't believe the church has been lying to us all these years. Women have been persecuted for centuries because of the lie.

Right there plain as day in Genesis 3. Eve gave Adam the apple and he ate it.

Abbey looked for a hiding place in the room but could find nothing satisfactory. How could she get the Bibles out of the room and to a safe place without Eck or anyone else seeing her? Several trips would be necessary. The books were too heavy to carry all at once.

Why not leave them where they were? The books had been hidden in the basement for many years. Maybe they should be left alone. They haven't been discovered all this time.

Abbey dismissed that thought.

The king could order a search at any time. If they were found, Eck would be executed immediately. With a new owner of the business in place, they might search just to prove Eck's loyalty.

No one would suspect her. As far as anyone knew, she'd never been in the building. Eck was her concern. Protecting her brother's life was the most important thing. He was the only family she had left... The thought of her mother brought tears to her eyes.

When her father died, her mom was obligated by the church to take a husband. Zwilling was their choice forced upon her. Her other option would have been removal from the church, which would have sentenced Abbey and her mom to a life of poverty and destitution. For the sake of her daughter, she chose what she thought was the lesser of the two evils. When she rebelled against Zwilling's harsh ways, he put her out with a writ of divorce, sentencing her and Abbey to a far worse fate.

Immediate imprisonment for her mom. Possible execution. No one knew for sure. Her mother hadn't been heard from in over a year.

The thought occurred to her that the information was even more important than their lives. Abbey's head spun with thoughts of the ramifications to the king and women everywhere on Mars if the information got out. A sudden weight fell on her shoulders.

How did the fate of the women of Mars become her responsibility?

This is so huge.

Her dad knew how big. Great care had gone into protecting the secret. Knowing him, he wanted to do something about it as well. He either didn't know what to do or died before he could do anything about it.

Abbey picked up one of the books and examined the printing. Definitely printed in their shop, although a different typeset than their normal machine. Another mystery. Where did he print it?

Her dad had invented the printing press when he was twenty-two years old and perfected it over the years. The invention revolutionized life on Mars. Businesses and trade could flow more freely with the advent of printing. Information was spread more quickly and accurately. It would have brought the written word to the masses had the king allowed it. Unfortunately, the invention only benefited the already rich. Dad often expressed his remorse about that fact.

There must be an original Bible somewhere. Dad didn't print it out of the clear blue.

Bibles had been transcribed by hand for years until they were banned. Her dad must have had a handwritten copy of a Bible, typeset it, and then printed the copies. Where would the original be?

Abbey's head was filled with ideas.

A book the size of the Bible would have many metal plates. In her dad's original idea for a printing press, he used wood blocks. The blocks made words and sentences and then made an imprint on the paper. When he decided to use metal instead of wood and a roller rather than a press, the idea allowed for large quantities of books to be printed much more quickly.

A tedious chore, each page of the Bible had to be on its own individual metal plate. The plates were covered with ink. A sheet of paper was placed on the plate with the words and sentences in reverse. The roller passed over the paper creating the impression from the ink.

The metal typesetting for all the books printed over the years were stored upstairs. No way her dad would have stored the Bible plates up there. Too easy for someone to discover. They had to be in this room. But where?

Abbey inspected the walls for a hidden compartment. She looked for any irregularities in the structure of the walls. Any indentation or crevice that looked out of place. Running her hand along every square inch of each wall, produced nothing.

The floor.

A pile of books lay on a rug in the center of the room. She frantically moved the books off the rug, careful not to make too much noise. Customers were still coming in and out of the store upstairs.

As she suspected, she found a small door cut out of the wooden floor barely wide enough for a man to fit through under the rug. She lifted the corner with her fingers and opened it. Below was total darkness. A ladder led into the unknown room. She would explore it later when she had some light. For now, it would serve as a good hiding place for the Bibles.

Abbey gathered them and carefully took them down the ladder two at a time and placed them on the floor at the bottom of the stairs, not daring to explore the room further. When the Bibles were safely in the room, she placed the rug back over the door and piled the books back on top of them.

A loud voice boomed from upstairs.

Josser Tomas Cornwallis!

She would recognize that voice anywhere. He delivered most of the sermons at their church. Anger rose up inside her. The Josser was the liar who'd been perpetrating the false story about the Garden of Eden for years.

What was he doing there? More importantly, how could she get out of there without being discovered? If he found her, the business would be closed, and she and Eck would be thrown in jail or worse.

Abbey considered opening the hatch and hiding in the room below. How could she cover the door in the floor? It would be obvious to anyone who walked in the room.

If she was quiet, maybe he would leave. Perhaps he was just picking up something for the king. Not likely. The Chief Minister of the Universal Church of Mars was not an errand boy.

Abbey had a bad feeling. She tiptoed closer to the door to see if she could hear what was being said.

Why was Eck talking in such a loud voice? He was soft spoken like her dad.

A signal... A warning they must be coming down to the basement.

At that moment, Abbey heard the distinct sound of people coming down the stairs.

What do I do?

3

This can't be good.

Eck's heart did a somersault when Tomas Cornwallis the Josser of the Church walked through the door unannounced.

He might be there to pay a bill. Eck was required to provide printing services to the church at a significantly reduced price, barely above cost. The church was notorious for not paying its bill, and it had accrued to an exceedingly high sum. Eventually, it would be paid, but Eck had to wait and let the church pay on its own timetable. Unlikely the josser would come to pay the bill. He never had.

He could be there to pick up the materials for the church. Again unlikely. The josser didn't run errands. Maybe he was there to order something sensitive in nature. Wishful thinking. Eck knew why he was there.

The josser was there to inspect his facility and assure himself nothing illegal was going on.

"To what do I owe this great honor, Josser." Eck tried not to let the anxiety welling up inside like a volcano to show on his face or in his voice.

"I've not been here since your father died. I wanted to express my condolences," the josser said as he scanned the room, clearly checking things out.

"The Black Plague has affected all of us. A very tragic thing," Eck said sorrowfully.

"The women have brought it upon Mars with their continued sin and rebellion. God is still judging all of us because of them."

Eck responded only enough to seem to agree. It was a strange feeling to be in the presence of a man who could throw you in jail, torture you, and take your life with just a simple command if you didn't respond to him properly. Great care had to be taken with every word and every action.

"Your father was a great man and did a great service to the church while he was alive," the josser continued. "I thought I should come in and personally thank you for his service. Can you show me around the shop? It's been several years since I've been here."

Anxiety turned to panic. Abbey was in the basement, and Eck had no way to warn her of the impending danger.

"I wish you'd given me some advance notice. The shop is a mess. Certainly not in the condition I would want to show such a distinguished guest. Perhaps we could schedule it at a time when things were more presentable for your honor." Eck immediately regretted saying that.

Eck knew the josser wasn't there to see the shop for personal reasons. This was an informal inspection. A lame excuse like a messy work area would not satisfy. It would only raise suspicion. The element of surprise was calculated to judge Eck's reaction as much as anything. He had to present the right tone. Any indication he had something to hide would only make things worse and bring on a much closer inspection.

As far as he knew, Abbey was the only thing illegal in the shop. Still, her presence there was enough to get them both thrown in jail if she were discovered.

Eck decided to take the initiative and see if the opposite approach might work. Before the josser could even respond Eck said, "Of course I would be happy to show you around, if you'll overlook the mess."

Maybe if he acted like he had nothing to hide, the josser would believe he didn't.

"This is the customer area where we store the metal plates for the books." Eck headed into the upstairs storage area, hoping the josser would follow him there.

Instead, the josser said, "I would like to see the downstairs."

Oh no!

Any hesitation on Eck's part would result in the josser detaining Eck, calling in the soldiers, and conducting a thorough search.

I hope Abbey is already gone.

"This way your honor." Eck raised his voice, hoping Abbey could hear him and had time to hide or get out the back door.

The stairway led to a large open room which housed the printing presses. An office was off of the work area. Abbey might be there. If so, she was trapped. The only way out was through the press room.

Customers weren't allowed downstairs, so she mostly worked there. If she were in the main area, as soon as Abbey heard voices coming down the stairs, she would slip out the back door to safety. Unfortunately, Eck had told Abbey to work in the back storeroom.

Of all days. If Abbey was back there, she might not hear them with the door closed. They could very easily surprise her. Eck kept speaking loudly, still holding out hope she had already left.

Distraction was the only thing that came to mind. "Have you seen our new roller technology? My dad developed it, and I've made remarkable improvements significantly increasing our production speed. We can now produce an entire book in a few hours rather than in a few days. Over there is our binding machine that puts the outside cover on the books. Let me show you how it works."

Eck walked over to the machine and pulled off a book in production.

"This is one we are working on for the church right now. Should be ready this week." The josser seemed uninterested. Eck was being too obvious. The josser was used to people being nervous around him, so hopefully he wouldn't think Eck had something to hide.

"What's in the back room?" He pointed to the closed door that led to the storeroom and possibly Abbey's hideout. Eck couldn't remember if the room had a hiding place.

"That's where we store our old discarded books."

"I'd like to see it."

Eck took a deep breath trying not to make his nervousness seem too obvious.

He walked over to the door and opened it. No other option came to mind.

"My apologies. This area is dusty and moldy. My son has been working in there," Eck blurted out.

A dim light barely illuminated the room. Abbey was sitting in a corner on the floor with piles of books around her. A cap covered her hair which was awkwardly stuffed into the cap. The room was dark enough she could barely be seen from the door. Not well enough to know she was a girl.

"Josser, this is my son Martin. We call him Marti for short."

"Pleased to meet you," Abbey said, lowering her voice slightly.

* * *

The Vandenberg Cathedral was located in downtown Boulder Bay. Next to various restaurants, cafés, and business shops, its majestic steeple dominated the sky. Beside the cathedral stood an obelisk with a statue of Henry III on the top. No buildings in the city were to be built higher than the statue. The largest city on Mars, it still only housed a couple of hundred thousand people who mostly lived on the outskirts. The middle-and upper class, lived in Boulder Bay. Her dad was privileged because of his invention of the printing press. Abbey had no idea why Zwilling was considered elite.

Boulder Bay was only a bay half of the year. In the spring and summer, the ice caps melted and filled the basin with water creating the most beautiful spot on the planet. The red mountains reflected off of the blue water and bright blue sky. The red sand accented the canvas of what was a picturesque and breathtaking area.

Abbey dutifully walked two steps behind Zwilling to the cathedral. Her arms were folded as her hands were still shaking from the encounter with the josser. Her father's predesigned plan had worked. Abbey was to always carry a cap with her while working in the shop. If discovered, she was to slip on the cap, and pretend to be his son. She was glad Eck had remembered the plan.

Eck pulled the name Martin out of thin air. The hope now was that the josser didn't think to check birth records. If he did, he would find Eck had no children. They would deal with that if the time came. For now, the josser seemed satisfied.

Another welp had formed on Abbey's cheek from another back-hand from Zwilling just moments before they had left for church.

"When you took a shower yesterday, you went two minutes over your allotted time," he had announced.

Abbey only shrugged.

A timer recorded the length of her showers. One a week was all allowed, and they could last no longer than seven minutes in duration. When she turned eighteen in two years, the time would go to ten minutes. At twenty-one, a man could take her as his wife by paying Zwilling a nice sum of money. He could always decline the money and take her as his own wife. She would rather die.

Fortunately, he'd never touched her inappropriately. Her value would be severely impacted, and Zwilling was above all else a businessman. If he tried, she would probably kill him first and take whatever consequences came her way. Maybe she could see her mother in prison before being put to death.

"I don't want to hurt you," he said almost sincerely. "You're just like your mother. Stubborn. I have to somehow break that..." His voice trailed off.

Abbey's fist had formed a ball ready to strike him at the mention of her mother. Before she could react, she was picking herself off the floor, stunned by a quick strike to the side of her head. The welp a reminder that she was legally his property. Women were property of men on Mars by order of the church which she had grown to despise and was about to enter.

Approaching the cathedral, Abbey separated from Zwilling and went to the back entrance. Only men were allowed to sit in the main church and enter through the main doors. Women and girls had to sit together in the balcony at the back of the church. Always crowded, with no good air circulation, the balcony was stuffy year round regardless of the weather outside.

Women couldn't participate in the church service other than to hear the teachings which were often directed for their benefit. They couldn't take communion, be baptized, or speak in church. Women weren't even allowed to sing the hymns. They were to remain silent at all times.

That was fine with Abbey. She had no interest in church and thought the whole thing was a waste of time. The men and the josser were hypocrites as far as she was concerned. What little she knew about Jesus's teachings were not on display by any man she'd ever met except her father. *And Eck.*

Her interest piqued, however, when the josser stood to speak and told the entire congregation his message would be taken from Genesis 3. He began reading from what was purported to be that passage. Abbey now knew it had been changed.

He began reading from the passage in a slow, deliberate, but authoritative voice. "The man and woman God created lived in the Garden of Eden. The man was named Adam, the woman named Eve. Eve came from Adam. First was man, then came woman. Man was given authority over all the earth including over women."

It's already not the same.

"God said to the man he could eat any apple of any tree in the garden except from the tree of the knowledge of good and evil. Adam instructed the woman not to touch the tree of the knowledge of good and evil or she would die."

Not true. It wasn't an apple. It was fruit. God didn't say she would die if she touched it. Only if she ate it.

"The serpent was craftier than any other beast of the field the Lord God had made. The serpent came to the woman and said, 'Did God actually say, 'You shall not eat of any tree in the garden?'"

"The woman, Eve, said to the serpent, 'We may eat of the fruit of the trees in the garden, but God said, 'You shall not eat of the fruit of the tree in the midst of the garden.' Adam, my master, said I should not touch it, or I would die.'"

The josser paused for effect, letting the words sink in. His already booming voice rose to its highest level of intensity.

Abbey sat on the edge of her seat, doing everything she could to not stand up and call the josser a liar right then and there.

"The woman saw that the tree was desirable to make one wise, so she took off its fruit and ate, and she also gave some to her husband Adam who was with her, but... he refused to eat it!"

Lies... All lies.

The josser pointed to the women in the balcony and said, "The woman ate the apple and brought sin and death into the world. Man refused to eat of the tree, maintaining his purity before God."

"So, God punished the woman," the josser continued. "In verse sixteen, God said to the woman, 'Your husband shall rule over you.'"

Abbey wanted to stand and shout at the top of her lungs, "You're a liar! That's not what happened!"

She was fidgeting and wringing her hands. Another of the older women, cautioned her to sit still. Guards stood at each corner of the balcony to make sure women were kept in line. They looked her way. Abbey sat back and took a couple deep breaths to try and calm herself down.

The josser continued with words that pierced Abbey's consciousness.

"God cast Adam out of the garden because of Eve. Man lost his position because of woman. Christ came to Mars to restore what man had lost." The josser was obviously enjoying himself.

He continued. "Let me read from several passages in the New Testament."

"Therefore, just as sin entered the world through one's *woman's* sin, and death came to man because of that *woman's* sin, so death was passed on to all men, because Eve sinned."

Abbey made a mental note to look for that passage and see if the josser had changed it. She was certain he had.

Each time the josser said the word "woman," he said it with strong emphasis. He would read a verse and then interpret it.

"It's women's fault," he said with a loud booming voice.

"Because of Eve, men must pay for her sin. Death entered into our lives because of women. But through one man, Jesus Christ, all men everywhere can be saved."

The men in the lower section clapped enthusiastically.

"Because of Christ, you no longer have to suffer from a woman's sin."

"There is no condemnation to any *man* in Christ Jesus."

"Every time Christ is mentioned, it says his death was for man, not for woman."

Another cheer went up. The josser put his hands up to silence the men.

"The serpent, the devil, still tries to tempt men through women. You must be strong like Adam. He resisted her wiles and refused to eat the apple. Women will try to entice you with their feminine ways and try to trick you into falling for them. You must resist them. Let God punish them with the curse. They must serve you. You must rule over them. It is God's will!"

The men stood applauding wildly.

When the roar died down, "You will know the truth," the josser said, "And the truth shall set you free!"

The josser stepped from the podium with both arms raised as the men applauded and shouted with fervor.

Abbey clenched her fist. Her jaw tightened and her eyes narrowed. Resolve built up inside her.

You will know the truth. It will set women free.

I don't know how, but I'm going to bring the truth to Mars.

* * *

The men exited the church first. The women dutifully sat in the balcony until the guards let them leave. Abbey looked around at the women surrounding her. A typical Sunday morning sermon. Bashing women. Blaming them for the sins of the world. Christ only died for men. The looks on the women's faces were that of resignation.

They'd heard it all many times before. A woman ate the apple. The man didn't. That's what they'd been told all their lives. They deserved their fate. It'd been ingrained in Abbey and every other woman almost from birth. For some reason, her father had never accepted that teaching. Abbey now had a better understanding why.

Adam ate the fruit too. She read it with her own eyes.

Abbey didn't know when her dad came in possession of the Bible and learned the truth. He'd always treated her kindly. He'd always encouraged her that she wasn't a second-class citizen. That God loved her, and Jesus died for her sins along with the sins of the whole world. He never specifically told her what he'd discovered in the Bible about Genesis 3, but she'd always known he was different from all the other men.

He was probably trying to protect her. Now he was gone. He couldn't protect her. Abbey wouldn't let that stop her. She had a purpose. A destiny. This path was chosen for her. She would die to get this truth out.

How?

How could one girl change the course of history? How could one sixteen-year-old stand against six centuries of teachings? How could she stand up to the king and the josser?

As she exited the building, she made her way around to the front entrance where she was to meet Zwilling. He was talking to someone at a distance. She stared at the doors to the church.

The entryway was made of stone with an arched entrance. Above the doors was a painting of Christ's crucifixion. Two men were kneeling at the foot of the cross. They were both holding what looked to be Bibles. Abbey had never noticed the entrance before.

Beautiful. Majestic. Not reflective, undeserving of the heresy being taught inside.

Words were written under the mural. She stepped closer—inside the rod iron fence where women weren't allowed. No woman had probably ever even stepped inside the fence for centuries.

Someone closed the heavy iron doors with a loud clang. Church bells rang out, signaling the end of the service. A man walked up to the door, attached a piece of paper to it, and walked away.

Abbey looked around. Not seeing Zwilling, she walked up to the door and looked at the paper. The note was a message for the university staff. Nothing more than a notice of the date and time of a meeting taking place at the church.

At that moment, an idea came to her. She stared at the door, thinking.

Was it possible? Could I do it?

Excitement welled up in her like a tidal wave.

The possibilities. The Bible... The printing press.

A hand on her shoulder jerked her back into reality.

"What are you doing up here?" a familiar voice said roughly.

Zwilling.

He began to drag her away.

Abbey looked back at the door.

This could work.

4

Women had a curfew on Mars. From sundown to sunup, women weren't allowed to be outside of their homes on the streets. Living on the equator, the sun was up exactly half of the time. A solar day lasted 24 hours, 39 minutes, and 35 seconds. Consequently, women spent half of their lives indoors while men were free to come and go as they wished. The only exceptions were the church prostitutes who primarily made their money for the church at night.

Abbey was breaking the curfew for the first time in her life and left her home at night headed for the shop. She would never be confused with a prostitute, so she carefully stayed close to buildings and out of the light as she made her way to the shop, carefully avoiding running into anyone. The two moons of Mars filled the sky with light making it harder to not be seen. The cap was in her back pocket in case she saw any soldiers. The disguise would only work if she stayed in the shadows of the buildings.

Zwilling finally fell asleep in a drunken stupor, which allowed her to slip out of the house unnoticed. The afternoon after church had been pure hell. Furious she had stepped inside the rod fence, which women were forbidden to do, he was determined to teach her a lesson she would never forget. The beating had been exceptionally harsh, and Abbey could still feel the aches and pains from it.

Discretion would insist she wait a few days before venturing out at night. Breaking curfew so soon after wandering into the forbidden area was a tremendous risk. But Abbey was so excited about her new idea, she couldn't wait to get started on it. Satisfied Zwilling was fast asleep, she slipped out of her bed and into her clothes and shoes, willing to take the risk.

Abbey instinctively touched her back pocket to confirm that the lightstick was still there. In her room, she'd hidden a lightstick and batteries given to her by her father for one of her birthdays. Thankfully, Zwilling had never found her hiding place. The lightstick was turned off. It would draw too much attention on a dark night. She would use it to explore the room with the hidden Bibles.

I can't wait.

A friend of her dad's had invented the lightstick along with the light illuminator and electricity. Few people could afford the luxury. The rich and the church were the only ones with electricity in their homes and businesses. The shop had electricity because of the printing press. The only streetlights were around the royal palace which made it easier for her to move around the streets without being seen.

The shop was only a few blocks from her house. The back entrance butted up to a hill and was cleverly disguised by her father. A short ten-minute walk, she made it to the back entrance of the shop without running into any soldiers. The only thing she saw were a couple of prostitutes standing on a corner, bored. They didn't even look her way.

She slipped through the backdoor unseen, carefully closing it so as not to make any noise. She turned on the light to the shop and went down the steps and into the area with the printing presses.

Having made it to the relative safety of the shop, Abby let out a sigh of relief. The windows in the basement were darkened, so she was free to turn on the lights. The church officials had questioned the darkened windows. Her dad told them it was necessary for printing. Light had no effect on printing. He just wanted to make sure no one saw Abbey working in there.

She opened the door to the back storeroom, having grown more accustomed to the smell of the musty books. She moved the rug away from the hatch and made her way down the ladder, anxious to finally discover what was there.

At the bottom of the stairs, she paused and scanned the room with the lightstick. Much larger than she expected, the room contained a printing press, cabinet, work area with various printing tools, a case with a glass top, and various metal plates organized in the corner.

A light fixture was affixed in the center of the room with a string hanging down. Abbey pulled the string, half expecting the light to be useless, and was surprised when the light came on and illuminated the entire room. She turned off the lightstick and walked over to the printing press to inspect it.

Clearly, this was where her dad had printed the Bibles. Inspection of the plates confirmed they were indeed the plates for the Bible. A rush of excitement brought a huge smile to her face. She had a printing press. One that could never be traced. No one would know where the printing had come from.

Her dad was brilliant. He clearly set up the room for that purpose but likely died before he could implement the plan. It gave her satisfaction that she could fulfill his plan.

Abbey inspected the hundreds of plates. It must have taken her Dad months to typeset all of them. The plates were in perfect condition, which she expected, considering her dad's meticulous nature and attention to detail.

The glass case caught her attention. She carefully opened the top of it. Inside were handwritten pages bound in a book form. Abbey scanned a couple of the pages, confirming what she suspected. A complete handwritten copy of the Bible written by a scribe or scribes was housed in the case. Judging by the paper, Abbey surmised the book was written in the first century, likely only a few years after Christ's death.

She carefully turned the pages that were still in remarkable condition considering their age. A date in the corner of the second page confirmed this particular Bible was scribed in 70 M.A. A.C., approximately seventy years after Christ's death. Abbey's mouth flew open in amazement. She touched it again, as if she were touching something sacred.

This original manuscript might have been written by someone who was an actual eyewitness to the accounts in the Bible. Abbey shared her father's love for books. The historical nature of the book was enough to bring tears to her eyes. Knowing it was about the life of Christ left her in complete awe.

A chill went through her spine at the discovery. Excitement and fear.

She would be burned at the stake if the book were discovered in her possession.

That wasn't going to happen. She would protect it with her life. It was too valuable to her dad and too valuable to her to let anything happen to it.

She would finish what her dad started. The original Bible, the metal plates, and the printing press were going to bring down the evil church and its leaders. Abbey was determined to expose them for the liars and hypocrites they were.

She inspected the press. Aside from needing oil and ink, it would work magnificently for what she had planned. Electricity was fed to the room, so she had power. Large stacks of paper lined the far wall. She would eventually need more, but it was enough to get her started.

This is going to be easier than I thought.

Don't be ridiculous. You have no idea what you're doing.

Her thoughts turned to the day's events at the church.

The josser's sermon. The posting of the notice on the door. The idea had come to her like a lightning bolt.

She would write a paper... A thesis.

Post it on the door of the Vandenberg Church. Late at night when no one could see her.

The church would be shaken to its foundation. The masses would be liberated as the word spread.

It would be a reformation of monumental proportions.

How do I write a thesis? *I can do it.*

Abbey had printed hundreds of theses written by scholars at the university. She knew exactly how to typeset them, including the format and layout. She could do it in her sleep. A copy of one of those would serve as an example.

Her limited knowledge of the Bible would be the biggest challenge. She would start with Genesis 3. That would be the first thesis. The church's account of what happened in the Garden of Eden would be exposed as fraudulent. Attached to the thesis would be copies of the original Bible verses in the hand of the scribes. She would nail them to the door of the Vandenberg Church.

Excitement pulsed through her veins as she thought of the possibility.

I can't wait to hear the josser's sermon after he gets the thesis.

How do I get it out to the people? Women can't read. The men won't believe it.

Multiple copies could be printed, but she had to get them in the hands of those who were not sympathetic to the king. Posting it on the door of the church wasn't good enough. The church would take it down and destroy it before anyone even knew it was there. Even if someone did read it, they wouldn't know it was authentic. The church would claim it was heretical and a forgery.

It had to be written with such authority that scholars who already disagreed with the king would give it credibility.

Take your time. Think this through. Worry about that later.

If God is calling you to do this, he will provide a way.

"I need to read through the entire Bible myself," she said to herself. "Take notes. Familiarize myself with the Scriptures. Write down every passage that refutes the church's teachings."

How will I nail it to the church door without being seen? The noise will attract attention. There were still too many flaws to her plan.

I'm only sixteen years old. I need help.

Maybe it's time to talk to Eck.

No. Not yet. Read the Bible first.

She walked over to the steps where she had left the Bibles from the upstairs room.

Her mouth gaped open in stunned disbelief.

The Bibles weren't there.

Abbey tried to get her bearings and process the information. She'd brought the Bibles down the ladder and set them next to the steps.

Right here. I'm sure of it.

She searched the entire room. They were nowhere to be found.

An overwhelming sense of dread came over her. Her heart pounded against her chest. She could feel every pulse in her ears. Her hands shook. She took the lightstick out of her pocket, clutched it in her right hand, and frantically searched the room for any evidence the Bibles had been there.

She began to cry as the stark reality set in.

Someone has been in this room and someone has taken my Bibles.

* * *

"The woman's name is Theba," Tomas said to King Henry X.

"What woman?" The king was distracted by a large turkey leg he was voraciously consuming.

"The woman who was bathing two nights ago across the street."

"Oh yes!" the king's eyes brightened. "I remember her. One of the most beautiful women I've ever seen."

"Only one problem," Tomas said with caution.

"What's the problem?"

"She's married."

"How's that a problem?" the king said with a frown.

"Her husband is a captain in your army. His name is Jeriah."

The king paused, pondering that new information.

"Perfect. He's at battle right now, right?"

"Yes. He's fighting the Cabenites."

"Good. Send for her and bring her to my chamber tomorrow night."

"With all due respect, Your Excellency, I don't think that's a good idea."

"Why is that?" the king said with his mouth full. Her husband was away in battle. There was no problem as far as he was concerned. The problem would have been if her husband had been in town.

"Jeriah is one of your trusted servants. For the morale of our men, I don't think it's a good idea for you to be sleeping with their women while they've gone to fight *your* battles. Let me get you a young virgin girl."

"No!" The king interrupted, his voice raised. "I want her. Swear her to silence. If she tells her husband, I will put both of them to death."

"The University scholars may rebel if they find out," Tomas argued. "There are hard-liners who speak out against adultery."

"It's not adultery," Henry said emphatically. "I'm the king. I'm the head of the church. I'm the maker of the laws. How can the one who makes the law break them? She's the only one who would be committing adultery."

Tomas didn't respond right away, clearly thinking about what to say without risking the wrath of the king. Apparently, he decided silence was the best approach.

"How much is the religious remission for adultery?" Henry said.

"Forty pounds."

"Change it to twenty."

Tomas opened his mouth, appearing to object.

"Also, give men absolute remission of their sin for the sum of twenty pounds for the sin of adultery," Henry continued.

The forty pounds gave the person forgiveness but didn't take away all their punishment from God. Absolute remission meant their sins were completely absolved without any punishment. The thinking had been that absolute remission for any sin for money would encourage the bad behavior.

"Plus, no one will ever know," Henry said. "If Theba says anything, the punishment for adultery for a woman is death. Theba will have committed adultery against her own husband. She won't say anything."

The king motioned for Tomas to leave him, signifying the conversation was over.

Tomas dutifully backed out of the room.

* * *

"Eck must have taken the Bibles," Abbey muttered out loud.

"Where would he have put them?"

She searched the downstairs room completely then went back upstairs and looked around but found nothing.

I need one of those Bibles so I can study it and prepare my thesis.

A sound startled her.

Abbey heard a noise coming from the room below. She listened carefully, not even daring to breathe.

After several minutes, she didn't hear anything. Cautiously, she made her way back down the ladder, still certain she'd heard something.

Abbey tiptoed over to the far wall to inspect it, careful not to make a sound. She reminded herself to breathe. To her right was a slight nook she hadn't noticed before. She shined the lightstick and discovered a door. A sliver of light came from under the door.

She wanted to take off running without looking back, but curiosity had gotten the best of her. Carefully opening the door, she peaked around the corner. A long tunnel extended from the door to as far as she could see. A lone light fixture illuminated the entire hallway.

She slipped through the door and cautiously walked down the tunnel. The left side of the wall of the tunnel was solid rock. Significant excavating had created this tunnel.

Where did it lead?

Several rooms lined the right side. The first room was a storage area with more paper and more printing supplies. The second room had a bed, nightstand, small lamp, and uneaten food on a table in the corner. Someone had clearly been in the room that night.

I must have disturbed them. Did this person take the Bibles? If so, she was going to find them and take them back.

She glanced around the entire room. The Bibles lay in the corner. Abbey walked toward them and picked one up, confirming they were the same ones she had found a few days before.

A door opened and closed. She heard footsteps in the tunnel. Getting closer.

She had nowhere to run or hide. The room had no closets, nooks, and no door to hide behind. A quick glance around confirmed there was nothing there she could use as a weapon. Frightened, she quickly assessed her options.

Was her entire plan thwarted before she ever started?

Abbey backed against the far wall and stood against it as the footsteps drew nearer. In the shadows so whoever it was might not see her.

A figure, a man appeared in the doorway. Slightly older than her, but not much. He walked past the entrance to the room.

Abbey tiptoed back to the door. If she had taken a breath in the last minute, she didn't remember it. Glancing around the corner, she caught a glimpse of him turn the corner and go back into the room with the printing press.

She looked back. Behind her was a door. The same direction he had come.

Was it a way of escape? Should she run?

Her father always said she was the bravest girl he'd ever met. Right now, she was feeling like the most foolish. Everything told her to flee. Her feet were poised to bolt out the door in the opposite direction of the man.

Curiosity wouldn't allow it. She had to know who the man was and what he was doing living downstairs in her father's shop.

A few seconds later the door opened. The man appeared from around the door. He closed it slowly and confidently.

The two of them stood face to face, ten feet away. They stared at each other. Neither said a word. Nothing from his expression gave away his intentions. Was he a friend or foe?

Abbey looked him up and down. He did the same to her.

Younger man. Probably twenty or twenty-one. Brown hair. Slight curl. Blue eyes. Mischievous grin on his face. Accented by dimples.

Really cute.

Stop it! You have to focus.

They stared at each other for what seemed to Abbey like a minute. Probably only ten seconds or so.

Neither moved.

Finally, he spoke. "Hi, Abbey. I'm Christopher. It's nice to meet you."

5

I'm scared.

Theba sat in the king's bedchamber by herself, clutching her hands together to keep them from shaking. Earlier in the day, soldiers had arrived on her doorstep and demanded she come with them. At the time, she had no idea why.

Upon arrival, she'd been taken to a room and given numerous beauty treatments and a special meal. A man named Morti oversaw her transformation. After a special salt bath, various lotions with sweet smelling fragrances were lathered over her entire body. Her silky black, flowing hair was washed and restyled. Nails were carefully cut, manicured, and polished with a bright red color. A satiny robe was placed around her to wear to the bedchamber. Had it not been for the fear of what she knew was to come, the pampering would have been one of the most pleasant experiences in her life.

I wish my husband were here. This can't be happening.

Morti told her what was expected of her.

Theba was appalled.

I'm married.

Her protestations fell on deaf ears. Morti and the others were servants of the king. Whether they sympathized with her or not, they never let it show. Theba had heard about the king's many wives and concubines, but she'd never heard of him taking another woman against her will.

It would be against her will.

She didn't want to be there. Theba loved her husband, Jeriah, with all her heart. He was a good man, one of the few who treated women well. Every day she thanked God for the blessing of such a wonderful husband.

Morti had said she caught the king's eye when she was bathing on the rooftop.

I should have been more careful. I didn't know anyone was spying on me. What a pervert.

Many thoughts raged in her mind like a wildfire.

How can I get out of this? Can I talk my way out of it? The king is disgusting. Theba had seen the king at a distance several times before. *Why would he do this to Jeriah? My husband is a captain in his army. Surely, the king wouldn't take one of his own leader's wives.*

Morti said it was best to obey the king's command. He warned her that Henry would kill her husband if she resisted.

The thought sent panic through her. *I can't let him kill Jeriah.* He would do it, too—kill her and Jeriah.

The king had his own wife, Queen Katherine, beheaded earlier in the day.

Theba, with all her nervousness, had hardly even noticed the room. Under any other circumstances, she would have been in awe to be in the presence of such luxury. The curtains were lush and made from the finest fabrics. Gold was everywhere. The bed was a large four poster with large fluffy pillows, with what looked to be fine satiny sheets and pillowcases. Thick, lush, animal skins, were neatly spaced on the floor throughout the room. The black bedspread looked to be made of some of the finest material and had the king's insignia in the center.

Theba shuddered at the thought of the king making her lie with him on that bed.

Maybe he won't make me do it.

She jumped when the door opened with a bang. The king laughed and talked in a loud voice as he entered the room. He stopped when his eye caught Theba sitting on a couch over in the far corner of the room. She had seen herself in the mirror earlier and admitted they had made her look beautiful.

"You are stunning," the king said, obviously pleased.

He walked straight toward her with a lustful look in his eye and a grin out of one side of his mouth. He reached out with the back of his hand to touch her cheek.

Theba instinctively pulled away.

"Playing hard to get, are you?" the king said. "I like that."

He grabbed her hair and pulled her head back.

"You're hurting me," Theba said meekly.

The king roughly released his grip on her hair. He took several steps over to a table next to his bed and poured two glasses of wine. He walked back to where Theba was sitting and handed her a chalice full of wine.

"Take a drink. It's okay. Relax. I'm not going to hurt you," the king said almost apologetically.

You already have. You're a monster. I hate you.

The wine tasted sweet and was aromatic. Theba took a big drink. Admittedly, the best wine she had ever tasted. The chalice was wooden with gold inlay. Probably worth more than everything in her entire house.

Theba took a bigger swig and downed the entire cup. Anything to dull the pain of what was about to happen.

Controlling the urge to flee, it took all her self-control to not bolt out of the room as fast as possible. The fear and anxiety were already turning to sadness, remorse, disgust, and regret. Her hatred for the king grew with every second alone with him.

The king placed his hand behind her head and kissed her aggressively. His breath was stale and tasted like fish. His kisses were undisciplined, wet, and sloppy, seemingly with no concern for her at all. She wanted to wipe them off her face. He was dominating her and had her pinned down. Letting her know fighting back was of no use.

He smelled of perfume obviously generously lathered on him right before he came into the room.

Theba tried to hold her breath. Trying not to gag.

He didn't seem to care or notice she was not kissing him back.

He abruptly picked her up and threw her over his shoulder as she let out a slight scream. He threw her down on the bed.

The only thing she knew to do was to think about Jeriah. She'd never been with any man other than her husband. The king was nothing like Jeriah. Her husband was a gentle and kind lover. Passionate, romantic. How she longed for his touch right then.

Almost as quickly as it started, it was over. The king rolled over and took another drink of wine, and kicked Theba out of the bed with his foot in the process.

"You weren't nearly as good as I thought you would be. Get out of my sight," Henry said angrily.

Theba tried to cover herself with what was left of the robe as she quickly made her way out the door. The clothes she'd worn to the palace were neatly piled on a chair outside of the room. A guard stood by the door. He didn't even look her way. Uninterested as if what was happening was commonplace. She slipped on her clothes.

Where are my shoes?

She didn't take the time to look or to ask. Without looking back, she ran down the stairs and out the door three blocks to her house.

God forgive me. Jeriah, please forgive me.

* * *

"Hi, Abbey, I'm Christopher. It's nice to meet you," he had said in a friendly manner.

The intruder stared at Abbey. She glared right back. She didn't know how he knew her name, but this was her father's shop, and he was a trespasser until he proved otherwise.

"I don't know how you know my name," Abbey said. "But this is my father's shop, and I'm his daughter. I demand to know why you're here. He's right upstairs. If you try anything, I'll scream, and he'll come running."

A wide grin came on Christopher's face.

Abbey wasn't grinning. She had a menacing look on her face, trying to seem as intimidating as possible on her one-hundred and five-pound frame. Her fists were in a ball. Shoulders tensed. Feet firmly planted ready to pounce or run, whichever the situation demanded.

"What's so funny?" she asked roughly.

"Your dad always said you were a feisty one. He was right."

"How do you know my dad?" she asked impatiently.

"Our dads were friends. My dad's name was Calvin."

"Was?" Abbey remembered her dad talking to her mom about a man named Calvin.

"Yes. The josser had my dad put to death for insurrection. He preached against the king and the church. The king ordered all the men in our family killed. I fled here and your dad hid me in this shelter. I've been here ever since. I can't go home."

Abbey unclenched her fists. While she didn't fully trust him yet, the story seemed to make sense.

Sounds like something my Dad would do.

She took a deep breath and allowed herself a moment to release some tension.

"Did you take the Bibles?" she asked, balling her fists again.

"My dad's the one who gave the Bible to your dad." Christopher explained. "Your dad was going to print them, and we were going to distribute them. Then my dad was killed, and your dad died..." His voice trailed off.

"Your dad treated me like his own son." He struggled to get the words out as tears welled up in his eyes.

At that moment, Abbey knew she could trust him. She unballed her fists.

"After your dad died, I tried to print some of the Bibles, but I didn't know how to use the printing press, and I ran out of ink. I've been hiding here for more than a year and sneaking out when I think it's safe. To scrounge for food. Not much food and water out there to find."

Abbey noticed how thin he was. Everyone on Mars who wasn't rich was thin. No one had enough to eat or drink. She made a mental note to sneak him some food.

"I just found the Bibles and the press. I didn't know they were here. Dad never said anything about them." Abbey spoke in more of a calm and disarming manner. "I was going to... Print the Bibles. Then... I had another idea," she said hesitantly.

Should I tell him?

Suddenly, the idea seemed foolish. Childish. *He'll laugh at me.*

"What was your idea?" Christopher asked sincerely.

She hesitated. Still not sure how much to divulge. If her dad trusted him, then she should too.

"I want to write a thesis," Abbey said firmly.

"What's a thesis?"

"It's a paper they write at the university on a particular topic arguing for an idea or philosophy."

"I never went to the university. I only finished the eighth grade. I know how to read and write, though," Christopher said.

"So do I."

Christopher's eyes widened in amazement. "You do? I've never met a girl who could read."

"Well, I can," Abbey said smugly. "I read really well. I know how to work the printing press too. I can print the Bibles and the thesis. I want to write a thesis on the Garden of Eden and explain to the people what really happened."

"That's a brilliant idea," Christopher said excitedly.

She was warming to Christopher. *He's nice.*

"We could write several of them."

"We?" Abbey said with uncertainty.

"Yes. I'll help. I've read the Bible several times. My dad taught me all about it. I know all the ways in which the church has changed the wording in the Bible. If you can write it, I can help you know what to write. If you can print it, then I can get it out to all the people who oppose the church and king. We'll make a good team."

Emboldened, Abbey said, 'I was thinking we could post the thesis on the door of the Vandenberg Church."

"Yes!" Christopher said. "We could post it on the door of all the churches. The people can finally know that what the church is teaching them is a lie. Abbey, you're a genius. Your father would be so proud of you."

"You too," Abbey nodded in agreement. "This is so great. I had no idea how to get my thesis out to the people. Sounds like you're just the person to do it." she started walking toward the press room.

"Where are you going?" Christopher asked.

"I'm going to get some paper and something to write with so we can get started."

As she was about to walk past Christopher, he took her arm and said, "I'm so glad I met you."

His touch sent a feeling through Abbey she had never felt before. Like a bolt of electricity flowing through her. For a moment, their eyes met. Abbey quickly looked away as she felt her face blush.

"This is going to be so fun," Abbey said as she skipped into the other room.

* * *

Two weeks later

"Here's the introduction to the thesis." Abbey read a printed document to Christopher.

"Out of love for the truth and the desire to bring it to light, the following is the actual account of what happened in the Garden of Eden with Adam and Eve. The following propositions about the role of women in the church and on Mars should be discussed and debated, and the truth taught to all the men and women of Mars."

"That's perfect," Christopher said. "Then you should say, 'Written in the name of our Lord Jesus Christ. Amen.'"

"Should we put that at the beginning or the end?" she asked.

"Put it right after the opening statement. That way, everyone knows this was written for the purpose of glorifying God. The church will call it heresy, but the people will know that God is behind this," he explained.

Abbey continued reading from the thesis point by point.

1. *God created man and woman both in his own image.*
2. *When the Bible uses the term "man," it's talking about mankind, including Adam and Eve.*
3. *Eve ate the fruit and then gave it to Adam who also ate from it.*
4. *The Bible says through "one man's sin death entered the world." Not one "woman's" sin. The church changed the original words.*
5. *God is no respecter of persons. Women and men were both saved and baptized under Jesus's ministry and in the early church.*
6. *Jesus had many "women" involved in his ministry. Seven women financed his ministry.*

7. *The early church had many "women" in leadership roles.*

8. *In the last days, young men and "women" will both prophesy.*

9. *There were seven "women" who were prophets in the Old Testament. God used women mightily throughout the Bible.*

10. *A woman is more precious to God and to her husband than gold or silver. Men are to treat their wives with gentleness and understanding and love their wives as Christ loved the church and gave himself for her.*

"What do you think?" Abbey said.

"Perfect." Christopher said. "I'll put all of the Scripture references next to each point and then you can begin printing."

"All theses' have to be signed by the author. What name do we want to put on the bottom? Abbey asked. "Any ideas?"

"This is for the people. What name means people?" Christopher asked, rubbing his hands together.

"Luther," Abbey said. "Luther means people." Abbey remembered reading that in a thesis several months before. "Let's sign it Luther. How about Martian Luther? That would mean to the people of Mars."

"I love it!" Christopher and Abbey jumped up and down like a couple kids. Which was exactly what they were.

6

The Vandenberg Church was packed.

So much so Abbey had to stand in the back of the already-sweltering balcony. Sweat dripping from her brow, she wanted to be anywhere else but there.

The josser had put out a decree of the king stating a special dispensation for the religious remissions of adultery would be announced this Sunday morning. The church was abuzz in anticipation. Abbey was interested only to the extent that it would provide fodder for another thesis. She and Christopher had two already completed and ready to distribute.

Abbey's mind was elsewhere. She had to keep reminding herself to wipe the smug grin off her face. She knew what was coming one week from today. The first thesis on the Garden of Eden would be posted on the church door next Sunday morning. Another on religious remissions would be posted the following Sunday morning.

Her mind was also on Christopher who had kissed her on her cheek when she had left the basement earlier that morning. Abbey reached her hand to her face and touched the area where he had kissed her, remembering how surprised she was but also how good it had made her feel.

The last two weeks had been a whirlwind. Christopher had already taken the twelve Bibles her dad had printed and distributed them around Middleton Bay, the Boreal Basin, the Sirias Major Plantum, and the Utopia Plenary regions of Mars. A distribution network had been set up with hundreds of people who opposed the king. So many people were involved, they could get the thesis out to the entire planet in just a few days.

Ninety-five churches in the regions would have the thesis posted on their doors. Those were the regions with the greatest pockets of resistance and the ones with fearless leaders who would faithfully distribute the message to the masses. A groundswell of support was building in the regions now they had some direction and leadership to the cause and ammunition to fight the heretical teachings of the church.

Abbey and Christopher had spent countless hours working on printing the thesis and the accompanying documents. Mostly at night. Zwilling had been away traveling to his brother's home in Yellowbird Cove. The reprieve had given her the opportunity to come and go at will, and Christopher had even snuck into the house a couple times.

Zwilling, of course, did not leave Abbey alone. A woman was assigned to watch over her with strict instructions to rule Abbey with an iron fist. But the lady couldn't care less what Abbey did or didn't do. The law said a woman couldn't be paid for work. So, Abbey's sitter was compensated with room and board, which she took advantage of by buying and eating lots of food and mostly sleeping. The extra food in the house gave Abbey the opportunity to sneak some to Christopher without the woman noticing.

When Zwilling returned from his trip, an illness had zapped his energy, and he spent most of his time in bed. Still weak, he managed to dress himself and make his way to the church. No one wanted to miss the day's announcement.

No one is going to want to miss our announcement next week either.

Attached to the thesis was a copy of the biblical account in the Garden of Eden and the corresponding passages related to each proposition in the thesis. The copies of the original would provide definitive proof of the validity of the Garden of Eden story and clear proof that the church had been misleading the people for centuries. Christopher had come up with the idea to add an additional sentence at the end.

The church will no doubt claim that the Genesis 3 account is a forgery. Demand that the church provides for everyone to view, the original manuscript written in the hand of first century scribes on the distinctive paper and ink from that time, proving the church's account is not a fabrication.

Abby couldn't wait to see the josser's reaction.

The crowd quieted as the organist began playing a hymn signifying the pompous entrance of the josser was imminent.

Abbey's thoughts went back and forth between the thesis and Christopher. A romantic bond was beginning to develop between them. Abbey didn't know what love felt like, but she was sure it was what she was feeling for him. Several nights ago, while working, she thought for a moment he was going to kiss her on the lips. Embarrassed, she turned her head away. She didn't know how to kiss. She had no sister or mother to teach her.

I won't turn my head next time.

Will there be a next time?

She felt her cheeks blush again. Thinking of Christopher sent goosebumps down her arms and butterflies to her stomach. A wide grin came over her face, which she quickly controlled. The guards might become suspicious. No woman has smiled or looked happy in church in decades.

The guards and other women looked in her direction. She couldn't draw attention to herself when they were so close to revealing the thesis. Abbey bit her lip and tried to look as sad as possible.

The happy feelings went away on their own when the josser entered the church to a large round of applause. He clearly loved the attention.

After several more hymns, the josser stood to speak. For forty-five minutes, he droned on and on about the importance of religious remissions. Abbey's feet hurt, her back ached from standing, and she was tired from a lack of sleep. Her clothes were drenched in sweat, and she couldn't wait until she saw Christopher again.

"God has imposed a penalty for sin upon man for Eve's act of eating the apple," the josser said in a loud booming voice.

Blah... Blah... Blah... Heard it already.

"God has entrusted the forgiveness of those sins to the Universal Church and specifically to the head of the church. God has ordained he determine the canonical penalties of sin and the cost of the removal of guilt."

The Josser continued. "Repentance of sin is not enough to remove the guilt. Payment for sin is required to receive full absolution and satisfaction for sin. Without payment of a religious remission, the sinner is condemned to hell."

There is no condemnation for those in Christ Jesus. Christopher had shown her that verse last week.

"The payment of religious remissions allows the church to construct these beautiful monuments of worship to God and fund the activities of the head of the church, our honorable King Henry X. The new remission I'm announcing today is going to fund the construction of a new church in Boulder Bay. A glorious structure, the likes of which Mars has never seen."

The men stood applauding, dutifully acknowledging the king.

In the thesis for religious remissions, one of the propositions Abbey and Christopher had written was, "If the king wants to construct a new church, why doesn't he use his vast resources rather than build it on the backs of peasants?"

"Man can only be saved by the religious remissions," Tomas expounded.

Heresy. Salvation only comes through faith in Jesus Christ.

Christopher had taught Abbey so much about the Bible and the finished works of Jesus dying for the sins of the people. She had seen the verses herself. Nowhere did the Bible say a man is saved by his own works. Nowhere did the Bible give the church or any man the authority to forgive sins. Jesus said only God can forgive sins.

The people hung on every word. It was clear why the church didn't want its people to read the Bible. They didn't want them to know the truth. They need them to stay in ignorance so they could fund their lavish lifestyles and maintain their power.

That is coming to an end.

The josser was clearly building to a finale. He needed to get on with it. The crowd was growing restless. Finally, the moment every-one had been waiting for. The josser was going to make the long-awaited announcement regarding the new religious remission.

"The church is announcing a change to the religious remission for adultery. From now on, the penalty for adultery will be twenty pounds instead of forty pounds!" The josser made the declaration in a large booming voice. The men stood to their feet, applauding wildly with approval. Several were slapping each other on the back and expressing tremendous jubilation at the unexpected news.

The josser did not try to quiet the crowd. He appeared to be rel-ishing in the adulation. The applause went on for several minutes.

When it died down, he said, "Further, upon payment of the twenty pounds, the sinner will receive full and complete absolution and satisfaction for his sin of adultery. No further payment for his sin will be required by God or his holy church."

The applause was deafening in the upper balcony as the clapping echoed off the walls from downstairs and bounced up to the ceil-ings. Of course, none of the women were applauding. They just sat in their chairs with numb looks on their faces.

When the din receded, the josser continued. "The punishment for women for the sin of adultery remains death."

* * *

The josser looked up at the women in the balcony with an angry glare as he pronounced that women would still be put to death for adultery. Several of the men looked up to the balcony as well. The women sat there with blank stares on their faces, showing no emotion at all.

Except for one woman. Her head was down, buried in her hands. Emotions flowing uncontrolled.

Sobbing... Terribly distraught... Fear... Guilt... Unable to hide the pain. No one knew what she was going through. They could never know.

Theba could hardly stand the shame.

I'm pregnant.

* * *

One week later, Sunday morning

The time to distribute the first thesis had come. Careful planning had gone into the distribution, and everything had gone smoothly. The thesis would be nailed to the door of the ninety-five churches throughout all the regions at three in the morning. Christopher would nail a copy to the door of the Vandenberg Church.

Eck would go with him to act as lookout for soldiers.

Eck had been brought into the plan several weeks before. The cost of the ink and paper was astronomical. Abbey couldn't take that much ink from Eck's normal supply without him knowing it. It was a great sacrifice for him to make but one he did gladly.

Christopher and Eck hit it off right away, and Eck was totally supportive of the plan. Tears flowed from both of them when Abbey showed Eck the note their dad had left for them. Eck considered it a privilege to be used by God in such a mighty way and to carry out the legacy their father had started.

They all knew the danger and accepted it willingly. This had become bigger than any one person. Bigger than even their father or Calvin could've ever imagined. They put a name to it— The Reformation. A name they hoped would create a cause everyone could rally around.

Abbey, Christopher, and Eck would not stop until the Reformation came to the people, or they died trying.

Abbey vehemently protested not being able to go with them to the church. Eventually, she gave in to the reasoning. Two men could walk freely at night and not draw any attention from the soldiers. A girl would draw immediate scrutiny. Too dangerous. As much as she wanted the satisfaction of watching her hard work nailed to the door of the church, discretion and common sense won out. Successfully nailing the thesis to the door was more important than her seeing it happen. She'd already imagined it in her mind a thousand times.

She wished them luck as they walked out the door through the tunnel exit armed with the thesis, a nail, a hammer, and tremendous resolve.

The completed thesis was a total of five pages. Christopher told Abbey that five was the number of "grace," in the Bible. More proof God was behind their efforts.

Abbey paced back and forth not willing to sit down until they returned safely. These were the two most important men in her life. She loved them both with all her heart. Rest was impossible until they were back with her inside the safe walls of the tunnel.

About an hour later, the door burst open. Eck and Christopher bounded in laughing and obviously signifying their mission was a success. Abbey ran to Christopher and threw her arms around him. Eck joined them. The three laughed and cried at the night's achievement. Abbey didn't have to ask to know things had gone well.

They didn't see a single soldier. Sunday morning had been Eck's idea. Perfect plan. Most people and soldiers were in bed asleep preparing for the Sabbath. If things went according to plan, it was possible no one would even notice the thesis until the doors of the church were opened later that morning.

More than a dozen copies of the thesis had been left on the doorsteps of prominent university scholars who were outspoken in their skepticism about some of the teachings of the church. A copy had also been left on the doorstep of the josser's personal residence.

Eck said goodbye and left to get a couple hours of sleep and to get ready to go to church. None of the three wanted to miss the reaction of the josser and the people when they arrived that morning.

Abbey and Christopher celebrated their success.

"We did it!" Abbey said.

"I'm so proud of you," Christopher said, as he took her in his arms, and hugged her tightly.

"I'm proud of you. Both of us." She could hardly contain the feelings of joy and love rising inside her.

Christopher started to pull away, but Abbey held the embrace. They faced each other, only inches separating them. She could tell by the look on his face that he knew what she wanted. Abbey was trembling, her mouth quivering. Her lips softened as he slowly moved toward her. Gently at first. Soft... tender. Carefully stealing her innocence.

Her heart flipped. Their lips parted, but Abbey pursued his. Kissing him harder. Instinctively. The room spun. An eerie quiet over the scene as if the entire world stopped while they experienced something God had planned for them.

His eyes were closed. Hers fixated on him. Unable to look away. Trying to sear the memory into her mind so she would never forget it. As their lips parted, she saw relief on his face. Apparently, this was something he'd wanted to do for a long time. They had passed the point of no return. No longer just friends.

Thoughts swirled around in her mind trying to ruin the moment. *What would we do about Zwilling? What if we were arrested and separated by jail or death? The church decided who married. The church would never bless our union.*

She quickly dismissed the thoughts. None of that mattered at that moment. What they experienced could never be taken away from them.

"You should probably get going," Christopher said sweetly.

"I will." Abbey said as she kissed him again. Passionately, not wanting the moment to end.

When it did end, she turned and headed to the door, looking back only to give him a smile and a slight wave.

* * *

The josser was having his morning breakfast, mentally going over his message for the church that morning. His message would be on covetousness and the sin of desiring to pursue worldly things and accumulate worldly possessions that were fleeting.

Tomas looked around at the worldly possessions he had accumulated. Actually, they'd been given to him by God as a blessing for being such a faithful servant.

The plates were made of the finest china. The utensils were solid silver. The chalice handcrafted by an artisan. His castle was bigger than two dozen peasant houses.

God had truly blessed him with every earthly pleasure.

A servant came through the door. Tomas raised his glass, thinking he'd come to refill it.

The servant handed him some papers.

"What's this?" Tomas asked.

His eyes widened and his mouth gaped open as he read the opening line of the thesis. Without reading further, he scanned to the end.

The signature.

Who is Martian Luther?

7

The josser carefully studied the thesis that had been left on his doorstep. Somebody had a copy of the Bible, and he was determined to find out who. The thesis left him with no definitive clue. He'd never heard of a man named Martian Luther. Attached were actual copies of Bible verses from an accurately inscribed Bible. Tomas was one of the few men who'd seen the originals and knew the truth about the Garden of Eden story.

How did they get an original? And who has it?

The Garden of Eden text had been changed long before him. When Henry I had been made king in the ninth century, he was a madman. Obsessed with power, he believed he was a sun god, and would walk the halls of the palace at night commanding the sun to rise. Suffering from epilepsy, much of his madness could have been attributed to his illness.

When he insisted that he be worshiped as a god, several Christian prophets confronted Henry, calling him a blasphemer and a heretic. Henry had them thrown in prison and then executed. Even his mother spoke out against him and gave him the name "mad emperor." Henry killed her by stabbing her to death with his own hands.

Over the years, his hatred for women and Christians grew. A fire in the city nearly burned down all the buildings of Boulder Bay and almost destroyed his reign. Blaming it on the Christians was the impetus Henry needed to crack down on them and have all Bibles seized. Most believed Henry started the fire himself for that very reason.

With all Bibles out of the hands of the masses, Henry was able to change the Genesis story to blame the fall on Eve and began a widespread crackdown on women. A set of decrees made it against the law for women to read, go to school, work, and hold any position of authority over a man. Through the centuries, the laws became more onerous to the point that women had virtually no rights on Mars other than those given to them privately by their husbands.

His predecessors simply continued the farce to maintain power and domination as women became more and more oppressed over the centuries.

Had Tomas been in charge, he wouldn't have changed the biblical text. He believed the argument for the superiority of men could be made through Scripture without changing the words. Verses could be taken out of context and used to make the arguments necessary. However, being the head of the church from a theological and doctrinal standpoint required him to stay consistent with the faith and continue to promote the lies of his predecessors, regardless of how ill-advised they'd been.

The document in his hands was a perfect example of why the people couldn't be entrusted with the truth. Verses could be pulled out of context for the purpose of making any argument. While Adam did eat the apple, Eve ate it first. Eve was to blame for all the wrath God had placed on man. Adam would not have eaten the apple had Eve not enticed him to do it. Even if the text taught by the church wasn't completely accurate, the truth was and that was the most important thing. Women were the cause of all the evil in the world and God had made man to rule over them.

Only those like him who were close to God could be trusted to interpret the Scriptures properly. The ignorant masses would only subvert the truth and twist it to oppose those in power. Men like Tomas knew what was best for them, and it was his job to make sure he protected them from themselves.

The king would obviously have to know about the thesis. Only after he could assess who had seen the document. As far as he knew, he held the only copy. He would hunt down the writer and deal with him harshly before it became a problem.

A servant entered the room, interrupting his thoughts.

"What do you want?" Tomas said.

"There's a woman at the door to see you. Her name is Theba. She said it's important."

What does that tramp want?

"Send her away. Tell her I'm busy." The servant backed out of the room without saying another word.

A few moments later, the servant returned.

"What?" Tomas said roughly.

"The woman insists she see you. It's very urgent."

"All right. Send her in," Tomas said with disdain. He had enough to worry about with the thesis. What could she want that could possibly be that important?

Theba walked into the room hesitantly, stopping just inside the door.

Tomas looked up. He was unable to speak for a moment, struck by her beauty. The king was right when he said she was one of the most beautiful women he'd ever seen.

Perhaps I can have her as well if I can do so without the king knowing.

"What was so important you had to see me? I'm extremely busy. I have a sermon to prepare for this morning." His tone was in between aloofness and seduction. He was torn between wanting her and not wanting to be bothered.

Theba approached him meekly and began speaking in a soft voice. So soft, he couldn't hear what she was saying.

"Speak up, woman. I can't hear you. What do you want?" Tomas said with a glare, recognizing there would be no way he could have her after the king had.

"I wanted to tell you I'm with child."

Tomas bolted from his chair and grabbed her arm, squeezing hard. Theba cowered, trying to pull her arm away. He was strong and tightened his grip.

"Is this some kind of trick? What do you want from the king? Money?" Tomas yelled.

"No, Your Honor. Do you think I wanted this?" Theba started crying.

"Does your husband know?"

"No. He's still at war. That's how I know it's the king's child. I didn't know what to do. I didn't know who to tell."

Tomas softened his tone and released her arm. He put his arms around her, smelling her hair as he drew her closer.

She's so soft.

He stroked her hair to comfort her. As his hand started down her back, she pulled away. Her mouth was agape obviously disgusted that his attempt to comfort her wasn't genuine.

His anger returned. Calling for the soldier standing guard outside his door, he had her seized.

She screamed. Theba resisted but was no match for the strength of the guard.

"Take her to the palace and place her in one of the rooms until I can come and decide what to do with her," Tomas said with authority.

Theba started sobbing.

"Let me go. I won't tell anyone." she implored, barely able to say the words between the sobs.

Tomas motioned for the guard to wait. He would have to think through this development carefully. It might be possible to make her disappear altogether, solving the problem once and for all. At the same time, the woman was carrying a royal heir. Regardless of how it happened, she was now royalty as well.

The fact she was married only complicated things further. The university scholars would strongly object if they found out the king had impregnated another man's wife. Now he had two problems. The scholars couldn't know about Theba or the thesis.

Theba was still crying. He tried to reassure her, softening his tone. He needed her to keep silent about the pregnancy. Needed for her to trust him.

"You did the right thing coming to me," Tomas said. "Don't tell anyone what you just told me. I'm going to have someone take you over to the palace and prepare a place for you. I'll come and see you later. I'll discuss it with the king and then come and see you."

Theba nodded and her tears stopped momentarily.

"Remember, not a word to anyone," Tomas said firmly.

Theba obediently nodded her head in agreement as the soldier led her out of the room.

I don't think I'll tell the king. She just needs to disappear.

* * *

A crowd of people gathered around the door of the Vandenberg Church as Abbey and Zwilling approached. Abbey knew why; Zwilling had no clue, and for the moment, didn't seem to notice. His illness had gotten worse by the day. Barely able to get out of bed and dress, he did so only because he would never miss church if he were physically able to make it. Faithful attendance covered a multitude of sins, according to church doctrine. Abbey hadn't missed a Sunday since Zwilling came into their lives.

Abbey tried to wipe the huge smile off her face but had a hard time controlling her delight. The crowd around the door was obviously gathered to read their thesis. Several university scholars in robes were carrying what appeared to be copies of the thesis as well. Tremendous satisfaction and pride welled up inside her as she admired the impact their handiwork already had. The hope was that the scholars would put pressure on the josser and the church to prove the thesis was a lie. That, they would be unable to do. While all the scholars supported the church and the king publicly, many were appalled at the excesses of the church and what many considered to be false doctrines being perpetrated on the masses.

Abbey had read enough of the theses of the scholars to know the opposition ran deep.

The new thesis on the role of women and the discrepancies in the Garden of Eden story might give the scholars the ammunition they needed to oppose the church and king. Having proof that the doctrines of the church were based on a lie might bring the church and king to their knees.

The thesis was causing a buzz. Abbey could overhear conversations and some of the scholars had serious and determined looks on their faces.

The josser would no doubt address it in his sermon.

I wonder what he'll say. I can't wait to watch him squirm.

* * *

Tomas entered the church through his usual back entrance, the thesis and Theba still weighing heavy on his mind. Thinking about it, he determined the primary suspect was the printer. Eck Whyburg had seemed awfully nervous the day Tomas had paid him the unexpected visit.

Comparing the typesetting on the thesis with the printing presses in Whyburg's shop wouldn't be hard. If the josser was right, this little insurrection could be put down in no time at all if Whyburg was the culprit.

He'd make another visit to the printer early this week.

Theba was a more complicated matter. No one could ever know about her. The scholars would claim that the change in religious remissions from forty pounds to twenty pounds was because of the king's adulterous affair. A national scandal would erupt. Calls would be made for the king to repent, and Tomas didn't see that happening. The king believed he was above the laws of the church, and no one had a right to question his behavior. A showdown between the scholars and the king would ensue. Who would win was anyone's guess. It had to be avoided at all costs.

The josser walked a perilous tightrope. While the king had unlimited power to run the church, he still needed the support of the intellectual class. The peons could be controlled by force. The scholars could as well, but diplomacy was always best. The church needed their support to continue the control of the masses.

If the scholars ever turned against the church and discovered the truth about the Bible, or the truth about Theba for that matter, many would turn against the king and begin speaking against him denouncing the affair and proclaiming the changing of Scripture as heretical. Tomas had to make sure the scholars never learned about the thesis. Some of them would believe it. If they demanded proof that the thesis was a lie, Tomas had no way to provide them with any. The Garden of Eden fabrication was the best kept secret that had lasted for six centuries and must last for many more to come.

He would worry about that when the time came. No one must ever know about the thesis or Theba. This morning's sermon would be business as usual and Tomas would act like nothing had happened. His sermon on covetousness was beautifully written and would be well delivered.

The blast of the organ playing was Tomas' cue to enter the church. His favorite part of Sunday church was entering to all the fanfare and adulation. A man of humble beginnings, he had risen through the ranks to the head of the church through sheer determination and superior intellect. Early in his career, going against the advice of his friends and family, he married a widow named Elise.

Technically, as josser of the church, he was forbidden to marry and was to remain celibate through his entire life.

His numerous indiscretions aside, the marriage was a much bigger problem which is why he had kept it hidden all these years. Not only his marriage to her, but her previous marriage. Once it became apparent that he might rise to the position of josser, Elise had to be dealt with. She would become a hindrance to him ever achieving his current position, so he quietly put her in a villa several hundred miles away and he changed the marriage records, so no one ever knew of it. They had no children, but she had a daughter from the previous marriage. He hadn't seen them for more than twenty years.

He wondered if he could remove Theba to a villa, miles away and could make her his mistress whom he visited periodically. He'd managed to keep his wife a secret all these years, so perhaps he could keep Theba a secret as well. Theba could raise her child there. He already had a plan on how to remove her husband from the picture.

His attention was quickly drawn back to the task at hand, as the last verse of the last hymn was concluded with a large blast of the organ whose massive pipes lined the wall to the side of him.

Tomas stood and slowly walked to the podium. He sat his notes down and looked out upon the crowd. He glared at the women in the balcony as was his custom. The women were a mixed blessing. He preferred that women not be allowed in church at all, but since they were, he took full advantage of using them as props to make his points about the evil and perverse nature of women and how they have destroyed God's will for the planet. As usual, the women were uninterested and not even looking his way.

As he looked out over the lower congregation, he immediately sensed something was wrong. The first rows of the middle section were reserved for the scholars. Several hundred of them sat in the pews with stately robes. He couldn't tell, but several of them had papers in their hands. The papers looked similar to the ones he had received.

Did they receive them as well?

Panic pulsed through his veins. Delivering the sermon, while scanning the scholars for more clues was difficult. He kept losing his train of thought. Was he imagining things or were some of the scholars scowling at him?

Say something about the women. Get the men applauding.

Before he could, a scholar in the second row stood to his feet. He had papers in his hand.

Holding them high in the air he said, "Your honorable, Josser. I demand to be heard."

8

Zwilling went straight to bed after church, so Abbey snuck out and ran all the way to the shop to tell Christopher what had happened. She began to relate the morning's events.

"I wish you could have been there. The josser was in the middle of his sermon, when one of the scholars stood up and demanded to be heard," Abbey said, and she started giggling.

A huge smile was on Christopher's face.

Soon she was laughing so hard she could barely talk. "You should have seen the josser's face," Abbey continued, trying to regain her composure. "He seemed surprised that anyone else knew about it. He must not have known it was on the door. It was still there when I left the church."

Abbey stopped to catch her breath. Christopher took her by the hand. That caused her to pause for a moment. They were sitting on the edge of the bed in the room off of the tunnel. Talking so fast, she was still gasping for air.

"Anyway, the scholar stood up and said, 'I have in my hand papers that purport that the Adam and Eve story is a fabrication.'"

Abbey started laughing again.

"He held up our thesis," she said proudly. "The man then asked the josser, 'Have you seen these papers?'

"I hadn't expected them to bring the thesis with them to the church," Christopher said. "Even better. I figured they would confront Tomas privately. I didn't think anyone would dare challenge him in public at the church."

Christopher sounded nervous as he said it.

"The josser looked like he'd seen a ghost," Abbey said.

"Brilliant idea Eck had to give the thesis to the university scholars," Christopher added. "What did the josser say then?"

"The josser denied it. He said they weren't real." Abbey's tone turned serious. Her disdain for the josser clearly coming out in her words.

"He said, 'I have seen the papers, and they are a forgery.'" Abbey did her best impression of the josser's voice. "That's exactly what you said he would say," she added.

"That's why we challenged the church to produce a copy of an old manuscript of the Bible. They can't. Their manuscripts say the same thing as ours." Christopher said. "Did the scholar challenge him to provide proof?"

"Yes. The scholar actually interrupted him and said, 'If this thesis is a forgery, then provide proof that the church's account is true. You have old manuscripts with the real biblical account. Just produce those and they will prove these papers are a lie.'"

"Perfect." Christopher said. "That's exactly what we wanted to happen. Let the scholars fight the battle for us." Christopher stood and paced around.

Abbey nodded in agreement. "Several of the other scholars voiced their approval, encouraging the one who was speaking." The smile returned to Abbey's face as she said it.

Abbey's forehead then furrowed as she got a serious look on her face again.

"But the josser wouldn't listen to them," Abbey said. "He said the Counsel would deal with it. 'We will capture the ones who've perpetrated this lie and bring them to justice—'"

"So," Christopher interrupted. "Did the scholars believe him and drop it," he asked anxiously.

"No. That was what was so great," Abbey said. "The scholars kept pressing him. Even accusing the josser of lying."

"Really?" Christopher said as if he was having a hard time believing the day's events actually happened. "This is more than we could've ever hoped for."

Abbey nodded and continued. "One even said, 'We don't trust the Counsel to deal with this honestly. You need to provide us with proof. Surely that's not hard for you to do, if the church account is accurate.'"

Christopher clapped his hands in approval. "Excellent," he said excitedly. "What happened next?"

"The josser was mad. Furious that anyone would defy him. So, he did what he always does. He tried to bully them."

"You dare to defy the Counsel and the king," Abbey's eyes burned with determination as she tried to mimic the josser's response. Christopher was obviously amused by her attempts to dramatize the events by getting into character, going back and forth between speaking like the josser and like the scholars.

"We want the truth. We demand the truth. Did Adam eat the apple?" a scholar shouted back.

"Of course not," the josser said. "The church account is the only true Bible. It's very clear what happened. Eve is the one who ate the apple."

"The manuscript attached to these papers say otherwise," the scholar said. "Attached is a copy of the Bible dated 70 M.A.A.C. The paper, ink, and writing seem to be authentic."

"That document is a forgery!" the josser insisted. "The perpetrators will be hunted down and brought to trial. You will learn the truth. The Counsel will bring them to justice."

Some in the crowd cheered. It seemed to Abbey like the crowd was turning against the scholars. She explained her perceptions as best she could to Christopher.

"Another scholar stood to speak," Abbey said.

Christopher hung on her every word.

Abbey spoke so fast, Christopher had to slow her down a couple times to clarify what happened. She barely stopped to catch her breath.

"The second scholar was even more adamant in reiterating what the first had said. The josser was sweating. The women were sitting on the edge of their seats listening closely. No one had never seen such a spectacle in church."

"What happened next was totally a shock," Abbey said.

"What happened?" Christopher said, scooting closer to Abbey in anticipation. Taking her hand again.

"'Your Honor,' the second scholar said. 'Is it true that the only reason the king changed the amount of the royal religious remission for adultery is because he committed adultery with another man's wife?'"

Christopher's mouth fell open.

"A gasp went over the entire crowd," Abbey said with emphasis.

"No, it's not true," the josser said in a loud voice. "The king received instructions from God to change the amount."

"'We have heard rumors that the king committed adultery with one of his soldier's wives,' the scholar said accusingly. 'Does the king think he is above the law?'

"An eerie silence came over the entire room. I wasn't sure what to think about the new development. Everyone waited for the josser's answer," Abbey explained.

"None came. Instead, he slammed his notebook together and stormed out of the chapel."

"He left?" Christopher's eyes widened. "It must be true then."

"Yes," Abbey said. "I think most people believed the scholars, and I think most people believe the thesis is true."

Christopher threw his arms around Abbey and kissed her. She kissed him back but then pulled away.

She sighed. She squeezed her eyes shut to fight back the tears.

"What?" Christopher asked. "What's wrong?"

"As everyone was leaving, the josser had the two scholars arrested. Soldiers came into the chapel, bound their hands, and escorted them out."

* * *

Tomas sat in his study on Monday morning, contemplating the previous day's events. Dreading having to tell the king about either of them. Thankfully, the king had gone hunting the day before and was unavailable until this morning, giving Tomas time to think through what he was going to say.

The news had only gotten worse. Overnight, he learned that a copy of the thesis was placed on the door of churches throughout the entire planet. Obviously a much bigger operation than he'd even imagined. If not contained, this document could spread like a wildfire throughout the masses and could threaten the very existence of the church and the king.

Not to mention the problem in the room down the hall.

"What a fool?" Tomas said aloud to himself. "Taking another man's wife. The king is an idiot. Now she's pregnant, and I have to be the one to fix it. I'm always cleaning up his messes."

A servant walked in, interrupting his thoughts, "The king will see you now, Your Honor."

Tomas gathered his things and strode down the hall to the king's office chamber. The king seemed to be in a good mood.

Not for long.

"Hello, Tomas." The king stood from his chair, walked around the desk, and embraced him. "How are you today, my friend?" he said as he slapped him on the back.

Tomas was slightly taken aback. Not that the king had never shown such affection, just that he was in this good a mood and that he would express it by touching him.

"I'm afraid I have some serious matters to discuss," Tomas said.

The king poured himself a chalice of wine and took a big gulp.

"What has you so distressed?" the king said. "You should have come hunting with me. We had a good time. Some shooting, some women..." the king laughed loudly.

"I have two problems I need to discuss with you today. The first is Theba." Tomas thought he should start with the easiest problem first. One in which he had a solution.

"Who's Theba?" the king's eyes narrowed, obviously thinking.

"She's the woman you saw bathing on the rooftop. You asked me to bring her to your chamber a few weeks ago."

"I remember now. A huge disappointment. Beautiful for sure. But... I would've thought she'd be more enthusiastic about sleeping with me. I am the king."

Tomas looked away, not wanting his face to give away what he was thinking.

"She's going to have your baby," Tomas blurted out, figuring he might as well get right to the point.

The king's reaction surprised him. He was in a particularly good mood.

"Splendid. If it's a boy, I'll make her my queen." The king had had several royal wives over the years, but none had ever been able to give him a son. The last was beheaded before she had much of a chance. He had seven hundred wives, but the church canon stated he could only have one queen. Any successor to the throne must come through a queen. If he were to die without a male heir, the whole church would be thrown into chaos.

Tomas fidgeted in his seat trying to think about how to word his next thought.

"You're forgetting that she's married," Tomas said.

The king paused and rubbed his chin. "I see what you mean. That does complicate things."

Tomas nodded. He pretended to be writing while he waited for a response.

"Just have her executed. That'll solve the problem," the king finally responded.

Tomas had anticipated that would be the king's first response. He was dreading this part.

"It's not as simple as that. The scholars know about her. They're accusing you of adultery."

The king stood up in his chair.

Finally, something to ruin his good mood.

"How dare they accuse me of a sin! I'm the head of the church. Appointed by God. That's blasphemy. I'll have their heads."

"They are being dealt with as we speak."

The king sat back down.

"Two of them have been arrested. They spoke up at church on Sunday. They accused you of changing the religious remission to cover up your sin."

"Well, that's ridiculous," the king said gruffly, apparently not remembering that was exactly why he'd done it.

"You see why we can't just have her executed. It'll give the impression the two scholars were right all along," Tomas said.

"We can't have that if we want to execute the scholars," the king retorted. "There will be an uproar if we kill them, but not if everyone knows they wrongly accused me. We have to make it look like they were wrong."

"You could just pay the twenty pounds and admit it," Tomas said hesitantly, knowing he was about to get yelled at. Thomas flinched in anticipation of what would come next.

Instead, the king said, "Who's her husband? Just say it's his child."

"His name is Jeriah. He's a captain in your army. Knows nothing about it. He's away fighting the Cabenites."

"Why did you let me sleep with one of my captain's wives?" the king asked brusquely.

Tomas ignored the comment, deciding it was better not to respond defensively. Too tempting to remind the king he'd tried to talk him out of it, so Tomas bit his lip. At this point, the king's wrath was on the woman not on him. He needed to keep it that way.

The king glared at Tomas to further make his point, but then moved on.

"Why don't we bring her husband back home?" the king continued. "Have him sleep with his wife, and then we can say the child is his. No one will ever have to know. We can deny I ever slept with her," the king said.

The smile returned to the king's face as he was in a good mood again.

"Where's the woman?" the king said before Tomas could respond.

"She's here in one of the bedrooms."

"Send for her."

Several minutes later, Theba was brought into the king's office. Shaking almost uncontrollably. Her lower lip quivered. She was biting it, seemingly trying to make it stop. Tears stained her face and the dress she was made to wear.

The king stood, came around from behind his desk and walked to where she was standing. He took her by the hand and led her over to a couch. He sat down and then made her sit on his lap.

"I hear we have a problem," the king said with a smirk. "What are we going to do about it?"

Theba's eyes glistened from tears building again. She tried to speak but didn't. Everything about her cried out in fear.

"I won't... say... anything... I promise," she finally blurted between the sobs. "Please don't hurt me or my husband."

The king stroked her hair. Tomas saw her flinch when he touched her.

"You are beautiful..." he said gently as he looked at her longingly.

"I have no intention of hurting you or your husband. We have a plan," the king continued. "We're going to bring your husband back home."

Theba's eyes widened and the tears stopped momentarily. A half smile formed on her face.

"When he comes back, you're to lay with him and tell him and everyone else that the child is his."

Theba nodded in agreement. She forced another smile.

The king threw Theba onto the floor and stood over her. Tomas bolted from his seat and took several quick steps toward them. Tomas thought for a moment that the king was going to strike her. Theba raised her hands in front of her head to try and block the blow, but it never came. Instead, the king continued yelling at her.

"If you tell him about what happened with us..." The king's eyes blazed with fury. "If you tell anyone, I'll kill you, the child, and your husband. Is that understood?"

Theba cowered and tried to slide back away from the king. Tomas stood between her and the king.

"Do you understand?" The king shouted at the top of his lungs as Tomas placed his hands on him to hold him back.

"Yes," Theba said with a hint of disdain. "I understand."

Tomas went over and helped her up. He led her to the door, needing to defuse this situation as soon as possible.

"Go back to your home. I'll have your husband brought back. Everything's going to be all right."

Theba nodded and quickly ran out of the room.

"Well that solves that problem," the king said smugly. "She won't say anything."

"I agree. That was a brilliant solution you thought of." It was the same thing Tomas was going to suggest, but better that the king think it was his idea.

"I'll send for her husband immediately. Once he lays with her, then you are in the clear."

"Such a shame. She would have made a good queen."

Tomas gathered his possessions and started to leave. *One problem at a time.* He headed to the door.

"You said there were two problems you needed to discuss," the king called after him. "What was the other one?"

Tomas closed the door, walked back to his chair, and sat down. He took a deep breath and then let out a huge sigh.

The king poured another chalice of wine. Tomas clinched his teeth and tightened his jaw. The king was not going to like what he was about to hear.

"So, what was the other thing?" the king said with a wide grin on his face.

He hesitated for a moment before speaking. "The scholars know the truth about the Garden of Eden. They know Adam ate the apple."

9

The Red Sea Scrolls were discovered in 1335 M.A. A.C., in a remote region on Mars, near the Red Sea. A group of nomads were exploring the Kamram caves on cliffs overlooking the sea, when they discovered an ancient fragment from one of the scrolls and reported it to authorities. The king at the time, Henry III, took control of the site and sent archeologists there to search for and recover the fragments.

They found 951 fragments of ancient texts of various books of the Bible written between the third century B.C. and first century A.D., and two complete manuscripts scribed around 70 M.A.A.C. Most of the fragments were so withered they were indiscernible, but the two manuscripts were in remarkably good condition. They were the only known complete manuscripts of the Bible.

Until now.

A third one obviously exists. I have to find it. Tomas looked across the table at Elmyr Fiori, the foremost expert on forging documents on Mars. Elmer was seventy-two years old, thinning hair, short and wiry, one hundred-forty pounds if wearing heavy clothes. He peered over his bent wire rim glasses examining one of the original texts of the Bible.

"Can you do it?" Tomas asked.

A man of very few words, Elmyr simply nodded while continuing to examine the documents.

While discussing the problem with the king, a plan had been devised to bring in a forger to recreate the Genesis 3 account to prove to the scholars that the document attached to the thesis was a fake.

Tomas chuckled to himself as he remembered how hard the king had laughed about the plan.

"We are going to create a fake document to prove that the real document is a fake. How ironic?" the king roared with laughter. "My subjects are so gullible."

Tomas wasn't sure the scholars were as gullible as the king thought. The document would have to be carefully crafted to withstand their scrutiny.

Elmyr was the perfect candidate. A former art forger, Elmyr had spent twenty years in prison for forging checks and official government documents. Given his freedom when he agreed to work for the church, he'd forged thousands of documents on behalf of the king and church over the past twenty years. His work was so good, no one had ever been able to tell a fake from the original. Tomas was hoping for that same result now.

"As you can see," Tomas said, "several of the pages are blank on one side. Always at the end of one of the books. I want to use one of those pages to create the forgery."

"What do you want me to write on it?" When Elmyr did speak, a squeaky, quiet mouse-like voice was the best he could muster from his tiny frame.

Tomas handed him a page with some writing on it.

"I want you to write the page from Genesis 3 on this blank paper from the old manuscript," Tomas explained. "You need to change verse six. It says in the original, 'So she took some of its fruit and ate it; she also gave some to her husband, who was with her, and he ate it.'"

Elmyr looked up at Tomas, obviously contemplating the ramifications of what he'd just read to him.

Tomas was counting on the fact that Elmyr had no moral compass and would do anything illegal for money. Or the threat of death, if necessary.

Elmyr studied the document. "Is this what you want me to change it to?"

Tomas nodded without responding.

"Just so I'm clear." Elmyr paused with purpose. "You want me to change it to, 'So she took the apple and ate it; she also gave some to her husband, who was with her, but he refused to eat it.'"

Tomas simply stared at Elmyr. What he wanted him to do was truly clear as far as Tomas was concerned.

Elmyr chuckled. "I can do it. Double my usual fee."

Tomas bristled. The church and king didn't negotiate. Most people understood their options were to accept the price or suffer the consequences. It hardly mattered. Elmyr would be executed shortly after finishing his work anyway.

They were sitting in a room underneath the royal chamber containing the treasury of the church. A large room, dark, almost cave like, with only a chair and table in the middle. Large chest-like containers lined the walls, overflowing with coins, jewelry, gold, silver, and other precious jewels. The manuscripts had been stored there for safe keeping for two centuries.

Elmyr looked around at all the opulent wealth and stated his fee as his eyes widened, giving away that he was either impressed to be in the presence of so much excess or disgusted. Tomas didn't know which and didn't really care.

"The church no longer has to say silver and gold have I none," Tomas said smugly.

"The church also can no longer say to the lame, get up and walk," Elmyr retorted.

Rage built up inside him at the obvious insubordination.

As if reading his mind, Elmyr waved his hand dismissively and simply said, "I didn't mean anything by it. Let's get back to business."

"No one can ever see this original," Elmyr said, changing the subject. "They'll know it's a fake by examining the ink. I can make this look like the original, but I can't duplicate the ink. You need to print this so that no one can tell it's a forgery."

"I can do that. But, you must have it done by this Thursday."

Elmyr only had two days to finish it.

"It's better not to rush this," Elmyr said. "I can't make a mistake. If I try to make a correction on this paper, it'll be obvious it's a forgery. This takes time and much care to get it right."

"You have until this Thursday. Your fee will be triple the usual amount if you have it done by then."

Elmyr continued poring over the paper. He looked slightly over his glasses at Tomas and said, "I can have it done by Thursday."

"Excellent. Get this done, and you'll be a rich man."

Elmyr started to stand and leave, but Tomas stopped him.

"You can't leave this room," Tomas said sternly. "The work has to be done here. I can't tell you how sensitive this is. No word can be spoken to anyone. No documents can leave this room. I will have food and drink brought down to you and a bed to sleep on. Understood? A guard will be placed outside the room. If you try to leave, you'll be arrested immediately."

Elmyr sat back down with a big sigh.

"Remember," Tomas said. "Not a word to anyone."

* * *

Faniel and Nathanial, generally known as Fan and Nate—the two scholars who had stood to challenge the Josser at church the previous Sunday—were locked in a dungeon at the lowest level of the prison.

Nate had been tortured on two different occasions. So far, Fan had been left alone.

"What do you think they are going to do to us?" Nate said nervously.

"I think eventually they are going to kill us," Fan said soberly. "You shouldn't have brought up the king's adultery. I told you not to."

"I know," Nate said, straining to look at the untreated wounds on his back. "The king shouldn't be allowed to get away with these things." The torturers didn't seem interested in gathering information, but only in making him suffer.

Fan had been spared the punishment because he had merely challenged the church's teaching. A punishable offense, but one they must prove first.

"The thesis proves the church has been lying. We just need to keep putting pressure on them to try and disprove the thesis. When they can't, maybe that will be enough to save our lives."

"I'm prepared to die," Nate said with resolve.

Fan looked at his protégé with admiration. He reminded him of himself when he was a younger man and much more naïve. Years of living under the rule of the tyrannical king and church had not so much weakened Fan's resolve, just his optimism.

"I am too, but I prefer it be for a good purpose." Fan's wrist and legs were bound in chains. Little food had been given to them by the jailers, but they were allowed visitors who had brought them some scant food and water. The visits had buoyed their spirits as they learned the thesis had spread throughout the territories.

The church promised a response to the thesis by this weekend. Everyone had been anxiously awaiting it.

"They're keeping us alive until they can disprove the thesis," Fan said. "We have to keep the focus on the thesis and not on the king's adultery. You threaten the king, and he'll make you pay. As you have already seen."

Nate winced.

Fan changed positions, trying to get more comfortable and then continued. "Just challenging them to disprove the thesis isn't enough for them to execute us. The scholars would rebel, and the church knows that. Not worth the risk. The king can't execute us all. However, they will likely try to make an example of us so others will be reluctant to challenge the king."

"Who do you think wrote the thesis?" Nate asked.

"I don't know, but the writing was brilliant. Christopher is behind it somehow. He's the one who delivered it to the churches out in the territories. Probably the one who put it on our doorsteps. He's in hiding. I knew his father, Calvin. He would be proud of him. If Christopher is anything like his dad, I think another thesis is on its way."

"I had a dream last night," Nate said. "There were two men in a certain town, one rich and the other poor. The rich man had a large number of sheep and cattle. The poor man had nothing except one little baby ewe lamb. He raised it, and it grew up with him and his children. It shared his food, drank from his cup, and even slept in his arms. It was like a daughter to him."

Fan listened intently to the dream, fascinated by its detail.

"Now, a traveler came to the rich man," Nate continued. "The rich man refrained from taking one of his own sheep or cattle to prepare a meal for the traveler who'd come to him. Instead, he took the ewe lamb that belonged to the poor man and prepared it for the one who had come to him."

"Then what happened?" Fan asked.

"I woke up. What do you think it means? Do you think it's from the Lord?"

Fan's heart beat a little faster as he thought about it for a moment. "I think it is from the Lord."

"What?" Nate asked, his eyes wide.

"I know what the dream means," Fan said. "The rich man is the king."

* * *

At two o'clock in the morning, Theba paced nervously around the house like a cat circling its prey. She'd been unable to sleep for two days as she anxiously awaited the arrival of her husband, Jeriah.

He should've been here by now.

Tomas told her they sent for Jeriah immediately. A two-day's journey, he should have arrived yesterday. Something must have happened to him.

Theba kept going to the window and looking out. A range of emotions pulsed through her veins each time she did so. Wanting and longing to see her husband, and yet fearful because of what she had done, the secret she had locked in her heart. Every time she went to the window, her heart raced. By the time it calmed down, she went to the window again. So many mixed emotions.

Anxiety. Dread. Fear.

Balanced with Love. Hope. Excitement.

Desire for her husband's touch. She nervously ran her fingers through her hair. So many times, she had lost count. Frowning that he wasn't there. Then Theba smiled through the darkness, excited to know he would be there soon.

He'll make me feel better.

Maybe worse.

Would he know something was wrong? *Can I hide it from him?* They knew each other so well. Thoughts were bouncing around in her head with no restraint.

While she couldn't wait for him to take her in his arms and make love to her, she dreaded her response.

Could she hide the shame and the guilt? She felt like damaged goods. The stench of the vile king was still on her. Theba could still feel his touch. Wiping her mouth, she made a face of disgust. She remembered his kisses, but was trying desperately to forget them. The memory was etched in her soul forever. Guilt rushed through her like a tidal wave.

What did she have to be guilty about? The king forced himself on her. Rape. That's what it was. She didn't give herself willingly. Never would she have cheated on Jeriah if it hadn't been the king forcing himself on her.

If she hadn't... King Henry would've killed both of them. Would Jeriah understand?

He must never know.

For what seemed like the hundredth time, Theba walked to the window and looked out. The two moons of Mars were full and illuminating the night's sky. Theba jumped when she saw movement out of the corner of her eye.

Jeriah?

No. A young boy. Wearing a cap. Hiding in the Zobria bushes. *Be careful. Those bushes will cut you.*

What's he doing? Why is he hiding? Who is he hiding from?

At that moment, four soldiers came around the corner and searched in the bushes and behind trash containers. The boy had a panicked look on his face. Fear gripped his eyes. Nervously, he glanced furtively, looking for a way of escape. If he didn't move soon, they were going to catch him.

He's in trouble. Maybe he stole something and deserved to get caught. Maybe she should tell the soldiers where he was hiding.

As the soldiers neared, the boy bolted across the street to her front yard and ran behind a large bush right in front of the window where Theba was looking. She stepped back behind the curtain so as not to be seen.

That's not a boy. It's a girl. I know her. I've seen her at church.

Why is she in trouble? Why are the soldier's looking for her? The soldiers hadn't noticed her when she fled across the street. Only a matter of time until they found her.

I have to do something.

Theba cracked the door, careful not to make any noise.

"Quick," she said to the girl. "Come in here. Before they find you."

The girl's eyes widened with surprise. She looked back at the soldiers who were drawing nearer. Quietly, she slipped from behind the bushes and inched over to the door. Theba widened it enough for her to sneak through. Once safely inside, Theba closed the door, making more sound than she intended.

The girl shook from either the fear or the cold. Theba put her finger to her lips to caution her to keep quiet.

Theba went back over to the window to look out at the soldiers.

They're coming this way. Panic rose inside of her.

They must have heard something because they were headed straight for her house. They would arrest both of them if they found the girl there.

"Go to the back of the house and hide in my bedroom," Theba said urgently. "Stay out of sight. Don't make a sound. I'll get rid of the soldiers. Get in the bed like you're sleeping."

Someone pounded loudly on the door. They both jumped.

"Open up by the king's command," a soldier said in a loud, commanding voice.

The girl looked like she was about to cry. Theba gave her a quick hug and sent her on her way, whispering, "It's going to be okay. I'll get rid of them."

The pounding on the door grew louder.

"Open up or we'll break the door down."

Theba opened the door slowly, cracking it only enough to look outside.

"What is the meaning of this?" Theba said sternly. "Waking me up in the middle of the night. My husband is a Captain in the king's army. Why have you disturbed me?"

The soldier's tone changed at the mention of her husband.

"We saw a boy in this area. He's suspected of having something to do with the thesis. We saw him running in this direction. Have you seen anything?"

"No. I haven't seen anything. I was sleeping."

Another soldier spoke up. "I saw your door close. If you were sleeping, how could your door have closed."

"I heard a commotion. I came to look and cracked the door and looked out. I saw you, but I didn't see a boy."

"Do you mind if we search your house?"

"Of course, I mind," Theba said with conviction. "That would be highly inappropriate. I'm a married woman, home alone."

"Where is your husband?" the soldier asked.

"He's fighting the Cabenites. He's due back home any day. Perhaps you should come back another time when he's here."

"We have orders from the king to find anyone who had anything to do with the thesis. We've seen this boy several times running through the streets at night, but we haven't been able to catch him. I'm sure he came in this direction. I insist by orders of the king that you let us search your house. It's for your own safety."

"My husband outranks all of you. He will not be happy if you violate his house. I gave you my word that no one is in here."

"We must insist."

"You dare to defy my husband, a noble servant of the king? I insist you leave this minute."

"You dare to defy the king?" the soldier raised his voice. "You're a woman. You have no right to defy us. You must do as I say."

"What is the meaning of this?" a booming voice said from a distance.

Jeriah!

10

"Why are you yelling at my wife in the middle of the night?" Jeriah said sternly.

The men immediately stood at attention at the appearance of a captain in the king's army. An imposing man, six feet, four inches, broad shoulders, muscular arms revealed by his sleeveless shirt. One hand on his sword sent the message he was ready to fight them if necessary.

The men looked at each other as if to see who would be brave enough to speak.

"We were chasing a young boy through the streets," one of the soldiers said hesitantly. "We... saw him run into your house." He looked at Theba with a slight glare. "Your wife refused to let us search the house. We have orders from the king to find this boy."

Jeriah looked at Theba and smiled.

Her heart did several somersaults as he looked longingly at her with his dark eyes. *He's so handsome.*

He exhibited a rugged, unshaven beard from the journey and his dark hair was unruly and wild. She basked in the smile revealing a slight dimple on his left cheek. His look was comforting even though Theba was panicking inside. She couldn't tell her husband about the girl hiding in their house. Already, so many things she had to lie to him about. Could she lie about one more thing? She had to.

"Is that true?" Jeriah asked Theba. "Is there a boy hiding in the house?"

Theba's eyes widened. *I don't have to lie.* "No, my dear," Theba said sweetly. "There is no boy in this house."

"That's a lie," one of the soldiers said.

A swift backhand to his face, sent the soldier flying onto the lawn where he landed roughly on his back.

"Don't you ever call my wife a liar!" Jeriah said sternly. "My wife said there was no boy in the house. So, there isn't. Leave here right this minute before I throw you all off of my property."

The soldier picked himself up off the ground and reached for his cheek where blood trickled from his upper lip. The other soldiers quickly rushed down the sidewalk and onto the street without looking back or saying another word.

Theba ran out of the house and into Jeriah's arms. He held her to his chest. Stroking her head, she began sobbing. Tears soaked his shirt. He held her tighter, reassuring her that everything was okay.

The emotions of the past few weeks were flooding her soul.

Jeriah's words were the most upsetting. *Don't ever call my wife a liar.*

Yet she was. The secret she held inside could never be revealed. They would both die. At times, over the past few weeks, she almost convinced herself death was a better fate. If it was only her, she would rather die than give birth to the king's child. But she had to consider Jeriah.

Her husband's life was more important than hers. A great man, a captain, a warrior, a leader of men. He'd accomplished more in his young life than most would in a lifetime. He must never know the secret. Jeriah would raise the child like it was his own. She knew he would. He would never suspect.

"I... There is..." Theba tried to make herself tell him the truth about the girl.

"What, my darling?" Jeriah said lovingly as Theba pulled away from him slightly. "What's wrong?"

"I did lie to you. Well not really. Sort of..."

"What?" Jeriah said with a smile.

"There's not a boy in the house, but there is a young girl. I don't know who she is. The soldiers were chasing her. She was so scared. I let her into the house. I couldn't let them take her away. I'm sorry I lied to you."

"You didn't lie," Jeriah laughed. "I asked you if you were hiding a boy, and you said no. You weren't hiding a boy. Those men shouldn't have been yelling at you in the middle of the night anyway. If you felt like you needed to help the girl, then I trust you."

Theba smiled, finally feeling some comfort for the first time in weeks. She took Jeriah's hand and said, "You must be hungry. Come inside out of the cold and let me fix you something to eat."

He didn't move. A somber look came over his face as his eyes narrowed and his brow furrowed.

"Come," Theba said more urgently, pulling on his hand even though he was much too strong for her to move him.

"I... can't," Jeriah said, shaking.

"What do you mean? You're home now. Come be with me."

"My men..." Was all he said.

"What about your men?" Theba asked, unsure what he meant or what they had to do with him coming inside.

"The battle's not over. I don't know why the king sent for me, but my men are still fighting. I can't sleep inside with you when my men are sleeping in tents away from their wives."

The panic returned. Fear. Anger as well. The plan... How would it work if he doesn't come inside? If they don't lie together, he'll know it's not his child. She can't have him believing she cheated on him. *I would rather die...*

"You're the captain. Your men will understand. You didn't choose to come back here. The king sent you."

"No." Jeriah said more strongly. He quickly softened his tone.

"I can't. I would give anything to be with you. I've missed you so much."

"I've missed you too. I can hardly stand it when you're gone for so long. I need you. Come inside and be with me." Theba kissed him passionately, trying to entice him inside.

He kissed her back giving himself to the moment. Then he pulled back firmly yet gently.

"You must come inside..." Theba said, her lip quivering, her body shaking as fear gripped her. "You just must—"

"*As* you live, and *as* your soul lives, I will not do this thing," Jeriah said with resolve.

"You always were a stubborn fool," Theba said with slight anger. She patted him on the chest. "There's no way I can change your mind?" she asked.

He looked at her lovingly and sat down on the porch.

"I will sleep out here tonight and then go back to my men to-morrow."

Theba knew her husband well. Nothing she could do or say would change his mind. This was what made him such a great man. A wonderful husband. Loyal. Dependable. Faithful.

The guilt returned with a flood. Here she was carrying another man's child. Why couldn't she have the resolve he had? Why couldn't she have said no to the king?

I'm so ashamed.

"Let me go and make you something to eat and drink." Theba said, composing herself. "I'll be right back."

Jeriah reached up and took Theba by the hand and looked deeply in her eyes. "I can't eat your food and drink your wine while my men have to eat the food out in the open fields. I have some rations with me and some water. I'll be fine. The war will be over soon, and I'll be home. I promise."

"Can I bring you a blanket and a pillow?" she asked, already knowing the answer.

"I'll be fine." Jeriah took a coat out of his backpack and put it on. He then used it as a pillow and laid his head against it. He smiled and then closed his eyes to sleep.

Theba only nodded, her shoulders sagged, her eyes drooped as intense sadness overwhelmed her.

"Know that I love you," Jeriah said, looking up one last time before Theba went inside.

"I love you too," Theba said as she closed the door. Tears overflowed her eyes as she sobbed uncontrollably. Doubled over, the pain knifed through her chest like a sword, tearing her up inside. Her heart was breaking and there was nothing she could do about it.

What am I going to do?

* * *

Abbey came out of the back room and walked toward the woman who'd saved her. She took her by the hand and led her to the couch to sit down. Abbey used her shirt sleeve to wipe away the tears.

"What's the matter?" she asked.

The young woman was too distraught to speak.

"Is it because of me? I'm so sorry. Did I get you in trouble?"

The lady tried to speak, but the words didn't come. She shook her head no.

"I heard a man's voice. Sounded like the soldiers were fighting with someone. Who was he?" Abbey asked with a sense of urgency.

The woman of the house started crying harder.

"That was... my husband."

"Oh." Abbey said, not fully understanding. "Where's your husband?"

"He's sleeping outside on the porch," she said between sobs.

"Are you making him stay out there because of me? I should go." Abbey started to stand, but the lady grabbed her hand.

"It's not safe. The soldiers are still out there looking for you. They're probably watching the house. You need to stay here. What's your name and why were they chasing you?"

Abbey hesitated.

"They said you were responsible for the thesis they read at the church. Is that true?"

Abbey looked away. If she wanted to hide it, she was unable to.

The woman's eyes grew big and her tears stopped flowing for a moment. She took Abbey's hand.

Abbey started to pull away, but she held it tight.

"Don't worry. Your secret's safe with me. I won't tell anyone. My name is Theba. My husband's name is Jeriah. I like what you did with the thesis. That took a lot of courage."

Abbey's countenance changed as she beamed with pride.

"My name is Abbey. Abigail Whyburgh."

Abbey then proceeded to tell Theba the whole story. The Bibles. Christopher. The thesis. Another one coming this Sunday. The story spilled out of Abbey like a dam bursting. Like she had been wanting to tell someone. Anyone. Theba seemed like someone she could trust.

Theba listened with a look of amazement on her face. "How old are you?"

"Sixteen."

"You are so incredibly brave for your age. How did you learn to read?"

Abbey explained about her dad, mom, Zwilling, and her brother, Eck. Her father died. Her mother was sent to prison. Zwilling was so horrible to her. The beatings. She hated him.

Then Christopher. He helped her write the thesis. Distribute them to the scholars. She was in love with him. He's twenty-one. Good looking. Kind.

"You would like him."

Abbey couldn't stop talking. Theba was dutifully listening to every word. Seemingly fascinated. If she was bothered, she didn't show it.

"What about you?" Abbey said. "Why were you crying? Why is your husband outside?"

Theba's turn to let everything spill out.

The king. Forcing himself on her. Disgusting. A child.

"My husband, Jeriah. The love of my life. He was away—Captain in the army." Theba struggled to get the words out. She told Abbey about the plan concocted by the King and the Josser.

"My husband won't come inside. He said it's his duty to remain outside. He said, 'how can I enjoy being with you when my men aren't home with their wives? It wouldn't be right.'"

"Wow!" Abbey said in amazement. "He's so loyal."

"He's as stubborn as a mule," Theba said affectionately. Proudly even, though the words didn't match the obvious pride she had in the character of her husband. A sober look came on Theba's face as her eyes drooped and her shoulders sagged again.

"The king will kill both of us." Theba started to cry again. Abbey stood and walked over to the kitchen and grabbed a towel to give to Theba to dry her eyes.

"Why don't you tell him the truth?" Abbey asked.

A look of fear came over Theba's eyes.

"He would kill the king," Theba explained nervously.

"Just tell Jeriah the truth. He'll understand. He won't kill the king if he knew the king would kill you."

"I'm so ashamed. What if he blames me?" Theba's hands were red from where she was wringing them.

"He won't," Abbey said reassuringly. "He loves you. It's not your fault. The king is a pig. He deserves to die. What he did to you was horrible? Explain it to Jeriah. He'll understand."

"What if he won't forgive me?" Theba put her hands to her face.

"There's nothing for him to forgive you for," Abbey said gently. "You did nothing wrong. Go talk to him," Abbey implored.

"Maybe you're right. If I tell him, he'll go along with the plan. We have to face this together. It was wrong for me to lie to him to begin with. I need to tell him the truth."

"Yes!" Abbey said emphatically. "Go tell him. I'll stay here with you. Tell him he has to come inside. Both of your lives depend on it."

Theba wiped away the remaining tears as her demeanor changed. Her shoulders broadened. She sat up straight with resolve and a determined look on her face. She clenched her jaw and pressed her lips together. Her eyes steeled to form a look of courage.

Theba stepped to the door, opened it, and started to go outside. "Wish me luck," she said smiling back at Abbey, closing the door behind her.

A few seconds later, the door opened and Theba burst back inside.

"What?" Abbey asked.

"Jeriah's gone."

* * *

King Henry poured another glass of wine and handed it to Jeriah. They were both showing signs of the effect of the strong drink. The king had sent a servant to Jeriah's house to make sure he'd gotten there safely. The servant returned and informed the king that Jeriah was sleeping outside of the house. Infuriated, the king sent the servant back to the house to bring Jeriah to him.

"I was told that you wouldn't go in your house and lay with your wife. That's why I sent for you," the king said with a grin. "I wanted to reward you for your faithful service on the battlefield. Your wife's beautiful..." The king paused momentarily, remembering when Theba had been in his chamber. Made him want her again.

I'll send for her again after he goes back to battle. Maybe the next time will be better.

Henry was jolted back to reality by Jeriah's words.

"My men are dwelling in tents, the servants of my lord on the battlefield are sleeping in open fields. They are eating the military rations. Shall I then go to my house to eat and drink and to lie with my wife? I would never do such a thing."

I would. I would sleep with your wife again in a second. You wouldn't have to ask me twice.

The thought caused the king to momentarily lose his train of thought. So, he didn't say anything.

Get him drunk.

Maybe he wouldn't remember he hadn't laid with his wife if he was too drunk to remember the night.

He poured Jeriah another drink. Jeriah refused.

"Thank you, Your Majesty, but I cannot indulge in excessive drink while my men suffer in battle."

The king admired Jeriah's loyalty to him but was annoyed that he was openly defying him. Then it occurred to him, Jeriah's loyalty was with his men not the king. Jeriah was in defiance of his king!

I'm commanding him to lay with his wife. How hard is that? It's not like she's ugly.

"Jeriah. I appreciate your loyalty to your men. I really do. But I'm commanding you to go to your house and lay with your wife," the king said sternly. "You don't want to defy me on this. I'm your commanding officer. I'm the king. This is an order. Do you understand?"

Jeriah nodded and stood to leave then bowed respectfully. The king embraced him and sent him out.

The king called for a servant.

"Follow him and make sure he goes back to his house and then report back to me."

A few minutes later, the servant returned.

"Well?" the king said as he took a large gulp of wine.

"The captain did not go to the house."

"What?" the king said. "He dares to defy me. Where is he?"

"He went to the barracks where your guards sleep, and he fell asleep there."

The king threw his chalice at the servant. He ducked in time, but the chalice banged against the wall, creating a huge stain as wine spilled on the wall and the floor.

"What a fool! I gave him a chance. Now he must die."

11

Abbey and Christopher were hard at work in the basement putting the finishing touches on the new thesis entitled *Religious Remissions: The Heresy of the Penitential Canons of the Church.*

The first thesis was spreading throughout the territories, and the two of them could barely keep up with the demand for more copies. Along with the ninety-five churches in the territories, they had to print more than three hundred copies for leaders of the rebellion throughout the eastern territory of Mars. In addition, a copy was printed for every scholar this time, not just for the select few.

Sleep was hard to come by, and Abbey felt the effects of the strain. The work was in addition to all her normal chores she had to maintain at home. Fortunately, Zwilling was still suffering from his sickness, and barely paid attention to her. Still, she had to be careful not to get caught out at night or the punishment would be severe. The king had significantly increased the number of guards making nightly rounds, which made it all the more difficult for Abbey to move around undetected, as her close call with the soldiers the night before had reminded them all.

"So, it's true. The king committed adultery with one of his captain's wives." Christopher said as Abbey told him her entire encounter with Theba.

"We have to get this information out to everyone," Christopher said excitedly.

"No. We can't. I promised her I wouldn't tell anyone." Abbey said.

"The king has to be exposed," Christopher said sharply. "Nate's in jail because he confronted the king. Word is that he's been tortured. He and Fan might even be killed. We must do something to stop them. This information might save their lives."

Nate said it so strongly that Abbey was offended. He'd never spoken to her that way before. Anger rose inside of her.

"The woman was raped," Abbey said angrily, pausing to let those words sink in. "She had no choice. She's embarrassed and ashamed. Her husband doesn't even know about it. If we tell anyone, he'll find out. I can't do that to her. I won't let you."

"You won't let me?" Christopher chuckled as he spoke sarcastically.

Abbey glared at him, sending daggers through Christopher. To the point that he physically stepped back.

"This information could bring down the king." Christopher wouldn't let it go.

"You're not to tell anyone. Promise me," Abbey said with resentment in her voice. "If you do, I'll never speak to you again. She's my friend. You've no right to tell anyone what she told me in confidence." She was unsure how to fight with Christopher. They never had before.

She stood and moved closer to where Christopher sat and glared down at him.

"Promise me, you won't say anything. It's none of your business." Tears were forming in her eyes.

Christopher held both hands up in a sign of surrender. "Let's just focus on the thesis. We have enough to do as it is," Christopher said as he turned his attention back to the papers he was organizing.

"Fine!"

Abbey stormed away, her loud footsteps echoing through the basement as she went back to the printing press to check on the final printing.

Still angry, but feeling bad. It wasn't Christopher's fault. Any other circumstances and she would have agreed with him. Theba was different. A bond had formed between them that night. They knew each other's secrets, and they both seemed to understand what the other was going through. Both had a common enemy—the king. Abbey wouldn't do anything to hurt her more than she already was hurting. Christopher would just have to understand. The thesis was their fight. The scholars already knew something about the adultery. Let them confront the king. Abbey was hoping they weren't successful, for Theba's sake.

Doesn't the Bible say not to gossip. She remembered reading something about that. She made a mental note to bring that up to Christopher. Telling others was tantamount to gossip, and the Bible forbids it. One more argument to keep in mind if she needed it.

Thoughts turned to Theba and their conversation. She felt so bad for her. Abbey was determined to be there for her to the extent a sixteen-year old can be for an older married woman with such a complicated and dire circumstance. Theba had no friends she could talk to. Where could she turn? Who could she tell? Even telling Abbey was a risk, which Abbey realized when she told Christopher what had happened.

I wish I hadn't. I was gossiping. I broke her trust.

A whole range of emotions pulsed through her. Sadness for her and Theba. Fear of getting caught. Love for Christopher that had no future. A battle with the king she didn't know if they could win.

I'm just tired. I need to make up with Christopher. Say I'm sorry.

The strain was getting to both of them. They'd hardly had a moment to be alone together when they weren't working.

A touch on her shoulder. Abbey turned. Christopher placed both hands on Abbey's shoulders and looked deeply into her eyes. "I'm sorry, I spoke to you so harshly. Forgive me."

Abbey rocked back and forth, embarrassed like the sixteen-year old girl she was. *Stop it.* Sometimes she was so mature and other times she acted like a little schoolgirl. She patted him on his chest and said, "I'm sorry too."

"Do you want to kiss and make up?" Christopher said with a mischievous grin on his face. "It's our first fight you know. Except the first night when you almost took my head off."

They both laughed, easing the tension somewhat.

The kiss was warm and passionate. Sending a feeling of euphoria through her starting from her heart and permeating every part of her.

A new wave of emotions stirred inside as if her love for Christopher had lain dormant in a kettle which was her heart and was being stirred vigorously. Abbey hadn't realized how much she'd missed his embrace. His touch.

A booming voice from upstairs blaring through the intercom interrupted the moment. Eck had set up an intercom system, so they could hear when someone came into the shop upstairs. An extra layer of protection. In this case, a warning. An alarm.

The josser just came into the shop.

* * *

In the morning, King Henry sent for Jeriah who'd been sleeping with the guards, having never gone back to his house. The king sat on his chair in his bedchamber while Jeriah stood dutifully.

"Jeriah," the king said, "the battle for the city is taking too long. I want you to lead a siege on the city."

"Your Excellency," Jeriah explained, "I don't think that's a good idea." Jeriah hesitated, obviously trying to say the words carefully. "We're outnumbered. The best thing is to wait them out. They'll eventually run out of supplies, food, and water. We've cut off all of their supply routes. Once we've weakened them, they'll surrender without us having any loss of life."

"I don't think so," the king said more strongly. "I have confidence in you and your ability to lead men. The Cabenites continue to defy me, and they must be made an example of. If not, everyone will think they can defy the king and just hole up like cowards and wait us out. We must destroy them quickly and violently. Kill and plunder everyone in the city. Men, women, and children. Don't leave anyone alive, and then burn the city."

"Kill everyone?" Jeriah asked hesitantly.

"Yes. Make an example of them all. Can you do it?"

Jeriah didn't answer.

"Can you do it?" the king shouted, his tone turning confrontive. "I thought you were a great warrior. Perhaps, I've overestimated your ability to lead my men."

Jeriah stiffened and stood at attention.

"No, Your King," Jeriah said with determination. "I'll lead your people to a great victory. Thank you for your confidence in me."

Jeriah started to leave, but the king stopped him.

"I want you to lead the way," the king said. "You ride at the front. Let the men see your courage."

The idea came to the king overnight, that he could order Jeriah into battle where he would certainly be killed. No way they could overtake the city. Too well fortified. Jeriah's strategy was the right one. They should wait them out.

The king had more important motives. If Jeriah were killed in battle, the king could take Theba as his own wife. He'd make her queen and then lay with her and when the baby was born everyone would think it was his and that she conceived after she became queen. If it was a boy, he could actually become the heir he didn't have.

A brilliant plan given to me by God.

The king knew Jeriah was too proud of a man and a mighty warrior to not follow his instructions.

As if on cue, Jeriah said, "You can count on me. I will make you proud and secure for you a great victory."

The king embraced him.

With any luck, you'll be dead soon, and I can have your beautiful wife.

* * *

Eck heard the sound of the bell notifying him of a customer entering the shop. He rounded the corner from his office where he'd been working on paperwork. The thesis had put him behind on his regular business. He tried not to react when he saw the customer was the josser carrying some papers.

A wave of fear exploded inside. Everything in Eck's being wanted to go back into his office and hide. He'd expected the josser might send soldiers to search the shop since he would be a prime suspect in the printing of the thesis. No search had ever come. The last thing he expected was for the josser to walk in by himself.

Further intrigue occurred when the josser locked the door behind him and turned the open sign over to closed.

"Eck, my dear friend," the josser said in a loud booming voice. So loud it was almost like he was giving his sermon at the church. The josser reached out his hand, and Eck took it in his as the josser shook it vigorously.

Why is he being so friendly? Is it a trap?

"Your honor," Eck said in his most friendly voice.

Why are you here? Get out of my shop, Eck wanted to say next but bit his lip hoping the josser didn't see it.

Instead, he said, "It's an honor that you have visited me twice in six weeks. What can I do for you today?"

Eck had heard that the josser suspected him of printing the thesis. At least at first. The josser had contacted all the suppliers of ink to see if Eck had purchased any large quantities. Anticipating the inquiries, Eck developed a formula for making his own. It allowed him to produce large quantities of ink from common ingredients that the josser would never expect or inquire about. Also, it cost a third of regular ink, saving them a lot of money.

Rumor was that the josser had scholars loyal to the king examine the thesis with other documents printed by Eck. When they didn't match, it further proved to the josser that Eck wasn't behind the thesis. The josser had no way of knowing about the hidden printing press in the basement where Abbey and Christopher were no doubt listening to them as they spoke.

Eck was pleased when he heard he'd been ruled out as a suspect and now, apparently, the josser needed him for something very important.

Eck would use to his advantage the fact that the josser trusted him. A good way to get information.

The josser lowered his voice slightly.

"Is anyone else here?" the josser asked leaning over the counter and peering around the corner to see into the office.

"No. I'm alone. And as always, whatever work I do for you is strictly confidential. Did you ever find out who printed the thesis?" Eck asked with the right amount of curiosity.

"We have not. I think it's being printed out in the eastern territory somewhere. Do you have any ideas who might have done this?"

Eck just shrugged his shoulders.

A grin came on Tomas's face. "You know, at first, I thought you did it."

The josser stared into Eck's eyes, obviously looking for any sign of guilt.

Maybe he doesn't completely trust me.

"Me?" Eck said with a grin and the right amount of dismissiveness. "I would never do such a thing. My father and I have faithfully served the king for years. It's outrageous that someone would produce a forgery and accuse the king of such despicable things." Eck put the emphasis on despicable. He got his point across at how despicable the king's behavior was without letting on that he really believed they were.

"Agreed," the josser said. "That's why I've come today. You can help me right this wrong." He pulled out some papers.

Eck glanced at them not trying to be too obvious about his extreme curiosity.

"What I have here is the original copy of the Genesis 3 story from a manuscript written in 70 M.A. A.C." The josser paused as he turned the page toward Eck.

Rather than touching it, Eck pulled out some gloves and carefully began inspecting it. He quickly glanced to verse sixteen and read it to himself. "She took the apple and ate, and she also gave some to her husband who was with her, and he refused to eat it."

Eck was amazed at the handiwork of the forger. Elmyr Fiori was the only one who could have produced such a work. Eck couldn't tell it apart from the original. If he didn't already know it was a fake, he would never be able to tell. The paper also came from that time period. He surmised that they took a blank page from the original. *Ingenious plan.*

The ink was obviously not the same, but he didn't dare say anything.

"This certainly disproves the thesis," Eck said. "What would you like for me to do?" Eck asked, already dreading the answer he knew was coming.

"I need for you to print copies for me to distribute to the scholars on Sunday."

"I don't know if I can have it by then." Eck was trying to think of something to delay the distribution. The second thesis would be distributed Sunday, and he didn't want a competing document that could disprove both. The document in his hand would destroy all the credibility of the writers of the thesis. Any further theses would be assumed to be heresy, and pressure would mount to find the culprits.

"That's unacceptable," the josser said as his entire demeanor changed. "I must have it by tomorrow."

"With all due respect, Your Honor," Eck explained, "if I rush this, the roller could damage the original. Something this valuable must be handled with great care."

Eck continued without giving the josser a chance to respond. "I also have to make sure the ink doesn't bleed through on this paper. I've never copied anything this old." Eck, of course, was lying. He had printed copies from the original his dad had stored without doing any damage to the original.

"The copy must show that the paper is older. I can do that through my printing press. We must take great care to preserve the document so we can disprove the thesis," Eck said as he narrowed eyes trying to put on his most serious face.

"I agree that care must be taken to preserve this document. Still, I must have it tomorrow."

"Of course," Eck said, not wanting to let the josser see the panic that was rising inside of him and would soon explode through his countenance.

You have to hold it together.

Just as quickly as he entered, the josser left. Eck locked the door behind him and kept the closed sign up. He turned off the lights, took the Genesis 3 page in his hand, and hurried to the basement.

We have less than twenty-four hours to come up with something. If I print this document, it will ruin everything.

12

"We can't print this," Abbey said holding the forgery in her hand. "It will ruin everything. All of our work would be for nothing. We can't let the king win. We just can't." Abbey stomped her foot as she said it with animated hand gestures.

Christopher was standing off in a corner with his hand to his chin deep in thought.

"I don't have a choice," Eck retorted. "If I don't print it, Tomas will have me thrown in jail or worse."

Nothing was said for a good minute or two. Abbey started to break the silence, but Christopher interrupted her.

"What if there was a way to sabotage the document?"

Abbey nodded excitedly in agreement.

"I thought about that," Eck said, "but how do we do that without me losing my head. I could ruin the document through the printing process, but the josser would be furious and blame it on me. They would just make another one and get someone else to print it."

"Could we delay it past Sunday?" Abbey asked. "We need to get the second thesis out. Tell the josser your printing press broke down, you ran out of ink, you... whatever." Abbey was speaking so fast and so nervously, it was almost incoherent at times.

"I tried that already. He said in no uncertain terms that it must be ready by tomorrow."

Christopher walked across the room and took the document from Abbey and studied it carefully then set it back down.

"This really is an amazing forgery. You can't tell it's not real. This is only Genesis 3. They didn't make a forgery of the other verses they changed." Christopher said.

"They don't have to," Eck said. "All they have to do is disprove one of our pages. Then they can say all of them are fake. The worst part is Fan and Nate will be executed after they distribute this. That will be all the proof the josser needs to kill them."

"The scholars won't believe him," Abbey interjected.

"Some won't. But most will," Christopher said soberly. "The leaders of the opposition out in the territories won't believe it, but they were already resisting the king. This won't make any difference to them. We can keep giving them theses and they will believe them, even preach them. We just won't get much help from the scholars. They don't want to end up like Fan and Nate."

"There must be something we can do," Abbey said with her lips quivering.

Christopher's eyes widened noticeably.

"What?" Eck said. "Do you have an idea?"

"Could we alter the document just enough to where it's obvious it's a forgery, but no one would know that we did it. Something so minute, so small, that the scholars would catch it, but the josser wouldn't."

"What do you have in mind?" Eck asked.

"Nothing," he said with exasperation. "I'm just trying to come up with something, anything..." His voice trailed off.

Abbey stood up and started jumping up and down excitedly.

"We could...I know what we can do...We can make a..." She was so excited she was making no sense.

"Just calm down," Christopher said with a smile. "Take a deep breath and tell us your idea."

Abbey took a deep breath and then started talking fast and incoherently again. Christopher took her by the hand and led her to a chair and made her sit down. She bolted right back up out of the chair and went over to the manuscript and picked it up.

Abbey took a deep breath. "We could put a comma in the manuscript."

Eck started to respond but stopped obviously considering the idea.

Commas weren't used in manuscripts until the sixth century when Josephilus used them for the first time to create pauses in sentences to make them more readable. Aristophanus used dots in the third century A.D. to separate words. The dot was placed at the top, middle, or bottom of the line. Josephilus created the mark that was commonly used today.

"Abbey, you're brilliant," Eck said.

"I know, right." Abbey was beaming with pride.

"Eck, can you duplicate the ink?" Christopher asked.

"Enough to where you can't tell a noticeable difference. All the better if you can tell a slight difference. More proof it's a forgery. All we have to do is place one comma in one spot that is not noticeable. The scholars are going to scour this document and examine it over and over again. Someone will catch it. We just have to hope the josser doesn't."

"He probably won't even look at it," Christopher said. "When he realizes what happened, he will think that the forger did it. He won't blame it on us. We just printed what he brought to us. He should have examined it more carefully."

"Great idea, Abbey," Christopher said. "That way there's no doubt that the document is a forgery."

They huddled together in a group hug.

"I'll get to work on this right away," Eck said.

"This is going to work," Abbey said excitedly.

* * *

Jeriah sat in his tent with Beno, his second in command, reviewing the orders from King Henry to attack the city where the Cabenites lived. Jeriah and Beno rose through the ranks of the army together and had been close friends since the training academy. Strong and courageous, Beno had killed eight hundred men by himself in one battle making a name for himself as one of Jeriah's mighty men.

"This is a suicide mission," Beno said throwing the orders on the ground in disgust.

Jeriah only nodded looking off in a distance.

"It says that you are to lead the battle. Why does the king want you to be in the heaviest fighting? You're much too valuable a captain. We should wait until the supplies have run out in the city and they will surrender," Beno implored.

"These are the king's orders," Jeriah said soberly. "Assemble thirty-seven valiant men and have them meet me at the front lines at the first light tomorrow. Choose men who don't have wives and kids at home."

Beno hesitated. "This also says you are to kill all the men, women, and children in Caben."

"I will not do that," Jeriah said strongly. "This is the first and last order I will ever defy of my king."

Jeriah moved closer to Beno so he was looking him directly in the eye.

"Listen to me carefully. I will not likely survive the battle. We probably won't be able to take the city either. However, if we should somehow succeed and take the city, I give strict orders that the men are not to kill the women and children. You are also not to loot their supplies. Leave them with enough food and water to survive. Don't burn down their homes..." Jeriah's voice trailed off.

"What if the king's wrath rises when I tell him you didn't follow his orders?" Beno asked.

"Just tell him, 'Your servant, Jeriah is dead also.'"

For whatever reason, the king wants me dead. That should appease him.

All the way back to camp, Jeriah had tried to figure out why the king had ordered him to attack the city. Nothing about the mission made sense. Taking the city was impossible at this time and the king knew it. While the king had done many irrational things before, this time seemed different. Like he specifically wanted Jeriah to be on the front lines and attack the city.

Like he wants me to die...

Was it because I defied him and wouldn't lay with my wife? It's all so strange that he sent for me anyway. He insisted I go be with my wife and was furious when I wouldn't. Why would he even care? He said it was to reward me, but that doesn't make any sense. It has to be something else. Everyone was acting strangely. Even Theba...

The thoughts still made no sense.

Beno didn't understand the orders either and kept resisting trying to talk Jeriah out of it. "Jeriah," Beno said, "you have a wife. Why should you be the only one with a wife in the front of the battle? This is not right."

Jeriah placed his hand on Beno's shoulder.

"You have always served me well, good friend. I'm making you a Captain. You will take over for me when I'm gone."

"No." Beno said emphatically, his voice cracking. "You're not going to die. As God lives, so shall you. Let me fight with you. I will die with you."

"You are such a good friend and brave soldier. The men will need you after I'm gone. You must lead them as I have. Stay here. If we are somehow successful and are able to break through the city gates, then attack. Otherwise, stay behind and report back to the king that the mission was a failure. Don't send your armies as reinforcements unless you see that we are successful. I don't want to destroy our entire army because of a foolish order."

Beno began to speak like he was going to protest. Instead, Jeriah reached into his pocket and pulled out a piece of paper and handed it to Beno.

"Please give this note to Theba," Jeriah said. "Read it to her. Tell her that I love her and I'm sorry I broke my promise to her." Tears welled up in Jeriah's eyes.

"What promise did you break?" Bono said.

"I told her I would be home soon..."

* * *

The thesis on Religious Remissions was nailed to the door of the Vandenberg Church and distributed to more than three hundred scholars. Hundreds of copies were printed and distributed in the eastern territory and more than a hundred were nailed to the door of churches throughout Mars. Christopher had fallen into his chair exhausted from the effort.

Abbey had a copy in her hand and was reading it aloud and admiring their handiwork even though they had read it dozens of times.

Religious Remissions, The Heresy of the Penitential Canons of the Church.

Out of love for the truth and from desire to elucidate it, Martian Luther, an ordinary lover of God and Mars presents the following statements and demands those who dispute them to present proof of their fallibility.

1. The king has no authority to remit any penalties for sin or remit any guilt, except by declaring and showing that it has been remitted by God.

2. The king acts ignorantly and wickedly, by imposing monetary remission to the church for remission of sin.

3. When the king uses the words "full remission of sins," he is only talking about the sins he has imposed himself.

4. Only God can forgive sins according to Jesus.

5. It is certain that when money clinks in the king's money chest, greed and avarice can be increased; but when a humble man repents, the result is in the hands of God alone.

6. Any truly repentant Christian has a right to full remission of penalty and guilt, even without religious remissions from the church.

7. People on Mars have erroneously been taught by the church to think that religious remissions are preferable to other good works of love.

8. Repentance of sin and absolution for guilt are available to all people on Mars, men, and women alike.

9. Christians should be taught that giving to the church is voluntary and not an obligation.

10. The king and those who forbid the teaching of God's word are enemies of Christ.

11. Christians should be confident in entering into heaven by faith in Christ rather than in works demanded by the church.

12. The true treasure of the church is the most holy gospel of the glory and grace of God.

Signed, Martian Luther.

"I can't wait to see the look on the Josser's face this morning at church," Abbey said with a wide grin on her face.

Christopher did not seem to share her excitement. Distributing the thesis had been much more dangerous the second time around. Soldiers were out in force and Eck and Christopher had to carefully avoid getting caught carrying the documents. Both had several close calls. Two soldiers were in front of the josser's house, so Eck didn't leave a copy this time. Too dangerous.

"Just as well," Eck had said. "Let him be surprised when he gets to church."

Sensing something was wrong Abbey stood and walked over to where Christopher was sitting and took his hand. "What's wrong?" she asked.

"Don't forget that the Josser will be delivering his fake document today," Christopher replied. "He's going to try and discredit both of the theses as forgeries." Christopher's eyes drooped as he said it and his shoulders sagged. "This battle is far from over," he said somberly.

"Yeah, but they will find the comma. They have to. When the scholars confront the josser about the comma, they will know that his document is the real forgery. That will be even more proof that the king and the church are lying."

Abbey was the optimist in the relationship. She often implored Christopher to not be so pessimistic. He always insisted that he was realistic, not pessimistic. Nothing could dampen Abbey's enthusiasm even Christopher's mood. He was just tired, and she was so proud of how hard he had worked.

"Let me rub your shoulders," she said as she stood and walked behind him and began rubbing hard wanting to release the tension in his shoulders and between them.

"We can't get overconfident," Christopher continued. "What we're doing is extremely dangerous. I worry about you every time you go out at night. What if Zwilling catches you?"

"He won't. He's still sick. Most of the time he stays in bed."

Zwilling still had a bad cough and was so weak he rarely came out of his bedroom. A nurse had been hired to care for him full time during the day. A strong medicine put him to sleep at night.

"How's Theba?" Christopher asked, changing the subject. Abbey quit rubbing his shoulders and pulled her chair next to him.

"She's worried," Abbey said. "She hasn't heard anything from Jeriah. Last night when I stopped by, she was crying. Something about a feeling she had that something was really wrong. She thinks the king is going to have Jeriah killed."

"I wouldn't put it past him. He's not going to let it go. I don't think he would kill Jeriah on his own. He has to have a reason. All of his army would rebel against him if he did something like that. The king is too smart to let that happen. Knowing him, he's plotting something. He'll probably try to make it look like an accident. Jeriah needs to be warned."

A look of fear crossed Abbey's face. "Theba would just die. She's already starting to show a little. I don't know what would happen to her if something bad happened to Jeriah."

"You're a good friend to her. Just keep telling her everything is going to be alright." Christopher said it as if he didn't really believe it.

Abbey's eyes widened as she bolted up from her seat.

"What time is it?" Abbey asked.

"I don't know, but it's getting close to sunrise. You need to get going."

Abbey gathered her things, kissed Christopher quickly on the cheek and headed for the back door at the end of the tunnel.

"Be careful," he said as the door closed behind her.

13

Fan and Nate were awakened by the sound of prison doors opening, as the steel doors clanging together sent a crescendo of dreaded noise throughout the prison. Still dark out, they could think of no good reason why the guards were coming to their cell.

Groggy and barely able to sit up from the untreated, infected wounds, Nate only mustered enough strength to turn his head to look at the prison doors.

Fan jumped to his feet and stood in front of Nate as if he could somehow protect him from the fate he'd long since resigned himself to. The torture had mercifully stopped, but they both knew the soldiers could come at any time to take them to their deaths.

When he saw the figure in the doorway—not a guard but the Josser himself—Nate found the strength to sit up.

The Josser held a handkerchief over his nose from the vile and rank smell of the prison with one hand. He held papers in his other hand.

"To what do we owe this honor?" Nate asked sarcastically. "Have you come to apologize?"

Fan glared at Nate as if to say that he was making things worse with his obvious scorn. They had argued about this. From Nate's perspective, things couldn't get any worse. Fan said that wasn't true. Things *could* get much worse. They probably were about to.

"I see you still haven't repented," the josser said with a sly grin on his face. "Doesn't matter. I have in my hands your death sentence signed by the king. I wanted to deliver it in person and see your faces as I give it to you."

Neither gave a reaction. They weren't going to give him the satisfaction.

If the josser noticed, he didn't say anything.

"I also have in my hands proof that the thesis is a forgery and a hoax. I wanted you to read it before you die."

The josser handed two pieces of paper to one of the guards and instructed him to give one copy to each prisoner.

Nate gingerly stood to his feet, his legs wobbly but determined to stand. Nate took the paper and began reading it. The forged copy of Genesis 3. A look of resignation came upon Fan's face as the two looked up from the paper and at each other. No words were necessary to know what the other was thinking.

"As you can see, this is a copy of the original manuscript of Genesis 3," the josser said with glee in his voice. "This proves once and for all the thesis is a lie, and Adam did not eat the apple. It will be distributed to all of the scholars today at church. The perpetrators of this blasphemy on the church will be hunted down like dogs and executed just like you are going to be."

"You lie," Nate shouted. "This document is a fake." The josser motioned for the guard to strike Nate which he seemed reluctant to do so he just pushed Nate to the ground. Chains eerily echoed through the dungeon. Nate started to speak again.

Fan held his hand in the air trying to silence Nate.

Nate paid no attention. "This is obviously a forgery," Nate said. "How'd you do it? You got someone to change the Bible so you could keep your lie going. I don't know how, but God will eventually expose your lies."

The josser was surprisingly restrained.

"I have a document in my hand." The josser waved it in the air. "It's a confession. Let me read it to you."

I Nathanial Beaumont swears by the almighty God that the thesis is a forgery, and I confess to my blasphemy. Adam did not eat of the apple, and I am guilty of high treason for opposing the church and its teachings and accept my fate.

"I will never sign that," Nate said angrily. "It's a lie. The thesis is real. This document you gave us today is the forgery."

The josser did not raise his voice but said sternly, "You see how grievously you have offended his Majesty. Yet he is so very merciful, that if you will lay aside your obstinacy and change your opinion, then your death will be swift and painless. If you persist and refuse to repent of your sin, then you, Faniel, will be thrown into the lion's den and will die a slow and painful death at the lion's hand. You Nate, will be drawn, quartered, disemboweled in the square, and burned at the stake."

Nate stood again to face his accuser, resolve building inside of him. "I'll never sign it. God has given me a dream about the king. I demand to tell it to him. The king must repent, or God will take his life."

The josser moved across the cell with amazing swiftness and struck Nate in the face, sending him sprawling backward, his chains clanging against the wall. For a moment, everything went black and Nate could not see to stand. The josser stood over him as rage filled his entire body; his shoulders tensed, his jaw clenched, his fist balled ready to strike again.

"You are an apostate. God would never give you a dream or speak to you. Your very words are blasphemous and condemn you to hell."

Nate shook his head from side to side trying to clear his senses. Fan reached for his friend, but the guard placed a spear between him and Nate. Fan stepped back.

The josser looked at Fan. "Do I assume that you refuse to sign it as well?"

A somber look came over Fan's face. "I would never blaspheme the king unless I was sure that he was wrong. I don't know which document is a forgery, yours or Martian Luther's. One obviously is. I cannot sign the confession not knowing for sure. My conscience would not allow it even if I were to benefit in my mortal body. I'm not afraid to die. If my cause is unjust, and my words blasphemous, the king will condemn my soul to hell, and I will have deserved it. If my cause is righteous, God will somehow reward me in the life to come."

"You're a fool. You have a wife and four kids. Sign this document, and I'll see that your death is quick, and your family won't have to see you suffer. The king has even agreed to absolve you of your sin and not condemn you to hell."

The josser shoved the confession into Fan's hands. "Sign it! Or I will have you thrown into the lion's den this very morning."

"With all respect, sir, I cannot sign it. I am the king's good servant, but I am God's first. I have been sentenced to die as a traitor, but none of this has been proven. If I had as many lives as I have hairs on my head, I would willingly give them all for what I believe in. Even if Genesis 3 is a forgery, the king has not dealt righteously with the people. He oppresses them with religious remissions. A second thesis proves it."

A look of surprise came over the josser's face as his eyebrows raised, obviously not knowing about the existence of the second thesis.

Fan continued, not waiting for a reaction. "Women are treated as property rather than as children of God. You cannot ignore the other truths of either thesis. For that just cause, I willingly die if it be God's will."

The josser tensed with increasing anger as Fan spoke each word.

"Seize him!" he shouted. "Have him thrown in the lion's den without delay."

With those words, the josser stormed out of the cell, ripping the confession papers in disgust.

* * *

Abbey slipped out the back tunnel, looking both ways to make sure no one was in the alleyway leading to the road. Soldiers were looking for a young boy wearing a cap, so Abbey tucked her hair into a thick coat. She carefully made her way from building to building, avoiding the main roads where the soldiers were patrolling.

The front of Theba's house was being watched carefully, so Abbey avoided that area. A backway had been discovered which allowed her to come and go without detection. She visited Theba almost every night, the time together bringing encouragement to both. However, the sun would be rising soon, so she had no time to stop by that night. She would see her in church in just a few hours when the new thesis would, no doubt, create quite a stir. Theba knew all about it and was as excited as Abbey to see more opposition to the horrible king.

Still no word from Jeriah, which was troubling to Theba. Often, weeks went by without hearing from him, so it didn't necessarily mean anything bad had happened. However, the word was that Jeriah was going to lead a siege of Caben. Abbey had tried to reassure her as much as possible. The captains were generally kept out of harm's way, so Theba tried not to worry.

Abbey tried to put those thoughts out of her mind. She needed to concentrate on getting home safely.

Soldiers were on nearly every main street as she attempted to navigate back to her house, having to take an indirect route, exposing her to the soldiers longer than she would have liked. The thought occurred to her that after today, when the new thesis was revealed, it may even be impossible for her to continue to be out at night. The odds of her discovery were too great.

Rain was rare on Mars, but clouds often filled the sky, and tonight they were blocking the light of the moons making her harder to see in the shadows. Abbey started to relax as she neared the road to her house.

Suddenly, a voice from behind yelled, "Stop!"

A soldier!

Abbey panicked but turned and faced the soldier. The night was colder than usual, and she tightened the coat around her which would be a normal thing to do given the frigid night.

Maybe he won't be able to tell I'm a girl.

"Sir," Abbey lowered her voice to try and sound like a boy. "I must hurry to the church. I am the josser's ring bearer, and I must get to the church and polish the bell before the josser arrives. I must hurry."

The soldier was shivering from the cold and didn't make a move toward her or ask any more questions. He seemed satisfied with her response.

He simply said, "You can be on your way. Let us know if you see anyone suspicious."

Abbey nodded and turned, letting out a slight exhale of relief. As she did, the hood fell off her head exposing her long hair. She quickly reached to tuck it back in, but it was too late. The soldier had already seen it. He reached for her and grabbed her arm but couldn't get a good grip because of the thickness of the coat.

She let out a scream and took off running. The soldier was right behind her. Abbey rounded a corner and slipped and fell from red sand that had gathered at the intersection. Fortunately, the soldier slipped as well. He tried to kick her with his right foot as he was falling, but she rolled away as the kick barely missed her head.

Anger temporarily replaced the fear and for a moment, she thought about kicking him but instead used the opportunity to run away, trying to put as much distance between them as possible as he struggled to regain his footing.

The soldier was bigger and stronger, but Abbey was quicker and more agile. Her light frame allowed her to serpentine through the buildings, making it harder for the soldier to get a good angle on her. For a moment, Abbey lost him as she ducked onto a side street behind several stone buildings. She might have been in the clear but two other soldiers heard the commotion and were coming toward her from the other direction.

Abbey was trapped in the alleyway.

She looked around, quickly assessing her dire situation.

The soldiers were cautiously approaching her. Two from one direction, and the first soldier from the other as he blocked her only way out.

Houses lined the alleyway. Abbey made the quick decision that her only chance was to scale one of the houses and get on the roof. Made of stone, the rocks on the side of the house provided small crevices that could be used for footing. At the same time, the rocks were smooth and slippery. She'd have to be careful or she'd slip off the rocks and fall to the ground.

She leaped onto the windowsill of the nearest house. The soldiers sprinted toward her as she barely climbed out of their reach. One reared back and threw his spear at her. Abbey let out a shriek. Seeing the spear coming toward her, she almost lost her focus and grip on the rock.

The spear bounced off her coat, causing a slight tear but not penetrating through to her skin.

A soldier was able to get onto the windowsill. He reached for her foot and gripped it. She kicked his hand off of her causing him to lose his balance and fall back to the ground. The height of the house was only ten feet or so, and Abbey was on the roof before the soldier could regain his footing and get back on the sill.

The houses were close enough together that she could jump from one to the other. They went in several different directions, so Abbey had the advantage. The soldiers couldn't see her and wouldn't know which way she was going. Had they followed her on the roof, they might have caught her right away. Instead, they searched from the ground and waited for her to jump off somewhere.

The pause in the chase allowed Abbey time to take a deep breath. Her pulse was racing, and her heart was beating hard against her chest. The breath energized and calmed her enough to not act impulsively. The soldiers were no doubt trying to set a trap for her.

The pre-dawn sun now made it easier for them to see her, but if she could hide long enough for the sun to rise, then she could walk normally down the street.

Thinking the soldiers would never suspect her to stay on the roof, Abbey jumped from house to house until she found a good hiding place. The soldiers would search for her on the ground and not on the roofs. She could hear them shouting in the distance, but none were near her.

Another concern was to not make too much noise on the roof. Her footsteps were no doubt echoing in the houses below. She didn't want a homeowner coming out to try and find the source of the commotion, giving away her position.

She turned her coat inside out. The inside layer was red. Not ideal. Red would draw attention to her. However, they would be looking for a girl in a blue coat, so red was better than the blue.

From her hiding place, she could see the square where a number of soldiers had gathered to organize a search. Within a few minutes, the soldiers left to take care of their other responsibilities that came with first light. They probably assumed she'd already escaped.

Panic set in again as Abbey realized she had to get home before Zwilling awoke. He generally slept late, but this was Sunday. He could very well get up early to go to church.

She couldn't hide any longer. *I have to get home.*

She went to the far side of the roof out of the sight of the soldiers and slipped off the side, allowing herself to fall the ten feet and landed with a thud. She rolled over, and tried to lessen the fall. Abbey stood and brushed herself off. Satisfied that she was okay, she set out walking to her house only a few blocks away. She slipped over the fence at the back of her property, and for the first time since she could remember, she allowed herself to relax. The lights were off in the house, so Zwilling was still asleep.

The back door was creaky and old, and she had to be careful not to make too much noise. She slipped through the back door and shrugged off her coat without a sound that might wake him. Even if he woke up, at that point, she could just pretend she'd been there all night and was making breakfast.

Tiptoeing, she walked down the hall and around the corner to the kitchen.

As she did, a figure from behind startled her.

Zwilling.

He grabbed her hair and threw her to the ground while maintaining his grip on her hair.

"Where have you been?" he said, his voice filled with rage, his grip tightening around her.

Abbey screamed as he dragged her by the hair into the other room.

14

The guard led Faniel out of the prison and across a large courtyard. As they neared a series of entrances that led to the area that held the lions, the beasts roared. Each entrance was for an individual room with a steel gate separating the room from the lions. Fan's hands were bound with chains, but his legs had been freed so he could walk unencumbered.

The guard was apologetic. "Fan, I'm sorry," Dar said, "You don't deserve this. Surely, you are a righteous man." His voice shook as he spoke the comforting words.

Dar had watched over Fan and Nate for several weeks. So moved by their faith, he had asked them to pray for his child who was near death. When the child recovered, Dar attributed it to their prayers and had become sincerely sympathetic to their plight. Even sneaking food to them at times. Convinced they were wrongly accused, he defended them to the other guards. How could men guilty of blasphemy toward God, pray to God and have their prayers answered?

Many of the other guards believed too, although some were skeptical. Dar had said, "Whether these men are sinners or not, I don't know. What I do know is that my daughter was near death, and now she is alive and well."

As fate had it, Dar now led Fan to his death. He seemed more distraught than Fan. Barely able to choke back the tears, he tried to find the words that would make things better.

"You're only doing your duty." Ironically, Fan tried to comfort Dar. "Don't be troubled. God will deliver me from the lion. Even if he doesn't, I trust my soul to God's hand. You're a good man, Dar. Serve the king dutifully but serve God and your family more faithfully. I will pray that God will comfort you and not hold this charge against you."

Fan attempted to lift his hands and place them on Dar's shoulder, but they were bound by the chains, and his movement was restricted.

Dar noted the gesture and nodded with a word of thanks.

Fan walked with his head held high and his shoulders back.

Dar was slumped over, his head hanging, obviously distraught. He lifted his hand to his face to wipe away a tear.

"It's okay, my friend," Fan said. "If you faint in the day of distress, how small is your strength! God will rescue the one who is unjustly accused. Either in this world or in the world to come."

"Look at me. I'm the one crying," Dar said, managing a slight grin. "You're the one comforting me, and I'm about to do this horrible thing."

Dar's eyes widened as he glanced furtively around the courtyard. "I could help you escape," he said in a whisper. Other guards were milling about but hardly seemed to notice them. "You're my prisoner," he continued. "No one would say anything if I walked you out of here. I could say that I have orders to move you somewhere else. Or I have orders to release you."

"No," Fan said emphatically. "The josser will execute you. You have a wife and kids. I'm resigned to my fate. I challenged the king, and I broke the laws of the land. Just pray for me. Pray that God will deliver me. The Bible says that many are the troubles of the righteous, but the Lord delivers them from them all."

Nothing more was said as they neared the lion's den. Fan was led into a small room with a steel gate at the far end. After giving Fan a strong embrace, Dar rolled a large stone over the entrance to the den. The orders signed by the king were placed over the entrance.

From inside, Fan looked through the gate and saw a dozen or so lions pacing the courtyard. He heard footsteps on the roof, and suddenly the gate was opened. The lions let out a huge roar and came charging toward Fan.

Fan knelt to pray.

"May the God, whom I serve continually, rescue me!"

* * *

Zwilling started coughing violently, and he released his grip on Abbey's hair as he doubled over with his hands covering his mouth.

Abbey scooted away, petrified. She reached for a poker sitting next to the fireplace and stood, waving it at Zwilling. He recovered enough to start walking toward her, ignoring the threat of the poker, his eyes ablaze with fury.

"Where were you, you little tramp? Were you with a boy?" Zwilling said.

Abbey waved the poker back and forth to keep him away.

He reached for her, ignoring the poker.

She dropped it with a shriek.

He advanced toward her.

She bolted out the door and ran to the other room, Zwilling's heavy breathing warned Abbey that he had followed her.

"Answer me! Where were you?" he shouted.

"I just went out for a walk. I wasn't with anyone. I couldn't sleep."

"You lie!"

Abbey rushed to the other side of the couch.

Zwilling circled to the left.

She matched his moves, keeping the same distance between them. Her options were limited. If she ran away, the authorities would search her brother's business. They would find the printing presses. She had to let him catch her and take whatever punishment he dished out. He wouldn't kill her. She was too valuable an asset. This angry, the beating would be severe.

Abbey decided to try to calm the situation.

"I'm telling the truth. I got up early and went for a walk," Abbey said as she struggled to fight off the panic.

"You've been gone all night!" he ranted. "I woke up in the middle of the night and looked in your bedroom, and you were gone. It's against the law for you to be out at night. We could both get in trouble."

"I'm sorry. It won't happen again. Let me fix you some breakfast. You're sick," Abbey implored.

Zwilling coughed again. Catching his breath seemed difficult. Abbey inched slowly around him. Running from him could only make things worse. As she passed by him, he suddenly grabbed her around the waist.

She turned her back to him to run away.

He easily picked her up off the ground as she flailed her legs back and forth, trying to loosen his grip.

Abbey attempted to scream as he began to squeeze the breath out of her. Her ribs ached from the pressure. Lungs burned from the lack of oxygen. A forced cream was only a breathy moan.

"Zwilling... Stop. You're hurting me..." Abbey managed to squeak out the words as she struggled for each breath.

He ignored her cries as he flung her from side to side, maintaining his vice grip around her waist.

As she began to black out, he suddenly threw her across the room like a rag doll, her head banged against the table in a corner.

Zwilling started toward her with his hands raised as if he were going to choke her.

He's going to kill me.

Would this be how I die? The printing press. Thesis. Christopher.

All those thoughts ran through her head and strengthened her resolve.

I have to live. Mars needs me. Christopher needs me.

She struggled to get to her feet, but he was on her too quickly, grabbing her leg and pulling her back toward him. Abbey gritted her teeth as she fought for a way out of this.

Fear. Anger. Hatred. *I hate you!*

Zwilling's rage brought back memories of her mother lying on the same floor, enduring the same beatings. Abbey heard her mother's screams from her room, too many times to count, unable to do anything about it.

You hurt my mother. You'll never touch me again. The resolve she needed.

Abbey kicked him hard in the shin. Zwilling led out a loud groan as he stumbled, trying to maintain his balance. He reached for her, but she was too quick and easily stepped out of his reach.

She looked for something to hit him with. Before she could find anything, Zwilling began to cough violently again. Shouting expletives at her between the coughs. He started toward her again but then stopped in his tracks. His hands went to his chest as pain and fear crossed his face.

He staggered. "Help me," he mouthed the words, barely able to make a sound.

Abbey wanted to run but stood and watched as Zwilling fell to the ground, his hands still clutching his chest. His head banged against the floor with a loud, cracking sound. The loud wheezing stopped. No movement at all. Zwilling's eyes were open, maintaining a blank stare of disbelief at Abbey, as life drained from his face.

She let out a yelp then held her breath.

Is he dead?

* * *

Dar went back to his post and sobbed, and ignored the stares of the other guards. He kept mumbling to himself, "God, please forgive me. Please forgive me."

He only hoped Fan hadn't suffered. It wouldn't take long. The lions were rarely fed, so they were always hungry. Sometimes, it would only take a few minutes for them to devour an entire person.

Dar dreaded going back there. He'd never been bothered by the ritual killings before. He'd seen hundreds of people fed to the lions over the years. Seeing the torn flesh and remains of his friend made this different. Personal. This time he felt guilty.

His friend had saved his daughter's life. Why couldn't Dar have saved his? If he were braver, he would have.

After a few minutes, he got up and hurried to the lion's den. When he came near the entrance, he stopped. No sounds. Usually, the lions fought over the remains and made all kinds of racket as the strongest fought off the weakest.

Dar approached the entrance cautiously. He called out to Fan in an anguished voice, "Faniel, servant of the living God, has your God, whom you serve continually, been able to rescue you from the lions?"

No sound. Even the lions weren't roaring. They always made a sound when they heard Dar approaching, believing he had for them their next feast.

Dar called for Fan again, this time louder.

Faniel answered, "My God sent his angel, and he shut the mouths of the lions. They have not hurt me, because I was found innocent in his sight."

Dar was overjoyed as excitement flowed through him at the unbelievable turn of events. He scrambled up on the roof. The lions were all standing by the gate with their mouths shut. They looked toward Dar when they saw him, but still didn't make a sound. Some pawed at their mouths trying to open them. Others rolled on the ground, rubbing their mouths against the ground, trying to pry them open.

Dar quickly shut the gate, scurried back to the entrance, and rolled away the stone. Fan walked out of the lion's den with his chains off. He held a piece of paper. Dar grabbed Fan and put him in a big hug. He looked him over and found no wounds at all, other than those that had been inflicted upon him in prison.

Before Dar could speak, Fan blurted out, "This paper is a forgery. I can prove it."

"What are you talking about?" Dar asked.

"The josser gave me this paper that is supposedly a copy of the original Bible account of Genesis 3. Look right here..." Fan showed Dar the paper.

"What? I don't know what you mean." Dar had never had much interest in the church or the Bible and wasn't aware of the controversy surrounding Genesis 3 until Fan explained it to him.

"Right here in this line is a comma," Fan said, barely able to contain his excitement. Words were coming fast and erratically. "Commas weren't used until the fourth century," he explained. "This was written in the first century. It has to be a forgery." Fan bounced around with excitement.

Other guards were looking their way, noticing the commotion.

Dar tried to silence his friend. "Stay right here."

Dar went into the lion's den and grabbed the chains. He brought them back to where Fan was standing and reattached them to him.

"The other guards are watching us. I need to make it look like you're still my prisoner."

"I have to go talk to Nate."

"Let me take you to my house. I can't take you back to prison. The josser will kill you."

"I'm not afraid of the josser. Obviously, he can't kill me unless God allows him to. Let's go get Nate. Can you get him out of prison?" Fan asked with a mischievous grin on his face.

"What are you planning? You have something in mind. What is it?"

"No time to explain. We have to go get Nate, and we have to go to the church. I need to confront the josser at the church. I need to show him and all the scholars that the document is a forgery. The comma proves it."

They started back toward the prison.

Fan said, "Hurry! We must get going. Church will be starting in a couple hours. I can't wait to see the josser's face when he sees that I'm alive."

* * *

Theba answered the door to discover Abbey standing there clutching a bag of ice against her side.

"Zwilling is dead," Abbey said to Theba.

"Are you sure?" Theba asked.

"I think so. When I left, he was laying on the floor with a weird look on his face." She tried to mimic what his face looked like. It caused her to let out a thin chuckle.

"His eyes were opened, and they were just staring at me. He wasn't coughing or breathing. I kicked him and he didn't move. I tried to shake him, but he didn't wake up. I didn't know what else to do, so I came here. I hope that was okay."

"Of course," Theba said, as she adjusted the ice pack on Abbey's sore ribs.

Abbey winced from the pain. "What am I going to do?" she asked. "They'll think I killed him."

"He's been sick. They won't blame it on you. They'll think he died of natural causes."

"They'll take me away. I'm only sixteen. An orphan. They'll put me in one of those homes or in the king's harem."

She shuddered at the thought of Abbey in the king's harem.

"Does anyone know Zwilling?" Theba asked. "Does he have any other family? Will anyone miss him if he just disappears?"

"What do you mean?" Abbey asked. "How can we make him disappear?"

"We can get rid of the body. No one'll ever know that he's dead."

Abbey nodded excitedly. "He had a nurse, but he got angry with her last week and sent her away. He doesn't have any family that I know of. No one ever comes to visit him. He was such a despicable man, and he didn't have any friends."

"Leave everything to me. After church, we'll go to your house and figure out what to do. I'll help you."

Abbey threw her arms around Theba's neck. Her eyes suddenly widened.

"What?" Theba said.

"Church... The thesis... We have to go to the church."

Abbey explained to Theba about the second thesis, the forgery, and the comma.

"You can get dressed here," Theba said. "You can wear my clothes. Go take a shower. You'll feel better. If anyone asks about Zwilling just say that he is away on business."

The shower lasted for more than twenty minutes.

* * *

Dar freed Nate from the prison and took Fan and Nate to his house where his wife fed them and treated their wounds. They took showers, shaved, and changed clothes.

The men thanked Dar and his family profusely and then left to go to their homes and get their scholarly robes to wear to the church. The second thesis was on their doorsteps. Reading it brought them great joy.

"Church is going to be very interesting this morning," Fan said to Nate with a wide grin.

15

The scholars all gathered around the front entrance to the Vandenberg Church. So deep in discussion, they didn't notice Fan and Nate approaching. Obviously discussing the second thesis which most held a copy of in their hands.

"Excuse me," Fan said. "Can anyone tell me how to get to the Vandenberg Church?" Fan asked with a huge grin on his face.

"It's right here, you idiot..." The scholar's last word trailed off as his mouth gaped open at the sight of the one asking the question.

"It's a ghost!" another scholar said excitedly as he pointed at Fan. They all looked up in unison.

"We thought you were dead."

"No sir. Here in the flesh." Fan wrung his hands together showing he indeed was very much alive. "Can't kill me that easily," he said with a chuckle.

They all gathered around Fan and Nate, hugging them, kissing them on the cheeks, and slapping them on the back.

Nate winced in pain.

"Be careful. My wounds are still very tender," Nate implored, happy about the zealousness with which the scholars were expressing how glad they were to see them but in pain, nonetheless.

"We were told you were thrown in the lion's den this morning. We refused to be seated in the church out of protest on your behalf."

Fan was touched by the gesture.

"I was thrown in the lion's den this morning, but God has seen fit to save me."

138

"The lion took one sniff of you and decided you weren't worth eating," Nate said.

The scholars roared in laughter. Nate doubled over in a combination of laughter and pain.

"The guard opened the gates, and the lions entered the den," Fan began relating the story.

The scholars were drawn to every word.

"I was on my knees praying to God to rescue me. A lion approached and tried to open his mouth but couldn't. God had closed it shut almost like it was sewn shut."

A collective gasp went up from the scholars.

Fan continued. "The lions started contorting their mouths trying to get them open." Fan mimicked the lions. His mouth tightly shut, Fan thrashed his head from side to side and pawed at his mouth with his hands.

More laughter as the scholars were clearly amazed at the story.

"But the lions couldn't open their mouths, so they just laid down in the den with me. One even came and laid his head on my lap."

"Whoa!" the scholars said in one chorus, some oohing and some aahing, their mouths competing with their eyes to see which could open the widest.

"God is good..." Fan said.

"Yes, he is." The scholars said in unison.

"What happened next?"

"The josser came to see us earlier that morning to try and get us to sign a confession. He gave us this document he said was the original copy of Genesis 3." Fan held the copy in the air. But the scholars acted as if they hadn't seen it yet.

Fan continued. "I sat in the lion's den reading it. That's when I discovered it's a forgery."

"It's not real?" one of them asked.

"No. It's a fake."

"How do you know?"

"There's a comma in it. Right here. A clear comma in verse twenty-two. I didn't notice it at first. Something didn't feel right about the document. I didn't know what it was. The josser obviously didn't catch it."

Fan was interrupted by the organ starting to play. Several scholars looked that way, but none moved to enter the church. They were focused on Fan's every word.

"When I saw the comma, I knew it wasn't real. This document is dated 70 M.A. A. C. Commas weren't around then, as you all know. The josser and the king clearly had this document forged. It looks like the work of Elmyr Fiori. I came here this morning to confront the josser with his lies."

The scholars all nodded and voiced their agreement.

"There is another thesis," one of them shouted out.

"We've seen it," Nate said. "It's a brilliant work, totally refuting with Scripture the whole system of religious remissions. Clearly, from the verses shown in the thesis, salvation is from grace by faith in Jesus Christ and not by any works imposed on the church. That is the gospel. We have to get that message out to the masses so they can be saved."

Applause erupted among the scholars. A look of determination and resolve came upon everyone's face.

"When should we go in and confront the josser?" one asked.

"Let's go in now. I can't wait any longer to see his face when we confront him with the comma."

Everyone agreed.

"I can't wait to see the look on his face when he sees that Fan is still alive," Nate said.

* * *

Theba couldn't help but notice how hard Abbey was shaking, so she reached over and grabbed her hand and squeezed tightly. They were sitting in the balcony of the church.

"How does she do it?" Theba wondered to herself.

Abbey had been through so much. Attacked by her stepfather. Then watching him die right in front of her. Somehow, she had the courage and intelligence to write an entire thesis that was confounding the entire aristocracy and challenging centuries of church doctrines and beliefs. Theba's admiration for Abbey was welling up inside of her to the point that she had to wipe away a tear.

"Where are the scholars?" Abbey whispered.

Only a dozen or so scholars were in their seats. The rest were empty. On the seats was a piece of paper. Probably the forged copy of Genesis 3.

"I don't know," Theba said. "We saw them when we got here. They were all congregated at the front door, obviously reading your..." Theba stopped herself. She didn't want to say anything about the thesis loudly enough to where someone else could hear.

The organ suddenly began playing, and the men in the lower section all stood looking at the door where the josser would soon enter. Nothing. The door never opened. The organist finished his song and began another as the entire group of congregants sat back down.

"Where's the josser? Where are the scholars? Where is everybody?" Abbey asked.

Theba's mind was elsewhere. *Where is Jeriah? I hope he's okay.*

* * *

Jeriah mounted his horse and rode alone, unarmed, toward the city of the Cabenites. As he neared, archers appeared on the roof with their weapons aimed directly at him.

"I have come in peace," Jeriah said. "I want to speak to your leader. I'm not armed."

"How do we know it's not a trap?" a voice said from behind the gates.

Jeriah sat up on his horse and looked all around him.

"Do you see any other soldiers? Are you afraid of one man? Open the gates and let me speak to your leader," he said with authority. "I am Jeriah, the Captain of the king's army. I come on the authority of King Henry X. Open the gate. You have my word that it's not a trap. I will do nothing to harm you."

Yet. Jeriah thought to himself.

A few minutes later, the large wooden city gates swung open. Jeriah rode slowly into the city. More of a small community than a city. Surrounded by large, impenetrable walls. Inside the gates, more than a hundred men immediately surrounded him. Jeriah dismounted his horse.

A man approached, nothing more than a peasant. Wearing poor, ragged clothes, but clearly the leader of the city. Jeriah looked at him with admiration. This man had successfully held off his siege for months with only a band of misfits, not very well armed but obviously very committed. Jeriah had often said that when a man was defending his house and home, he was able to do things seemingly beyond his capability. These men were living proof of that fact, and Jeriah regretted that they would all soon die. The men anyway. Jeriah had given strict orders that the women and children were not to be touched.

As the man approached, Jeriah held out his hand. The man shook it reluctantly.

"My name is Jeriah. I am the captain of the king's army."

"I know who you are. My name is Cab. What do you want?"

"I have come to negotiate a truce. The fighting has gone on long enough. I have commanded my men to retreat. You will see them leaving later today."

A shout went out among the men who were listening. Cab raised his hand to quiet his men.

"How do we know that this is not a trap?"

"Because, later today, I'm sending you a gift. A wooden horse. A gift from the king. My men have spent three days constructing it. It's made of valuable cedar wood. A symbol of peace between us. The most exquisite and beautiful gift you will have ever seen."

Cab didn't say anything for a few seconds, obviously contemplating this unexpected development. Finally, he spoke. "Like you, we are tired of war," Cab said. "Peace is welcomed here. War with the king was not something we ever wanted. We just want to be left alone to live our lives. I accept your gift. There will be peace between us. We're all Martians. Let's live in harmony and peace together one with another."

"Amen," Jeriah said as he reached out and embraced Cab and hugged him warmly. He turned, mounted his horse, and rode away back out the gate he had just entered from.

As he left, Jeriah looked around the city at the faces of the men, women, and children, for a moment feeling pity for them.

They have no idea what is about to happen to them.

* * *

Tomas sat at his desk at the church, the organ resounding for the second time, signaling his cue to enter. Word had reached him that the scholars were not in their seats. Tomas had placed the forged Genesis 3 paper on their chairs earlier that morning, and he wanted them to read the document before he made his grand entrance.

They are ruining everything.

The scholars were protesting the death of Faniel and were refusing to enter. Tomas had sent guards to order them in. One of the guards had brought back another thesis which had been nailed to the wall of the church.

Tomas was furious. The thesis had challenged the authority of the king to issue religious remissions.

Blasphemy. Heresy.

They would pay with their lives. Yet, he was no closer to finding the people behind the theses. Several messengers carrying and distributing the theses had been captured and tortured but none would talk and give any information even with the threat of death. Whyburgh was still a suspect, but he'd been very cooperative in printing the Genesis 3 story for him. Obviously, he wasn't the one printing the theses.

Who could it be?

His thoughts were interrupted by a knock on the door.

"Come in," the josser said rudely.

One of the guards entered the room.

"Your Honor, I wanted to inform you that the scholars have taken their seats in the sanctuary."

He smiled. "Excellent." His threats had obviously worked, and they had come to their senses. This morning would be a glorious victory for the truth and for the king.

"Tell them I will be in shortly. I want to give the scholars time to read the paper on their chairs."

The guard turned and departed. The josser stood, faced a mirror, and adjusted his robe and tie, brushing off any lint.

"Fan is dead," he said to himself. "The forgery proves the first thesis is not real. That, in and of itself, will discredit this second piece of trash." The josser threw the thesis into the trash can, grabbed his notes, and walked out almost strutting as he made his way down the big hall to his entrance. No music was playing. Anger rose inside of him as the whole morning he'd planned so carefully was disrupted by the rebellious scholars. He must enter to music.

The josser grabbed one of the young men who served him as an altar boy and yelled for him to go tell the organist to play a hymn for his entrance.

When the music began, the josser strode into the sanctuary with his shoulders pushed back and his nose high in the air. Rather than taking his seat, he went directly to the pulpit, opened his notes, and signaled for the organist to stop playing.

"A great hoax has been perpetrated on the holy church and our king," he said in a firm and deliberate voice. "Several weeks ago, a document was circulated among the churches and scholars falsely claiming that Adam ate from the tree of the knowledge of good and evil. The document was a forgery. Godless and corrupt men blasphemed the name of our lord and our king in an attempt to deceive you and lead you to believe a lie. In your seats today, you will find proof that Adam refused to eat the apple."

The josser held the document high in the air and waved it back and forth. "Let me read from the true account of Genesis 3 from God's Holy Word." He held the paper in front of him and read in a clear, almost haughty voice. "So, she took the apple and ate it; she also gave some to her husband, who was with her, but he refused to eat it."

The josser raised his voice to a fever pitch. "Eve ate the apple and Adam refused. This is a true copy of the original manuscript written and dated 70 M.A A.C. that was discovered at the Red Sea. The blasphemers who prepared the thesis filled with lies will be punished."

The josser expected applause, but none came. Anger rose inside of him at the insolence of the scholars. He raised his voice in anger as he said, "One of the blasphemers, Faniel, has been sent to his death today. Any scholar or any man who dares to defy the king and the teaching of the church will be killed."

Sudden movement distracted Tomas. A man, a scholar, stood. Tomas blinked his eyes twice not believing what he was seeing.

Faniel.

And Nathaniel sat next to him.

What he saw was not making sense. He'd seen them with his own eyes earlier that morning in the dungeon. In chains. Now they were dressed in robes.

How could it be?

Faniel began speaking with authority. "I'm very much alive, Josser. You tried to kill me. I was thrown into the lion's den, but God has chosen to rescue me."

Murmuring resounded through the sanctuary. "It is not the thesis that is a forgery," Fan said, raising his voice to a crescendo. "It is your document that you've given us today that is the forgery." Faniel waved the document in the air.

"You lie!" Tomas said. "Read it yourself. It's right there in front of you. Clearly, it states that Adam refused to eat the apple. Do you dare to deny what you can see with your own eyes?"

Faniel calmly stated, "I draw your attention to verse twenty-two. There is a comma in that verse. Why would there be a comma in a document written hundreds of years before commas were invented?"

The josser scrambled to look at the document. Panic rose inside as he began to comprehend the gravity of what Faniel said.

It's not possible.

There it was, plain as day. A comma. *How did I miss it?*

Now, lest he reach out his hand and take also of the tree of life and eat and live forever...

Fiori... Elmyr that snake! He tricked me. He put the comma in there so everyone would know it was a forgery.

Tomas slammed his hand on the pulpit, gathered his belongings, and stormed out of the sanctuary.

The entire crowd sat stunned, a collective gasp of disbelief echoing throughout the entire church.

16

Beno saw Jeriah come galloping over the hill from his trip to Caben and let out a huge sigh of relief. No one knew exactly how the Cabenites would react. Would they seize Jeriah? Kill him? Use him as leverage in negotiations? Or would Jeriah's carefully laid out plan work. Jeriah had insisted upon going alone. Beno, his second in command, had anxiously awaited his return.

"How did it go?" Beno said as Jeriah dismounted.

"They didn't suspect a thing," Jeriah said, patting Beno on the shoulder. "Is the wooden horse ready?" he asked.

"Yes sir. They finished it while you were gone. It looks magnificent." His tone turned more somber. "Do you have to be one of the ones to enter the city in the horse? You should stay back and lead the men. Let me go in the horse."

"I'll be fine," Jeriah said with a slight grin of resignation. "The king has commanded me to lead the siege. For whatever reason, he doesn't want me to succeed. I intend to win a great victory for the throne. I might even survive it," he said half-heartedly—almost jokingly.

Jeriah entered his command tent with Beno following, struggling to keep up.

"Gather the men, I want to speak to them," Jeriah said as he drank some much-needed water.

Beno abruptly turned and walked out of the tent.

* * *

Jeriah sat down for a minute to rest, letting himself think about Theba and home.

"It's going to be a long and eventful night for me," he mumbled to himself. "I wonder what Theba will be doing."

She'll probably have a very boring night at home.

* * *

Theba and Abbey struggled as they dragged Zwilling's lifeless body onto a large piece of carpet. They rolled the carpet around the corpse and secured it with several strands of rope, both out of breath from the effort. Eck and Christopher were to arrive soon with a wagon pulled by a horse to transport the body to dispose of it.

"What about all his clothes and possessions?" Abbey asked. "Should we get rid of them?"

"You should keep those," Theba said. "That way if anyone should ask, you can say he's away on a trip. You can even show them all his belongings if you are questioned. Just a precaution that's probably not necessary. Hopefully, no one will miss him."

Abbey grimaced.

"I hate to have anything in the house that reminds me of him."

"I know, honey. At least he'll be gone. That's the main thing. Where does he keep his register to pay his bills?"

"Back in the office," Abbey said as she headed that way.

They both cautiously walked into the room as if they were doing something wrong. Theba began rummaging through his desk until she found a large black binder with a register along with numbered pieces of paper that could be used for currency. The currency was called marrii. The church controlled all of the marrii on Mars, but the elite were issued the papers which they used to buy and sell and conduct commerce. The peasants mostly bartered possessions for whatever they needed.

Theba didn't know how to read, so she handed the register to Abbey.

"Does it say how much marrii he has in his account?" Theba asked. "I hope it's enough to pay the bills, or the church will come and seize the house and discover he's gone."

Abbey's mouth dropped open as she read the number.

"I've never heard of anyone having this much marrii. This would last me a hundred lifetimes. This is unbelievable," Abbey said.

"What is?" Eck asked.

Theba and Abbey jumped, startled when Eck and Christopher unexpectedly walked into the room. They hadn't heard them come in the house.

Abbey handed Zwilling's register to Eck. He looked up with a puzzled look on his face after seeing the same number Abbey saw. Christopher took the black register out of Eck's hands. He looked up in shock as well.

"This will fund all of our work," Christopher said enthusiastically.

"We can print thousands of Bibles with this marrii," Eck added.

"How ironic?" Abbey said with her voice trailing off. "Zwilling's marrii is going to fund the entire Reformation," she said, laughing.

The other's joined in. Except for Theba.

"Isn't there something wrong with that?" Theba asked. "Isn't it sort of stealing?"

"The Bible says that the wealth of the sinner is stored up for the righteous. This is God's provision to fund the Reformation," Christopher answered. That seemed to satisfy Theba.

"Zwilling won't miss it," Abbey said with disdain. "At least some good will come out of his horrible existence," she said, thinking about her mother.

Christopher rummaged through the desk and pulled some papers out of the drawer. Old receipts with Zwilling's signature, he said.

"We can use these to forge his signature on the remittance papers. The church will never know. We'll take the marrii out a little at a time, so no one will suspect anything."

"Let's get Zwilling out of here," Eck said to Christopher while walking out of the room. The others followed.

Eck walked over to the roll of carpet and checked the bindings to make sure the body was secured. As far as anyone would be able to tell, they were simply transporting an old roll of carpet to be disposed of at the dump.

"Where are you taking him?" Abbey asked.

"Better you don't know," Eck said.

Christopher kissed Abbey on the forehead. Together, Eck and Christopher lifted the body and took Zwilling out the door and out of Abbey's life forever.

***

Jeriah stood before the assembled group of soldiers and addressed his men.

"Let those who have been gathered here today now go against the infidels and end with victory this war which began long ago. Let those who have been serving for small pay now obtain the eternal reward. For your efforts over the next few days, your king has absolved you from all of your sins."

A roar went up among all of the troops.

Jeriah signaled for them to be quiet as he continued.

"Let those who have been wearing themselves out in both body and soul now work for double honor. Over there," Jeriah pointed to the city of Caben, "are the enemies of our king and our God. Let us fight with honor and dignity in service to our king."

A shout went out throughout the throng.

Jeriah stepped down from his perch.

"Are you ready, Beno?" he asked. Beno simply nodded, his other commanders stood behind him and nodded as well.

"Have all the men pack everything as if they are leaving. Make sure that the Cabenites see the red dust to make them think you are really leaving the area. Once you're a good distance away, sneak back after dark, but make sure they don't see you. Stay far enough away out of the line of sight but close enough that you can reach the gate quickly. Once we open it, we will not be able to keep it open for long. We'll fight them off as long as we can."

The commanders nodded in agreement.

Jeriah continued. "Show mercy to them to the best you can while still taking the city. No women or children are to be touched. If the men surrender, don't kill them. Take them prisoner. Kill anyone who tries to kill you but try to take their leader alive if at all possible. His name is Cab. If I survive..." The words stuck in the back of his throat.

"If I survive," Jeriah said, regaining his composure. "Bring Cab to me. I hope we can spare as much bloodshed as possible. Maybe we can work it out where we can spare the lives of his men and still occupy the city."

Jeriah embraced his commanders. "God be with you," he said.

"And with you," they replied in unison.

The thirty-seven mighty men were already assembled at the horse. Jeriah paused upon seeing it for the first time. A magnificent work. Jeriah had instructed Epus to design and construct it. Forty feet high and twenty feet long, it weighed close to a thousand pounds. Wheels were constructed at the base and ropes attached to move it. More than a hundred men were needed to transport the horse to Caben.

They built a secret compartment underneath by which the men could enter and hide. Hollow inside, the men sat on the floor of the horse, and the bottom was sealed so it couldn't be seen except by close inspection. Hopefully, no one would think to look that closely.

The horse was immediately wheeled to the city so they could make it there before dark. A small hole in the side allowed Jeriah to see and hear what was happening on the outside.

Cab ordered the men to stop as they neared the gates.

"We are unarmed," one of Jeriah's men said. "Please accept this gift as a token of peace from the king."

"Leave it here," Cab said. The men let go of the ropes and scrambled away from the horse. They turned and started walking back to their camp.

Cab ordered his men to move the horse inside the city, and they quickly closed the gates behind them.

Once inside the gates, Cab walked around the horse, inspecting it carefully, although not thinking to look underneath it.

"Let's burn it," one of his men said.

* * *

Jeriah and his men heard the words and began to fidget nervously. He motioned for them to stay quiet. Jeriah always knew his plan might not work, but he hadn't thought about the possibility of being burned alive.

"No," Cab finally said. "We have defeated the great king. This is a great victory for us. The horse will be a reminder of our victory. Prepare a feast. Tonight, we'll have a great party."

A loud cheer went up among all of the Cabenites. Jeriah wanted to cheer as well, but he simply let out a huge sigh of relief. His men took their hands off their weapons, sat back, and allowed themselves to take a full breath for the first time since entering the city gates.

When night fell, the people of Caben reveled for hours, drinking heavily, and celebrating the end of the war by overindulging in food and drink. Jeriah hadn't anticipated this development but was pleased. The drunken men would be more easily defeated by his trained and well-rested army.

When they all fell asleep, Jeriah and his men slipped out the bottom of the horse and onto the ground below.

About a dozen guards were at the towers. Only two guarded the gate. Jeriah sent most of the men to take out the other guards, while he and four of his men easily overpowered the ones at the gate, killing them and hiding their bodies.

Once the other guards were disabled, all the men met back at the gate. Jeriah climbed to the top of the city wall and signaled his troops to move on the city. The men opened the gates and then set up a perimeter around the inside of it to fight off anyone who would try to close it.

The large gate made a loud sound as it was opened. Enough that it roused many of the men. Some were still drunk and sleeping, but several hundred made their way to the courtyard, moving quickly toward the commotion.

Faster than Jeriah had anticipated, considering the extent of the revelry the night before.

Cab was one of the first.

Jeriah glanced out the city gate to see how close his men were. Coming quickly but still a distance away.

I hope we can hold them off.

Jeriah estimated it would take them close to ten minutes to get to the city in a full-out sprint, wearing armor and carrying weapons. He instructed his men to spread out so they wouldn't be such an easy target.

Cab didn't order his men to attack at first but chose to organize them, buying Jeriah and his men some valuable time.

Jeriah would've done the same thing, even though it was a mistake.

He'd played out this battle in his mind a hundred times. The archers would go to walls of the city so they could shoot down on them. The Caben's armed men on the ground would spread out and attack Jeriah and his men from both sides and the center, trying to outflank them.

The archers were the main concern. His mighty men could fight off hundreds of men in hand-to-hand combat. At least long enough for the other men to arrive. Especially these peasants who weren't as well trained and battle tested.

They would be sitting ducks for the archers.

Cab finally ordered his men to attack once the archers were in place.

Jeriah ordered his men to hold their positions. "Stay as close to the gate as possible," he shouted. "We have to keep them from clos-ing the gate. Our men will be here in five minutes. We can hold them off that long." Jeriah knew it would probably be more like seven or eight minutes, but in a battle, no one could judge time. The men wouldn't know the difference. Didn't matter anyway. However long it was, was how long they had to fight to keep the gate open.

The first wave of Cabenites met stiff resistance from Jeriah and his men. Jeriah killed more than a dozen men in the first minute. Slashing his sword and knife by instinct in every direction, trying to keep from being overwhelmed by the larger numbers.

Jeriah could see the entire battle in his peripheral vision even as he fought desperately. Most of his men were just as successful as he, killing many more of the enemy than they were killing his men.

The archers rained down their first barrage of arrows, and Jeriah instinctively ducked. Most missed as they didn't have the right range of distance. Some even hit the Cabenites who were fighting in close proximity to his men. The second barrage would be more accurate.

Several of his men were struck down, but most fought valiantly. Jeriah moved to the back of the fighting nearer the gate. Not to get away from the action but so he could be the last line of defense and do everything in his power to keep the gates open.

Jeriah slashed the ropes to the gate with his sword, successfully rendering one side inoperable. It could still be closed but would have to be closed by hand which would take more time. Jeriah could hear the shouts of his men sprinting toward the city but didn't want to be distracted by looking back to see how far away they were.

The sound emboldened him and must have his men as well, as their intensity increased even more. A good soldier fought harder the longer the battle. More than a dozen of his men had fallen, and others were wounded, but they were fighting hard and killing dozens of men for every one of them that were killed.

All Cab's men were engaging them at the point of battle. Another critical mistake. Jeriah would have had some of his men head straight for the gate and ignore the battle had he been the commander of the Cabenites. Closing the gate should have been the first priority, even over defeating his men.

Cab may have been realizing the same thing, because he now shouted something at the top of his lungs, but his men weren't heeding his words. A sign that their men were not as well trained in battle.

Someone threw a spear at Jeriah. He ducked as he fought off three men at once, killing them and avoiding the spear. A blow to his back knocked him to the ground, but he quickly regained his feet in time to evade a sword thrust at him. He tried to keep his back to the gate and his body facing his attackers.

Harder to do as their numbers were dwindling and wave after wave of the enemy kept coming upon them. Only a dozen of his men were still standing. Every muscle in his body burned from the exertion. His breathing was heavy and labored. The adrenaline was the only thing that kept him going. He must dig deeper.

An arrow... He saw it out of the corner of his eye. Too late. Excruciating pain.

It struck Jeriah in the chest, just above his armor which had come loose from the battle. Near his heart. His strength left him as he fell to the ground. His hand was no longer able to grip his sword.

The last thing he saw were his men charging through the gate.

The victory is ours... Then everything went dark.

* * *

Hundreds of miles away, Theba bolted straight up in her bed where she'd been sleeping soundly. Sweat poured from her brow. Shaking. A sense of dread had come over her.

What's wrong?

"Something has happened to Jeriah," she said aloud to herself as she began sobbing uncontrollably.

17

Josser Tomas Cornwallis was beheaded in the fields of Giles, with no advanced notice, no publicity, and virtually no fanfare. A dozen or so people were in attendance.

His replacement, Jon Morgan Erasmus II sat in the office of the king and notified him of the news that his orders had been carried out. Tomas was dead. Chosen because of his reputation for high integrity and general tolerance of dissenting opinions, Jon was the perfect compromise with the scholars. A pious but practical man who believed in the supremacy of the throne but not its infallibility. Therefore, debate should always be encouraged as long as it was with respect for the king and his position as head of the church.

"Let me read back the statement you wish me to release to the scholars. I want to make sure it's correct," the new josser said.

Sir Tomas Cornwallis was executed for the crimes of heresy and sedition. Upon investigation, the king learned that Cornwallis and a forger named Elmyr Fiori conspired to create a fake copy of Genesis 3 and then tried to perpetrate the fraud by distributing it to the scholars. All of this without the knowledge of the king. Cornwallis was sentenced to death. Fiori has been sentenced to ten years of hard labor in prison. The investigation is ongoing, but the king believes they were the only two involved in the scheme.

Josser Jon suspected the king knew of the plot, but he was a humanist and believed all people were basically good and should focus on good works. Therefore, the end justified the means if the end result was something good. No good could come out of admitting the king's involvement. Weakening the king's authority in the church would not help his cause as he embarked on his new position of josser.

"That's perfect," the king said. "Distribute that immediately. What do you think of Martian Luther?"

"He offends all of my cultured sensibilities," Jon said with disdain.

"Then you agree he should be hunted down and executed."

"I do. He went too far when he questioned the authority of the king. I encourage dissent. In some ways, he has done Mars a great service by exposing the fraud being perpetrated on the people of Mars by the false teaching that Adam didn't eat the apple. I also sympathize with many of his views on women. However, the second thesis on religious remissions was sedition when he blatantly abased Your Majesty."

Jon believed the people should have access to the Holy Scriptures and should have some freedom to interpret them on their own. However, Scriptures were clear that God chose and installed the kings and gave them authority over the people. He had written his own thesis a few years before called *Dissent but Obey*. The scripture was clear, "Remind the people to be subject to rules and authorities, to be obedient, to be ready to do whatever is good."

At the time, Cornwallis had thought it treasonous, but it was well received among the scholars. It espoused Jon's humanistic beliefs perfectly. "Be a good person" above all else. Being good meant not questioning the authority of the king. His prevailing philosophy was that salvation came through good works.

Jon continued his thoughts on Luther. "If Luther had written more moderately, even though he had written freely, he would have honored himself and done more good for the world."

The king looked bored.

Jon decided to change the subject. "I propose the following changes to women's rights."

The king sat up in his chair, obviously more interested.

"The church should officially admit that Adam ate the apple. I am prepared to deliver a sermon on it this Sunday. Nevertheless, the Bible is clear that husbands should rule over their wives. It doesn't say that the church should rule over the wives, only that they should be subject to the edicts of the church. I suggest that we be more liberal with women and let the husbands decide their rules."

"What did you have in mind?" the king asked.

"Let's end most of the rules imposed on women. The ban on reading, for instance. The curfew. Prohibition for working. Let the husband decide those things for his wife and girls. If a wife becomes single by divorce or by her husband's death, the church should still take authority over her. If a girl is unmarried at her eighteenth birthday, and there is no one willing to pay the amount of the dowry to the church, then she should become your wife and serve you and the royal household."

The king was listening intently. His eyebrows were raised.

Jon thought he was still skeptical, though. "These new rules will have a lot of benefits. It takes a lot of manpower to enforce them. For instance, our prisons are full of women. We should release those who have not committed a violent crime. That would save us a fortune. Women working will bring more money into the treasury through religious remissions imposed on the husbands. Let the husbands punish their wives as they see fit."

The skepticism left the king's face when Jon made the case for the financial benefit.

"What is our position on women and salvation?"

"The early church clearly allowed women to be baptized and be members of the church. Think of how the king would ingratiate himself to the masses and to the women if you became more liberal and allowed women basic rights and access to salvation and the church. You would not be violating Scripture, and you would become an extremely popular king among the people. Makes them easier to control."

The argument was clearly resonating with the king as he nodded his head in agreement.

A knock on the door interrupted their conversation.

"Come in," the josser said.

Beno walked in, bowing as he entered.

"I beg the king's pardon. I have news from Caben. News of a great victory for the king."

King Henry stood to his feet as a frown came on his face, obviously not pleased. A strange reaction, the josser thought, upon hearing the news of a victory in battle.

Beno explained Jeriah's plan for the wooden horse and the attack in the middle of the night. The city was secured by the king's forces and the Cabenites surrendered.

The king slammed his hand on the table in disgust.

"I do have bad news," Beno continued. "Your servant Jeriah is dead. He was felled at the hand of an archer. He lived long enough to see the great victory."

The king's mood immediately changed as a smile came on his face. He walked quickly to Beno, and took him in his arms in a huge embrace.

"That is good news. Well done. What became of the Cabenites? Were they all destroyed as I commanded?"

"No, my king. Jeriah ordered that their lives were to be spared if they were willing to surrender to the throne. On his deathbed, Jeriah met with Cab, the leader of the Cabenites and insisted on his complete surrender. Cab agreed, thinking he and his men would still die but the women and children would be spared. Instead, Jeriah ordered that even the men be spared. The king's flag flies over the city."

Rage filled the king's face as his eyes rolled, his jaw clenched, his face turned red. His hands were raised in fists. He stormed back behind his desk.

"I ordered that everyone in the city be slaughtered. They defied me for months. They must all die."

The josser spoke up hesitantly. "Great King. This is your opportunity to show mercy and earn favor with the people. How will you collect religious remissions from the people if all the men are dead?"

Jon was learning that arguing the financial benefit was the most effective tact with the king.

The king's tone softened. He poured himself a chalice of wine. Raising the chalice in the air, he said, "Let's toast to a great victory." The king did not offer any wine to the josser or Beno, so they simply raised their arm in a gesture of a toast.

"Hooray to Jeriah," the king said sarcastically and with disdain.

Before anyone could speak, the king said, "Someone needs to tell his wife, Theba."

"I'm going to her now. Jeriah gave me a note to give to her," Beno said.

"Tell her that she has seven days to mourn her husband, and then she is to come and see me," the king said as he waved for Beno to leave the room. Beno backed out and closed the door behind him

"Prepare for Theba to become the Queen. I'm going to take her as my wife," the king said to the josser.

Obviously noting the puzzled look on the josser's face, the king continued. "Jeriah has won a great victory for the throne. I must do this for him. I can't stand to see his wife abandoned and without a husband. You said it yourself earlier. The church needs to take authority over widows. I want to honor Jeriah by making Theba my Queen."

Questions swirled around inside Jon's head. How did the king know Jeriah's wife's name? Why was the king so happy when he learned Jeriah was dead? Are the rumors true? Jon already knew the answer. The pieces of the puzzle started to come together. This could become a scandal that would test his resolve as the new josser. He knew of the king's indiscretions before he took the position. Much different perspective now that he was the josser. His piety would be challenged now that he was responsible to cover up the king's sins.

But... The end justifies the means.

* * *

A knock at the door startled Theba. The house had been cleaned for the third time that morning. Anything to take her mind off Jeriah and the uneasy feeling in the pit of her stomach.

Tears started to form as she walked to the door.

Is this the news that I've been dreading?

Her worst fears were realized when she opened the door and saw Beno standing there. The somber look on his face told her everything she needed to know.

She fell into his arms sobbing. His arms were the only thing holding her upright. He held her tightly, trying to speak words, but none came at first.

"He was thinking about you when he died," Beno finally said.

Theba fell to the ground at his feet. Beno helped Theba to her feet and led her into the living room. About that time, Abbey entered through the back door. Seeing Theba crying, she ran to her taking her in her arms.

Theba kept saying over and over again, "He's gone, Abbey. The king killed him."

Abbey took Theba's hand and led her over to the sofa where they sat down. Beno stood at the door just inside, obviously not sure what to say or do.

Theba struggled to fight back the tears and regain her composure. She had already said too much in front of Beno.

He must never know. No one must ever know.

Theba stiffened her neck as anger for the king raged inside of her overwhelming the grief. She stared into Abbey's eyes with a steel look of revenge.

Abbey met her stare with resolve.

Theba reached out her hand and motioned for Beno to come to her. "Thank you for coming to tell me. Jeriah thought so much of you. He talked about you all the time."

"Jeriah won a great victory for the king. You would've been proud of him." Beno explained about the wooden horse, opening the gates, the city surrendering.

Theba's heart softened as she thought of Jeriah fighting the battle and winning.

"Jeriah defied the king," Beno said.

"How so?" Theba questioned. Her face brightened as a slight smile formed.

"The king ordered that everyone in the city be slaughtered. Men, women, and children."

A look of disgust came on Beno's face. "But Jeriah refused and ordered all the people to be spared."

Theba looked at Abbey with a grin that was hard to muster but was reflective of her admiration for her husband. "That sounds like my Jeriah."

"Were you with him when he died? Theba asked soberly, tears starting to well up in her eyes again.

Beno told them the whole story. "He was unconscious when I found him. When the battle was over, the leader of Caben insisted that we take Jeriah to his quarters and place him in his bed. We did all we could for him, but the wound was too great. Jeriah woke for just a few minutes. He called for Cab to come to him. Cab was the leader of the Cabenites."

Abbey and Theba nodded with understanding. Abbey still clutched Theba's hands.

"Jeriah ordered that none of the Cabenites were to be killed as long as they would agree not to fight against the king anymore. The leader agreed and a truce was formed. They even embraced. It was quite a sight. Two warriors embracing each other after a fierce battle."

"What happened then?" Abbey asked.

"Jeriah told everyone to leave the room. Except me..." Beno's voice shook and his lips quivered as he struggled to speak.

"Jeriah told me to bring you this note." Beno pulled out a folded, worn piece of paper. "He told me to read this to you." Beno took a deep breath, his hands shaking as he started to read.

"My dearest Theba. If you're reading this, then I've broken my promise to you. I told you I would be home soon. I'm so sorry that I can't keep that promise."

Beno looked away as he wiped away tears, unable to continue reading. Abbey stood, walked over to him, and took the note from his hand.

Theba recognized a look of surprise on Beno's face as his eyes widened when Abbey started reading the note with the passion and intensity by which it was written. Beno might not have ever seen a woman read before.

Abbey read Jeriah's words, "You are the best thing that ever happened to me. I always said that I would love you for an eternity. Know that I will be anxiously waiting until I see you again in heaven. With all my love, Jeriah."

Abbey handed the note to Theba. She clutched it to her chest. Wiping her eyes, Theba said to Beno, "Where is my husband now?"

"I brought his body back with me. It's being prepared for burial. The king said to tell you that you have seven days to mourn your husband's death, and then you are to come and see him."

Theba bristled at the audacity of the king to tell her how long she could mourn her husband's death.

I will mourn his death for the rest of my life.

She bit her lip so that she wouldn't say anything. She knew this day was coming. The king would kill her husband and then take her as his wife. If it weren't for the child she was carrying, she would take her own life and go be with Jeriah in heaven immediately.

Maybe God can work something good out of this with me as Queen.

* * *

That day the angels came to present themselves before the Lord, and Satan also came with them. The Lord said to Satan, "Where have you come from?"

Satan answered the Lord, "From roaming throughout the mars, going back and forth on it."

Then the Lord said to Satan, "Have you considered my servant, Abbey? There is no one like her on the mars."

"That's why I've come today. She is just the person I want to discuss with you. Why are you protecting her? Every time I try to kill her, you put a hedge of protection around her. The soldiers had her in their grasp, and she got away. I thought her stepfather, Zwilling was going to strangle her to death, but then he died of a heart attack. I can't catch a break."

"She's so brave," God said with tenderness in his voice, "and she has been so faithful to serve me to get my Word out to the people with no regard for her own life."

"Does she fear you for nothing?" Satan replied. "You have blessed the work of her hands. Let me strike everything she has, and she will curse you to your face."

"You are not to harm her in any way," God said sternly. "But you can take her into the king's harem."

Satan turned to leave. Before he did, he said, "Tomas Cornwallis wants to talk to you."

Then Satan left the presence of the Lord.

* * *

The Lord went to the gates of hell and stood outside of them and called for Tomas to come to him. Michael the archangel accompanied him. Tomas was in Hades where he was in torment.

"Why am I here?" Tomas said. "I served you faithfully for all of those years. I preached hundreds of sermons on your behalf."

"Not everyone who says to me, 'Lord, Lord' will enter the kingdom of heaven, but only the one who does the will of my Father who is in heaven. Many will say to me on that day, 'Lord, Lord, did we not prophesy in your name and in your name drive out demons and in your name perform many miracles?' Then I will tell them plainly, 'I never knew you. Away from me, you evildoers!'"

Tomas was downcast. He looked up and pointed toward heaven.

"Look at Jeriah in heaven. Have pity on me and send Jeriah to dip the tip of his finger in water and cool my tongue because I am in agony in this fire."

God replied, "Remember that in your lifetime you received your good things, while Jeriah received bad things, and you sent him off to battle to his death and away from his wife. But now he is comforted here, and you are in agony. And besides all this, between us and you is a great chasm that has been set in place, so that those who want to go from here to you cannot, nor can anyone cross over from there to us."

Tomas answered, "Then I beg you, send Jeriah to my family and to all the people of Mars. Let him warn them so that they will not also come to this place of torment."

"I already have someone in place to warn them," God said, as Tomas remained in the flames, his shrill screams reverberating throughout all of Hades.

***

"Who have you chosen to warn them?" Michael asked as they were leaving.

"Theba and Abbey are the two I have chosen to bring my Word to the people," God said.

"But you gave Satan permission to seize Abbey and become part of the king's harem. Theba is about to become Queen. That's exactly the evil Satan wants."

God said, "No. That is exactly what I want. What Satan intends for evil, I intend for good."

PART TWO

"Here I stand; I cannot do otherwise, so help me God!"
Martin Luther

18

Two months later

A warrant had been issued for the arrest of Martian Luther. Additionally, a reward in the amount of 10,000 marrii had been offered to any information leading to his arrest.

"Does this look like me?" Abbey said to Christopher, laughing facetiously.

Abbey was standing next to a "Most Wanted" poster hanging on the wall of a building on the city streets of Boulder Bay. An anonymous tip provided to the church authorities had led to an artist sketch of a sixty-year-old man, approximately five feet-ten, two-hundred pounds, brown hair, hazel eyes, long beard, and even longer hair. Presumably, a description of Martian Luther from a tip provided to authorities by Christopher.

Ironically, the poster had been typeset and printed by Abbey for her brother Eck who had been hired by the church to design and print them. The three of them couldn't stop laughing over their hilarious scheme.

"I love it when you laugh," Christopher said. "You seem so happy."

"I am happy." Abbey said, taking Christopher's hand as they walked down the street toward a restaurant where they had reservations for dinner. Their first official date.

"Happy to be with you," she said affectionately.

"Look at the beautiful sunset," Christopher said pointing out across the bay.

Summer had come to Boulder Bay, and the sun glistened off of the water. The red sandy beach magnified the colors of the navy-blue sky, bright yellow sun, and glistening light-blue, almost green water. Dark black volcanic rock lined the rocky shoreline on the north side of the bay.

Vegetation and greenery were only present on Mars in the summer months because of the cold, and everyone looked forward to the two months when the trees bloomed, and flowers appeared bringing with them warmer temperatures and better moods among the people. The only downside was the increased winds which blew the red sand everywhere, getting on all the streets, buildings, windows, and doors, along with clothes and shoes which had to be dusted off before entering any building.

"Since the new josser took control, everybody is happier," Abbey said. "The women especially. Seems like men are having a harder time with women having more rights," Abbey said, poking Christopher in the ribs.

Christopher jumped away and then moved back toward her and tickled her ribs. Smiling every step of the way as the troubles of the past were distant memories. At least for a little while that night.

Abbey and Christopher walked into Max & Erma's café. They were given a seat at the window with a view of the lake. Christopher had stopped by earlier in the day and reserved the best seat in the house. The café used to be called Max's café. Two months before, women were not even allowed in the restaurant. When the king lifted the ban on women in business establishments, Max added his wife's name to the sign out front. Women were now free to dine there, and Erma free to work there which she was doing as she busily bustled around the restaurant barking orders to the staff and seating guests in a warm and friendly manner.

One of many changes rapidly spreading through at least the more developed areas of Mars. Along with that, now Christopher and

Abbey could come and go as they pleased at any time of the day or night. Women no longer had any regulations, and authorities were no longer seeking to arrest Christopher. Newfound freedom of which they were taking advantage of at every opportunity.

"What a beautiful view and a beautiful restaurant." Abbey noted as Erma led them to their seats.

A white ceiling with a large chandelier dominated the middle of the restaurant. Small but quaint. Red chairs, with off colored table-cloths. The floor was tiled with patterns. Crystal glasses were pristinely polished as was the silverware which sat on soft, satiny napkins. Every aspect was elegant but nondescript, not overdone. No detail missed. Abbey had never been in that nice of a restaurant before.

"I hope you like it," Christopher said with a sly grin. "Tonight is a special night. I have a surprise for you."

"What's the surprise?" Abbey asked like a little schoolgirl. She quickly tried to control herself. Over the past few months, she had matured so much and was trying to shed her still-childish manner-isms that surfaced occasionally, especially when she was excited. Abbey looked older than she was as her stunningly beautiful wom-anly features were blooming as rapidly as the flowers.

"You are stunning," Christopher said.

Abbey reacted shyly, shrinking her shoulders back. She fidgeted with the lace attached to the shoulder of her dress. It was bright yel-low, slightly above her knees, a modest neckline, accessorized by a cross necklace accenting the dress with noble simplicity. Abbey's natural long hair gracefully flowed and silhouetted the silky blue scarf tied around her neck.

A dress that was a year's wages for some people. Purchased earlier that week at a designer shop courtesy of Zwilling and his abundant trust fund he unknowingly left to Abbey when he met his untimely demise. As far as she was concerned, payment for her months of cooking, cleaning, and waiting on him hand and foot. Not to mention, enduring the general indignities of his presence which were now a distant memory rarely revisited.

"What's my surprise?" Abbey said.

"You have to wait," Christopher said playfully. "After we eat."

"Let's hurry up and order then," Abbey said looking around for the waiter.

* * *

"That may have been the best meal I've ever eaten," Abbey said rubbing her stomach.

The meal consisted of an 8 oz. beef tenderloin roasted to juicy perfection, with slowly baked onions, carrots, tomatoes, and celery bathed in a spicy cream sauce. Dessert a bittersweet chocolate silk pie, with chocolate shavings, a brownie on the side, with heavy cream on top. One they shared and were unable to finish.

"Someone needs to carry me back to the house," Abbey said as they left the restaurant. She suddenly stopped walking. "Wait a minute. What's my surprise?" Abbey asked. "You said after dinner. It's after dinner. I can't wait any longer."

"Just one minute longer," Christopher said.

They walked along the main trail back toward her house when Christopher suddenly veered off and onto a trail that led to an overlook. The sun had set, and the two moons of Mars were now reflecting light off of the water creating the appearance of four moons, two in the sky and two in the water. An unusual sight only seen at that time of the year. Abbey had learned one of the moons would experience an eclipse the next day. She made a note that they should come to this same spot to view it.

A shooting star flew through the sky, drawing Abbey's attention.

Christopher stopped walking and went down on one knee. He reached into his pocket and pulled out a small box.

Abbey put her hands to her mouth and let out a slight squeal. "Abbey, you're the only one I want to spend the rest of my life with. When I look into my future, the only thing I see is you. When you know what you want in your future, you want your future to start as soon as possible. Abbey, will you marry me?"

Abbey rocked back and forth with her hands clenched together up by her chest. She was unable to speak from the excitement.

"Will you make me the happiest man in the universe?" he asked again.

Abbey looked up in the sky and let out a little scream of delight.

"Abbey are you going to answer me?" he implored.

She bent over and threw her arms around his neck.

Christopher stood to his feet and wrapped his arms around her.

The kiss. Electricity. Passion. Intense love.

"I'll take that as a yes," Christopher said when the kiss finally ended.

"Absolutely, yes," Abbey said, kissing him again. She broke the kiss to tell him what's in her heart. "Of course, I'll marry you."

Her mouth flew open again. "I want to see the ring." She realized they were so focused on each other, the box with the ring was still unopened.

Christopher slowly opened the box as Abbey's mouth remained wide open. Her heart was pounding. Her cheeks flushed. Breathing was fast with shallow breaths.

"It's made of Trylicite." Christopher said.

"So beautiful. It must've cost a fortune." The joy brought tears to her eyes as Christopher was treating her so sweetly and gently.

Trylicite was a rare mineral that was formed from high temperatures and silica likely from years of volcanic activity. Only the elite could afford a ring this rare and valuable. The best they could deduce, Zwilling had invested in a Trylicite mine in the northern polar area of Mars. A very productive investment that had earned him a fortune and provided a significant monthly income. The ring had probably come from a stone from Zwilling's mine.

Christopher slipped the ring on Abbey's middle finger where engagement rings were traditionally worn.

Abbey let out a loud ahhh as she held her hand out from her and admired the beauty and significance of the ring. She was so in love with Christopher. *How did I get so lucky?*

"What's wrong?" Christopher asked. "You don't like the ring?"

"No, it's not that. I love the ring!" she said, trying to reassure him patting him lovingly on the chest. "I was thinking of my mother. I just wished she could be here with me. I miss her."

* * *

Theba was officially the Queen of Mars.

A private ceremony officiated by Josser Jon in the king's royal ballroom was attended by only a small staff and a few royal officials. The last aspect of the great deception was finalized. The king could now argue that the child was legitimately his. The adultery would never be discovered.

The only consolation to Theba was that, if it was a boy, he would be the heir to the throne. Theba was determined to raise him with the qualities and integrity of what should have been his real father, Jeriah. Vowing that her son would change the course of history on Mars, she would dutifully play her part as queen. If it was a son, her reign would be secured. She didn't know what would happen to her if it was a girl.

Better not to worry about it.

Theba was in her royal bedchamber, surrounded by handmaidens and opulence beyond what she had ever imagined possible. The room was twice the size of her whole house. She would give it all up to go back to her previous life with Jeriah. The wound was still fresh and unlikely to go away anytime soon.

A guard came to the entrance of the bedroom and announced, "The josser is here to see you, My Ladyship."

"Send him in," Theba said as she adjusted her dress to ensure modesty after standing to greet him.

Jon entered the room, bowed, and then crossed to where she stood, taking her hand, and kissing it as she greeted him warmly.

"How are you doing tonight?" he asked, obviously happy to see her.

A most unusual bond had formed between them. Theba hoped it wasn't turning romantic on his part. It certainly wasn't for her.

"I'm very well, thank you," Theba said trying to keep it friendly but properly distant. What did you want to see me about that couldn't wait until tomorrow?" Theba immediately regretted the tone and hoped he didn't take it the wrong way. She looked forward to his visits as much as he did. The alliance had been greatly beneficial to an agenda Theba was forming in her mind. One in which josser Jon would be immensely helpful in bringing about, even if unknowingly.

"Our usual business can be discussed tomorrow," he said. "I have news on the other matter you asked me to look into."

Theba and the josser met several times a week to discuss matters of importance to the church and the throne. The king had lost interest in everything except hunting, drinking, sleeping, and chasing women. Their marriage had been for appearances sake only. Thankfully, the king hadn't touched her once. She'd only been alone with him twice and only to discuss minor requests. He'd never shown the least bit of interest in anything other than her bearing him a son.

The king had granted the josser almost free reign to run the church and the kingdom and he was doing so skillfully. Unbeknownst to anyone, he had turned to Theba for ideas on how to make life easier for women and how to ingratiate the throne to the working and peasant class of which Theba was once a part. Her advice had been invaluable. Or at least she hoped his inclusion of her was sincere and not based on an attempt to get closer to her. So far, he had implemented most of her suggestions, and they were making a difference for the people of Mars. Particularly the women.

"What is the news?"

"Very good news, my lady," he said with a smile. "You'll be very pleased."

The queen simply nodded, awaiting the good news.

"I have found the woman, Elizabeth Whyburgh. The woman whose husband Zwilling had imprisoned with a writ of divorce. She's very much alive. I had her brought to the royal palace. She's right outside the door. Would you like to meet her?"

Theba bolted from the sofa where she'd been sitting.

"Yes. Bring her in right away. Hurry."

The josser quickly went out the door and was back in a moment. On his arm was a thin and haggard-looking woman whose hair was mussed, her clothes ragged, and her face worn from the year of obvious abuse in the prison. Her beauty was still obvious to Theba, who was able to see through the pained look. Abbey's mother was obviously once a beautiful woman and her daughter looked just like her.

Theba immediately took her in her arms and embraced her.

"That will be all, Jon," Theba said, dismissing him, noting the disappointment on his face. She quickly added, "Josser, thank you. I'll see you tomorrow."

A smile returned to his face as he left.

Theba took Elizabeth by the arm and sat her down on her sofa with no concern that the dirt and grime might get on her royal couch.

"May I get you something to eat or drink?" Theba asked.

"Something to drink," Elizabeth said weakly.

The queen motioned for a maid to get them both something to drink. Elizabeth was looking around the room, clearly in awe of what she was seeing compared to what was likely the horrendous conditions of a prison cell that had been her home for the past year.

"I'm so sorry this has happened to you, Elizabeth," Theba said. "May I call you Liz?"

"Yes," she said. "But why am I here? What do you want with me?"

Theba smiled. "I don't want anything from you other than to reunite you with your daughter, Abbey."

"How do you know Abbey?" Elizabeth's countenance immediately changed at the mention of her daughter's name. "Is she still alive? I have no idea what has happened to her. I left her with that miserable man, my husband, Zwilling. I have no idea what he has done to her. Is she okay?" Liz asked the questions in rapid fire, not waiting for an answer. Questions that had obviously been haunting her for a year.

"Zwilling is dead," Theba said. "Abbey is fine."

A look of relief flashed across Liz's face. The picture of Abbey and herself rolling Zwilling's dead body into the carpet flashed through Theba's mind. The emotions of elation and disgust competing against each other for supremacy inside her. No reason to tell Liz any of that story. She and Abbey had agreed to take their part in the disposing of his body to their graves. Theba didn't know where Zwilling was buried and didn't want to know. She doubted Liz cared at all about Zwilling, other than she was probably glad to hear he was dead.

The queen continued. "Your daughter has been a good friend to me. You have an amazing girl."

"I know," Liz said. "Can I see her, or do I have to go back to jail?"

Theba laughed.

A confused look came across Liz's face as her eyes narrowed.

"Liz, you never have to go back to jail again. I've been searching for you. You're free. Free from prison, free from Zwilling. You'll find that a lot of things have changed for women on Mars since you've been gone. Your daughter has had a lot to do with that. So has your son, Eck?"

Liz looked amazed as her head tilted to the side. "You know my son, Eck?"

"I do. You would be proud of him as well. You have two amazing kids. Let's get you out of these clothes and cleaned up."

Theba motioned for her maids. "Take this woman and bathe her in cream and find something in my closet that will fit her. Do her nails, hair, and makeup. Bring her back to me."

They stood to their feet. Theba gave Liz another hug. This time Liz responded more warmly.

"I can't thank you enough." Liz said, tears forming in her eyes and then running down her cheeks. Theba wiped them away with the sleeve of her dress. She took Liz's hand and put it in her maid's hand and said, "They will take incredibly good care of you. I'll see you soon."

* * *

Two hours later, the maids led Liz back into Theba's royal bed-chamber. Theba's breath momentarily left her as she gazed at the women who had been transformed beyond her wildest imagination.

I see where Abbey gets her beauty.

Liz stood there looking awkward with her face dominating, over-whelming even, the opulence of the room.

Theba filled a chalice of wine and gave it to her to drink.

Sipping it slowly, Liz's shoulders relaxed, the tension leaving her face with each drink.

"You look lovely," Theba said, taking her arm and leading her over to the couch. "Your daughter looks just like you."

A smile came across Liz's face.

Abbey has that same smile.

This was why she agreed to be the Queen. There's so much good she can bring to Mars.

Theba called for the guards.

"Go to Abigail Whyburg's house." Theba gave them specific directions. "You will find a girl named Abbey there. If she's not there, wait at her house until she comes home. Then bring her to me at once."

The guards bowed and left the room.

Theba looked at Liz and smiled.

"Abbey is going to be so excited to see you."

19

Abbey and Christopher walked arm-in-arm down the streets of Boulder Bay toward Abbey's house. A huge smile on her face, Abbey couldn't quit holding her left hand out in front of her, gawking at the ring, and saying, "I'm promised," which on Mars meant she was promised to be married.

They passed two soldiers on the street and barely noticed them. Things had certainly changed on Mars. Two months before, Abbey ran for her life on these same streets, jumping from rooftop to rooftop. Not that long ago, Zwilling stood over her about to strangle her to death.

Today, she was walking down the street with the love of her life, all the marrii they should ever want or need, and with all the bad people out of her life forever.

"Nothing's going to spoil this moment with you," Abbey said. "This is the best night of my life. I'll never forget it. I love you so much."

Christopher nodded, the huge grin on his face confirmed he was as happy as she was. "I love you too," he said sweetly.

"Where are we going to live?" Abbey asked as she took a couple of skips alongside him while still clutching his arm with both hands.

"Not Zwilling's house. I'm going to buy you a big, beautiful house," Christopher said emphasizing the word *big*. "It'll have a big kitchen. A big backyard so all our kids have a place to play."

Abbey stopped walking at the mention of the word *kids*. She hadn't thought that far ahead.

"How many kids do you want?" She asked somewhat shyly. The most they'd ever done was kiss. The realization of what it meant to be married hit her all at once, replacing the excitement with nervousness at the thought of kids and what would happen between them to make kids. Theba had explained it to her as she and Christopher had gotten closer.

"I want a bunch of kids," Christopher said with a grin. "How about you? How many do you want?"

"I don't know. I haven't thought about it."

"Why don't we have twelve? Like the twelve disciples," he said, grinning.

"Twelve!" Abbey released his arm. "How am I going to have twelve..." stopping in mid sentence as the picture of twelve kids running around the house and yard was playing like a nightmare in her mind.

"I'm kidding," Christopher said. "I think I want four or five."

Abbey let out a huge breath. Four or five still seemed like a lot. "We aren't even married yet. We have lots of time to think about that," she said, regretting that she had brought up the subject.

Abbey shivered slightly. Maybe from the cold, maybe from the thought of twelve kids. Christopher apparently noticed and took off his dinner jacket and wrapped it around her, drawing her closer to him, warming her with his body next to hers.

"I don't care how many kids we have as long as I have them with you," she said affectionately as she leaned over and gave him a quick peck on the cheek.

As they rounded the corner and neared Abbey's house, they both stopped in their tracks at the same time. Two soldiers stood on the steps in front of her house.

Abbey abruptly turned around and pulled Christopher with her as she headed back the direction from which they'd come.

"Why are soldiers in front of my house?" Abbey asked in a whisper.

Christopher shrugged his soldiers.

Terror gripped Abbey like a vice. "They're going to take me away to be in the king's harem," she said with a look of disbelief as the pace of her words quickened. "Maybe they found out Zwilling is dead. Oh my God. They're going to arrest me."

"I won't let them arrest you," Christopher said resolutely. "Let's not jump to conclusions. You don't know why they're here." Christopher stared off into the distance, obviously thinking.

"Maybe they discovered the printing press and that I'm Martian Luther," Abbey said with panic in her voice. "They're going to kill me." Tears started to run down her cheeks.

After the second thesis, the decision was made not to write any more. The josser had preached a sermon on religious tolerance, effectively ending the threat of persecution for dissent. With the changes happening on Mars, they didn't see the need to write more theses. Dozens of them had been written by scholars over the past couple months debating the merits of what they had written in the two. The word was spreading without them, and they were still contributing by legally printing papers for the scholars.

The downstairs press had been dismantled and all evidence hidden or destroyed. The authorities were still looking for Martian Luther, but no one suspected them, and they made sure nothing could be tied to them. Now, soldiers were in front of her house, and Abbey had no idea why.

"Let's go back to the shop," Christopher said. "You can stay downstairs with me until we can figure out what's going on." Christopher stopped to face her and wiped the tears off her face and away from her eyes. "I won't let them take you. Nothing is going to happen. I promise." Christopher said it with his hands-on Abbey's cheeks, staring directly into her eyes.

"That's a promise you can't make," Abbey said as she broke the embrace and started walking a backway to the shop. The memory of the beautiful evening together—the proposal, the ring, the dinner—all forgotten at least for the moment.

Things suddenly felt like they did two months before.

* * *

Theba wondered what was taking her guards so long. They should've been back with Abbey by now. Elizabeth had finally gone to sleep with assurances from Theba that she would wake her as soon as Abbey arrived. Theba barely slept, waking every time she heard a sound. The sun was now up and no sign of Abbey or the soldiers.

As if on cue, the two guards arrived at her door. Abbey wasn't with them.

After bowing, they said, "We knocked on the door of her house, but no one was home. We stayed all night like you told us to, but no one ever came."

That's strange. Abbey always stayed at her house at night. Maybe she fell asleep at the shop.

"Are you sure you have the right house?" Theba asked.

They described it, confirming it was definitely Abbey's home. Elizabeth walked in at that moment.

"Is Abbey here?" Liz said.

"No." Theba answered, giving her a quick hug of reassurance. "She didn't come home last night."

"Where would she be?" Liz asked nervously.

"She probably stayed at the shop or over at Eck's house. They've been working really long hours." Theba turned to the guards and said, "Go to the Pharis University Press. Do you know where it is?"

They both nodded.

"It's not open yet but will be soon," Theba continued. "Wait until it opens, and then go inside and ask for Abbey. She'll probably be downstairs but the person at the counter will know where she is. They might be afraid of you. Try to reassure them that you are friendly. If anyone asks you why you want to see Abbey, say that you are a messenger of the queen and that the queen would like to speak to her at once. Tell them it's especially important."

Theba didn't want them to mention her mother. That was going to be a surprise.

The guards nodded, backed out of the room, and closed the door behind them.

Liz's face was frozen in a state of confusion and fear, her eyes flitted from side to side, and her mouth contorted in pain.

Theba took her by the hand and said, "Everything's going to be all right. Let's have some breakfast. They'll find Abbey soon."

"I want to go home," Liz said. "I can wait for Abbey there."

That sounded like a good idea to Theba. She made sure Liz had something to eat and something to wear and then had one of her other guards accompany her to her house.

After Liz left, Theba felt the same sense of dread she felt when she knew something bad had happened to Jeriah. She tried to dismiss it.

What bad thing could possibly happen to Abbey?

* * *

The king had signed a decree.

Let a search be made for beautiful virgins for the king. Let commissioners in every province of his realm bring all these beautiful women into the harem of the citadel of Asus, which is a royal retreat on the other side of Boulder Bay across from the lake. Let them be placed under the care of Morti, who is in charge of the women; and let beauty treatments be given to them. Then let them be brought to the king one at a time to see who finds favor with the king and who he will take for his wife.

Morti read the decree silently to himself and then reviewed the names of the young virgins that had been provided to him by the commissioners. The list had been too long, so he'd cut it down to a few dozen girls. All of the girls had been gathered and brought to Morti's office. They would be transported to Asus later that day where they would be kept for ninety days in seclusion away from everyone.

A name on the list of excluded girls caught his eye.

Abigail Whyburgh, Boulder Bay.

Morti sat the list aside, but a penetrating thought kept searing his conscience like a hot poker.

You need to include this girl. Abigail Whyburgh. Send for her.

Where was that thought coming from? As much as Morti wanted to resist the thought, it was too powerful. This had never happened to him before. For some reason, he was drawn to that name.

Morti called for two soldiers.

He gave them Abigail's address with the instructions, "Go to her house, pick her up, and bring her to me. If she resists, arrest her." He sent the soldiers on their way.

Strange.

Almost like there was a supernatural force controlling him, compelling him to include Abigail in the group of virgins.

* * *

Christopher was in the main shop preparing to open the business for the day.

Abbey slept downstairs from the stress of the activities the night before. She resisted sleep for hours until finally succumbing in the wee hours of the morning from sheer exhaustion.

Christopher had quietly sneaked upstairs to the office, hurrying to get everything ready for the arrival of their employees.

PUP's business was booming. Zwilling's money had allowed for a major expansion. The backroom where Abbey had first discovered the Bibles was now filled with four printing presses. Ten employees had been hired and trained. Nine women and one man. Abbey had been teaching the women how to read.

The bulk of the expansion was to meet the demand for the printing and sale of Bibles. When the king decreed that Bibles were no longer banned, hundreds of orders flooded PUP to the point where they were constantly behind the demand. The presses ran constantly as more than a hundred were printed and bound each week.

Eck was over in the eastern territory developing a distribution channel and setting up salespeople to take orders. A warehouse would store the Bibles, and a group of delivery men would take them to customers throughout all of Mars. An aggressive undertaking but worth the tireless effort. Driven as much by wanting the Word of God to get to the masses as the motive for substantial profit which would go back into the business. As the demand continued to grow, Eck was able to lower the cost of printing and increase the profit even more.

Christopher had been made a partner in the business, and now he would be Eck's brother-in-law as well.

I can't wait to tell him we are promised.

Christopher unlocked the door and turned the sign to *Open*. Two soldiers appeared at the door, startling Christopher, and sending a wave of panic through him as they entered the room.

"Good morning," Christopher said, not wanting to sound at all uneasy.

The guards acknowledged the greeting with one of their own. One of them said, "We're looking for Abigail Whyburgh."

Christopher's heart pounded at an increasingly rapid pace. "She's not here right now," he said, glancing back to the stairs leading down to the work area. Instinctive, yet he immediately regretted it, not knowing if he'd somehow given away that she was there.

"It's extremely important that we talk to her."

A resolve rose inside of Christopher. A defense mechanism. *She's promised to be married to me,* he wanted to say as he pictured himself throwing them out. Wisely, he simply said, "What do you want of her? I can get her a message when I see her."

The soldier responded. "The queen has need of her. She wants to see her at once."

Theba.

A huge sigh of relief came over Christopher. If the soldiers noticed the huge exhale, they didn't acknowledge it. Christopher felt it at once as his whole body relaxed.

"I'm sure Abbey would love to see the queen. I'll give her the message. Tell the queen Abbey will come and see her at once."

"We need to accompany her. It's the queen's order," the soldier said with authority.

Christopher thought about it. Abbey would want to change clothes and shower before she met with the queen. He also had no way of going downstairs to get her without giving away the existence of their hiding place.

"Go to Abbey's house later this morning," Christopher said. "I'll have her meet you there. Then you can take her to the queen. Abbey... uh, Abigail will be really excited."

The soldiers left. Christopher locked the front door and hurried around to the back entrance to give Abbey the good news. The soldiers weren't looking to arrest her. Queen Theba wanted to see her.

I knew it wasn't anything bad.

* * *

Elizabeth was hard at work in her kitchen rearranging everything that was out of place. Although happy to be home, it wouldn't feel like her home until everything that reminded her of Zwilling was removed from the house. And until Abbey was there safely.

Elizabeth had already started a pile of Zwilling's clothes and personal effects outside in the backyard. A large bonfire would rid Zwilling and everything associated with him out of their lives completely. His memory was reduced to nothing but ashes. The anticipation of the satisfaction of seeing the fire drove her to get everything out of the house as soon as possible.

A knock on the door startled her.

Abbey? No, she wouldn't knock.

Two soldiers stood at her doorstep. The memory of the last year of her life—soldiers and prison bars—flooded into her mind. Momentary fear instinctively pulsed through her. She suppressed it. A skill she'd learned in prison.

These must be the queen's soldiers. Who else could they be?

Liz allowed herself to relax and breathe and opened the door.

"We are here for Abigail Whyburgh. The king has need for her."

"She's not here right now. I expect her at any time."

"We'll just wait for her here on the front steps," one of the soldier's said coldly.

"That's fine," Liz said as she closed the door and went back to the kitchen. She returned to washing and arranging the pots and pans.

Something the soldier said nagged at her.

What was it?

"The king has need for her." She quit what she was doing as she was reminded of the words.

Why didn't they say the *Queen* has need for her? They must have misspoken. Why would the king send for Abbey? Liz dismissed the thoughts but couldn't shake the uneasy feeling welling up inside of her.

She dropped the pan in her hand that landed on the floor with a loud bang that echoed throughout the kitchen. These weren't the same soldiers in the Queen's bedchamber. She remembered their faces clearly.

How can I warn Abbey?

* * *

Abbey quickened her pace as she wanted to get home, change, and go see the queen. She hadn't seen Theba since she became queen, and she desperately wanted to see her and find out how she was doing. Feeling foolish that she'd let fear get the best of her. They should have talked to the soldiers the night before. They would've already taken her to see Theba.

She glanced down at her ring. *I can't wait to tell Theba that I'm promised to Christopher. She'll be so excited.*

Abbey saw the soldiers off at a distance walking away from her house. She waved to them. Having gotten their attention, they started walking her way. She kept her pace and bridged the gap between them in no time.

"Hello," she said in her most friendly voice.

"Are you Abigail Whyburgh?" the soldier said matter-of-factly.

"Yes, I am. I hear the queen wants to see me. I just need to shower and change. I'll just be a few minutes."

"You have to go with us now. We have our orders," the soldier said rudely. Grabbing Abbey by the arm roughly, he bound her hands behind her back.

"You're hurting me," Abbey said angrily. "Why are you doing this? The queen is going to be so mad at you for treating me this way."

The soldiers ignored her as they pulled her down the street.

Abbey kept looking behind her at her house. One soldier on each side made resistance futile.

What's going on? Why are they treating me this way?

Her worst fears were realized when the soldiers walked past the entrance to the royal palace and continued down the street and into one of the royal offices. They took Abbey through a set of double doors and down a long hallway into a room with only a couple of chairs and a desk.

A thin, middle-aged man sat behind the desk. Silver hair made him look older than his features. He wore wire rimmed glasses. Was meticulously dressed. His nails were perfectly manicured, which was unusual for Abbey to notice except that they were painted. He looked up from his papers at Abbey and smiled with a look of approval. A feminine manner evident as he began to speak.

"What's your name?" he asked.

"Who wants to know?" Abbey replied.

"You have spunk. I like that. The king will like that..."

Abbey bristled at hearing the man mention the king. Suddenly, it all made sense.

The harem. Concubine. Abbey's worst fear.

Christopher. I'm promised.

One soldier spoke up, "She said her name is Abigail Whyburgh."

"Hello Abbey," the man said as he stood and walked around the desk. "My name is Morti. We're going to become incredibly good friends."

20

Queen Theba was concerned that if the child she was carrying was a girl, the king would displace her, and she would meet the same fate as Queen Katherine... or worse. Worse would be having to lay with the king again as many times as it took to give him a son as an heir. She and the josser had discussed it several times, and she intended to bring it up again at their daily morning meeting which had just started.

She didn't have to.

"I have a solution to the problem we discussed, My Ladyship," Josser Jon said. "The problem of what to do if your baby is a girl."

"What is your solution, Jon?" Theba had begun calling him by his first name. She was still My Lady, My Ladyship, or My Queen. Not that she cared. Informality would've been better as far as she was concerned. Jon had insisted.

"I've written a new royal decree," he said. He pulled out two pieces of paper. Handed her one and began reading from the other.

Upon the death or permanent incapacity of the king, the oldest living son will ascend to the throne. In the event that the king has no living son, the oldest living daughter will ascend to the throne. If there are no living heirs, the reigning queen will ascend to the throne.

Theba almost jumped out of her seat. "The king will never sign that," she said.

"He already has," the josser said with a sly grin.

"What have you done?"

"Look at the paper in your hand."

"You know I can't read."

"I know. Look at the signature line." The josser leaned over the desk and pointed to a line on the paper, brushing her hand slightly, sending a slight chill through her. Their relationship was one of necessity and survival for her. Nothing more. If she could use his attraction for her to her advantage, she would. It could never progress beyond that. Jeriah would always be the only man for her.

"Right there," the josser pointed. "That's the king's signature. Next to it is the royal seal making it official." Jon sat back down in his chair with a satisfied look on his face.

"Why would he agree to that?" Theba asked.

"Well... He didn't exactly agree." Jon ducked his head sheepishly and shuffled his feet.

"Jon... I ask again. What have you done?" Asked this time slowly and with more emphasis.

"I have a confession to make," he explained. "The king asked me to set up another harem of virgins. Which I did." Theba nodded. She knew about the virgins. Couldn't care less what the king did other than the horror she felt for those young girls, most of whom actually considered it a great honor and opportunity. A possible escape from their miserable lives into royalty. A cold acceptance had formed in her as she learned to be indifferent to the king's boorish behavior as long as he left her alone. His child was growing inside her. Nothing more to it than that. She intended to use that to her advantage in every way possible.

Jon continued. "They are in Asus as we speak. The king signed the decree authorizing Morti to select a group of virgins, train them, and then bring them to the king in three months. As you can imagine, the king was more than willing to sign that decree. Was even excited about it. So excited, he didn't notice the last page. He just signed it without reading it. It's now the law."

"How does that help me?" Theba asked. "If my baby is a girl and the king is alive, he'll still behead me."

"We just have to make sure he's not alive." Jon said only slightly above a whisper.

Theba looked the other way, not wanting Jon to see the smile that had formed on her face as she thought about what he had just said.

* * *

At first, Christopher was only annoyed at Abbey. Now he was a little angry. Two days she'd been gone without the courtesy of a note or any word. Not that he was worried. Abbey was no doubt partying with the Queen. Living it up. Good for her. She deserved it. Happy for her, but he could use her help at work. Honestly, he missed her. Things weren't the same when she wasn't around.

The bell on the shop door rang.

Abbey.

Christopher walked out of the back office to the sound of a familiar voice.

Eck. He'd returned from his trip to the eastern territories.

"Christopher, how are you?" Eck said warmly as he set down some boxes and wrapped his arms around Christopher in a friendly embrace. "Anything eventful happen while I was gone," Eck asked.

"I got promised to your sister," he wanted to say. Abbey would be so mad. She would want to be there when they told him. Instead he said, "Nothing to speak of. How about you? Was your trip a success?"

"Very much so. I can't wait to tell you all about it." Eck pulled out a handful of papers.

"Are those orders?" Christopher asked as his eyebrows raised.

"They are, and there are many more to come. I hired more than a dozen salespeople. We're going to need more help around here. Speaking of help, where's my sister?" he asked with a grin.

A flash of anger jolted through Christopher's body which he immediately tamped down.

"She's at the palace visiting the queen. You know how it is. Personal friends with the queen. She doesn't have time for us common people," Christopher said half joking and half sarcastically.

Eck laughed, clearly taking it only as a joke.

"When is she going to be back?" Eck asked.

"I have no idea," Christopher said with a faraway look. "No idea."

*　*　*

Of all the girls, Morti liked Abigail the best. She pleased him and won his favor in the first two days. Something was special about her, even beyond her stunning beauty. He immediately provided her with special beauty treatments and more refined food. Abigail was to be bathed every day for six hours with oil of myrrh and various perfumes and cosmetics. Seven female attendants were assigned to her, and she was moved to the best place in the harem along with them.

Every day Morti walked back and forth from the courtyard to the harem to find out how Abbey was and how she was doing. Abbey had been complaining incessantly. She wanted to go outside. Wouldn't eat the food. Demanded to see the queen. Wanted to go home.

Morti was there to address her complaints. "You have a lovely figure and are very beautiful," he said to her, admiring her stunning looks which were already significantly improved even after only two days. "Are you enjoying the baths?" he asked.

"Seriously?" Abbey said with an attitude. "How long do I have to sit in a bathtub for six hours a day? It's only been two days, and I'm about to lose my mind."

"Most girls love the pampering."

"I'm not most girls," Abbey said sarcastically.

"That's very obvious," Morti said with an affectionate smile.

"I want to go outside," Abbey demanded. "I'm bored."

"You can't go outside. The sun and the cold wind will dry out your skin."

Abbey made a face of disgust as a frown formed and she squinted her eyes. She wiped her arms with her hands like she was trying to get something sticky off of them.

"I feel like a stick of butter. I'm all greasy and oily."

"That's the point. It's good for your skin. The finest oils in Mars are used to make you feel and look like a lady."

"Morti, you have to listen to me," Abbey said with more urgency. "There's been a mistake. I'm not supposed to be here. I'm promised to another man. I can't marry the king."

"Are you still a virgin?" Morti asked.

"Yes... I mean no. I'm not still a virgin," Abbey said, clearly lying.

She's smart too.

Morti shook his head to let her know he knew she was lying.

"Okay..." Abbey said sheepishly. "I'm still a virgin. I lied," she admitted. "But I am promised to another man. That's the truth. They took my ring." Abbey held out her hand to show Morti as her eyes began to water and a sad look came over her face.

Childlike, yet mature well beyond her years.

"It's the truth, I *am* promised. His name is Christopher." Abbey said, folding her arms together tightly.

"I'm sorry. I really am," Morti said sincerely. "But you're the best one by far. Maybe the best I have ever worked with. The king will be incredibly pleased with you."

"How long do I have to stay here?"

"For three months," he answered.

"Three months! I can't stay here for three months. Morti, I'll just die." Her look turned fearful.

Morti tried to reassure her. "There's nothing I can do, but I like you Abbey. I want to make your stay as pleasant as possible. I want to be friends."

"I know the Queen. I demand to speak to her. Queen Theba will see that I'm released from here."

"There's nothing the queen can do for you. The king has decreed this. He'll throw you in jail if you disobey him. The best thing you can do is just to make the best of it. I have a feeling the king is going to pick you over all the other girls. Think what that would mean for you and your family. Marrii, fame, a life of opulence."

"I don't want that. I just want to go home. I have marrii. I have Christopher. He loves me."

Morti sat next to her and put his hand on her shoulder.

"I have something for you," he said as he brushed her hair back and wiped away some of the tears.

"What?" Abbey said between sobs.

Morti pulled out her promise ring and held it in the air so she could see it.

"My ring!" Abbey said excitedly as she bolted up to a sitting position, the tears went away as quickly as they had come upon her.

"You can wear it but not on your promised finger. Wear it on one of your other fingers. Don't wear it in the tub though. The oils will damage it."

Morti leaned in and whispered to Abbey, "You can wear it on your promise finger at night when no one else is around."

She threw her arms around him. "Thank you so much!"

"You're welcome. Like I said, I like you Abbey." It was a genuine feeling. Morti wasn't just using her. The king would be pleased with him for sure. Morti took a personal interest in the girls. Often grew to love them. Abbey was special. He saw it immediately in her.

He spent the next hour telling her what was expected of her and what it would be like before the king. He stopped when dinner was brought to her room.

"I'm not going to eat your food and drink your wine," Abbey said defiantly.

She is a feisty one.

Morti was more impressed with Abbey with every minute he spent with her.

"What's wrong with the food and wine? It's the best in all of Mars."

Abbey walked over to the table and picked up a big slab of pork ribs bathed in sauces by the end bone. She held it in the air before throwing it back on the plate in disgust.

"I can't eat this. I'll look like a fat pig in three months if I eat this every day."

Morti could sympathize. He weighed a hundred and forty-five pounds soaking wet and ate like a bird. Pork ribs had never touched his lips. But the king liked his girls shapely.

"I'm afraid of my lord the king," Morti said. "He has assigned your food and drink. Why should he see you looking worse than all the other young women your age? The king would have my head because of you."

"Test it for ten days," Abbey said. "Give me nothing but vegetables to eat and water to drink. Then compare my appearance with that of all the other girls who eat your royal food and drink your wine. Treat me then on the basis of what you see."

So Morti agreed to this and to test Abbey for ten days. He ordered that all of her choice food and wine were taken away and that she was only to be given vegetables and water instead.

"I like you Mortimar," Abbey said with a huge grin. "Can I call you Mortimar?"

"Not if you want me to answer," Morti said with a grin.

* * *

Two days later, Eck and Christopher had still not heard from Abbey. Christopher had gone to the palace to ask to see the Queen.

"They wouldn't let me in," Christopher told Eck upon returning. "I tried to tell them who I was, but the guards didn't seem to care. I told them to give the queen a message, but I don't think they will."

"Something's wrong," Eck said. "Abbey would've come back here by now. No way she would stay gone this long."

"What should we do?"

"Let's go to her house."

"I went there yesterday. The door was locked. I banged on the door. The curtains were all closed. Didn't look like anyone was there."

"I have a key. Let's go have a look around. See if we can find any clues as to what happened to her."

* * *

Elizabeth was petrified. Frozen in fear. She didn't know what to do. Abbey never came home. She considered going to her son's shop but was afraid of being captured by the soldiers. Women weren't allowed in places of business. She'd been there many times when her husband was alive. Now... Who knows what they would do to her?

I can't go back to that prison.

The nightmares. Guards. Beatings. Barely enough food and water to live.

She was home but still felt like she was in prison. All the curtains were drawn. The lights kept off. The banging on the door yesterday sent fear pulsating through her body. Fear that had never left her. It was with her constantly. Elizabeth was afraid to open the door. Even look out the window. It might've been the soldiers coming for her.

Was the Queen nice to her so they could capture Abbey? Queen Theba seemed so nice. So genuine. Was it all a ruse? A trap. Did she unknowingly lead her daughter right into the trap?

Where was Eck? Why didn't he come to see her? Was he dead? In prison. Eck would come here if he knew she was alive.

I know he would. So would Abbey.

They're both in prison, she concluded. The only explanation. *They'll come for me too. I have to keep hiding until I can figure out what to do.*

Elizabeth suddenly stopped what she was doing. Footsteps. Then a rustling was at the door. Voices. The doorknob was jiggling.

Elizabeth looked around for something to use as a weapon.

I can't fight soldiers.

I have to hide.

She went to her bedroom. Her husband had constructed a room behind a bookshelf. He called it a safe room. A place they could hide if someone was robbing them or had come to arrest them. So well hidden no one would notice it. Also soundproof. They couldn't hear her. She couldn't hear them.

She quickly made her way into the room and closed the door as she heard the front door opening.

I'll be safe in here. No one will find me.

21

Eck had not taken a breath since before he started unlocking the door to Abbey's house. He became aware of it when his lungs began to burn reminding him to take one. Searching the house of a loved one who'd been missing for several days seemed like a good idea at the time but was causing a tremendous amount of anxiety now that they were about to open the door. Especially, not knowing what they would find on the other side. Still a good idea, but nerve wracking, nonetheless.

The first thing that struck Eck was how neat and organized the house was. Not like Abbey at all to keep the house that clean. Everything was in its place, pristine, not a speck of Mars red dust on anything even at the entrance. Reminded Eck of back when his mother kept the house. Back when she was alive.

Eck opened the front curtains letting sunlight flood the room. Christopher opened the back curtains.

"Look at that," Christopher said pointing to a pile of things on the back lawn.

"Looks like Zwilling's stuff," Eck said with disdain.

"I thought Abby was going to keep those things in case someone started asking questions."

"I guess she changed her mind."

It didn't take long to search the house. Only four rooms.

"No one's here," Christopher said.

"Someone has been here though," Eck said from the kitchen. "Come look at this."

Eck pointed to a slice of uneaten bread on a plate. Christopher picked it up. Smelled it. Tapped it lightly on the counter.

"It's not stale," he noted.

"Somebody was going to eat this, and not too long ago," Eck said.

"Why would Abbey be staying here and not come to the shop to see us? Doesn't make any sense," Christopher stated as his chiseled face contorted. His upper lip curled with an obvious look of puzzlement, perhaps disappointment if Abbey didn't have a logical explanation.

Christopher had finally told Eck about the promise, the ring, and the night together before she disappeared. Eck had suggested that maybe she got cold feet. Too much too soon. Christopher dismissed that thought. He was certain she felt the same way about him that he did for her. For now, they were just focused on finding her.

"The queen is the last person we know who saw Abbey. We have to see the queen," Eck said.

"The guards won't let us in."

"Grab that box over there." Eck pointed to a box near the back door. A quick look through it confirmed that it was more of Zwilling's things that were headed for the trash heap.

"What are we going to do with that?" Christopher asked.

"Come with me. I have an idea."

They left the house, locked the door, and headed for the palace.

* * *

They arrived at the entrance to the palace in less than five minutes. Several guards greeted them at the entrance.

"Let me do the talking," Eck said to Christopher as they approached.

The guards lowered their spears, so that they were in front of them. Not exactly threatening, but a warning. Standard procedure to warn the approaching men to keep their distance until instructed to proceed further.

"I have a delivery for the queen," Eck said in a friendly tone. The guards didn't change their demeanors at all.

"Leave it with us and we'll see that she gets it," the soldier said with authority. The response Eck expected.

"The queen instructed that it was highly sensitive, and I must deliver it to her personally."

"Wait here," one of the guards said as he left his post and disappeared inside of the building. He returned several minutes later.

"The queen's assistant said that she wasn't expecting a delivery for the queen. Just leave it with me."

"Tell her it's from Eck Whyburgh. Pharis University Press."

The soldier left again.

Christopher motioned for Eck to move back away from the entrance far enough so the guard couldn't hear what he said. "If this doesn't work, distract the guards and I'll run past them," he said with nervousness in his voice. "Maybe I can make it to the queen before I get caught."

"That's the dumbest idea I've ever heard," Eck said. "You won't get ten steps before the guards will be on top of you. Then I'll have to worry about you and Abbey. Let's just wait and see what they say."

Christopher had a disappointed but resigned look on his face. It was a dumb idea that had no chance of working. He seemed desperate, more so with each passing minute Abbey was missing.

In reality, there was no chance they could get in the palace undetected. Built to be impenetrable, at least for a couple of unarmed and untrained commoners like them. This time the guard was gone for almost twenty minutes. When he arrived back, the new Josser was with him.

"You have a delivery for the queen from PUP," josser Jon asked.

"Yes," Eck said with emphasis.

"Is it from Abbey?"

Eck paused. How does he know Abbey? How should he answer that question?

He decided to take a chance.

"It is from Abbey. She's my sister."

"I know," the josser said. "Come with me."

How does he know she's my sister? Eck wanted to ask him the dozen questions that were running through his mind. The josser didn't say anything more, so they didn't either. Besides, they were too busy turning their heads from side to side admiring the royal palace which neither of them had ever been in.

The palace seemed to go on forever. Guards were everywhere along with marble floors, plush carpets, ornate tapestries, and statues of the king, lining every hallway. Red everywhere. Carpets, curtains, chairs with velvet red cushions were all royal red. Large portraits of past kings and the present king lined the walls along with famous paintings from the most talented artists on Mars.

After several turns, they arrived at a foyer with two large high doors that looked to be twelve feet tall. Two guards were standing at the entrance directly ahead of them. Another man sat in a chair next to them.

"These two men are here to see the queen." The josser was speaking to a man in tight leotards with a rooster shaped hat with a large feather sticking from it. Eck had heard of the notifiers but had never seen one in person.

The notifier stood, walked over to them, and asked their names. With the information, he ordered the guards to open the doors and bellowed in a loud voice the arrival of guests for the queen.

Yelling wasn't really necessary. When the large doors opened, standing just inside was Queen Theba in a full length formal white dress, her beauty lit up the room and caused Eck and Christopher to pause for a moment. The last time they had seen her, she was in peasant clothes, sweating, her hair mussed as she helped load Zwilling's body onto a wagon.

Wearing her tiara and a big smile she motioned for them to enter. "Come in," she said warmly, taking them both in her arms and hugging them profusely.

"Is Abbey not with you?" she asked looking past them into the foyer.

Eck looked at Christopher. Christopher returned the look with a confused one of his own.

"We thought she was with you," Christopher said.

"I sent for her, but she wasn't at her house." Theba paused obviously thinking. "She must be with your mother."

"My mother's dead," Eck said somewhat angrily. He thought Theba already knew that.

"What happened to her? I didn't know she was dead," Theba stated with her voice quivering.

"She died over a year ago. You knew that. Zwilling had her put away with a writ of divorce. At least we assume she's dead. We haven't heard anything in over a year."

"She's very much alive. I saw her just a few days ago," Theba retorted.

"You saw my mother! She's alive." Eck's eyes began to water.

"She was in prison," the josser interjected. "I found her at the queen's request and brought her here."

"I wanted to surprise Abbey and I sent my guards to find her," Theba explained.

"Right," Christopher said. "The guards came to the shop and said that you wanted to see Abbey. They didn't say why. Nothing about her mother."

"I'm sorry about that. I wanted it to be a surprise to Abbey and to you, Eck." The queen was obviously distraught.

"I told Abbey you wanted to see her, and she left the shop to go to her house," Christopher explained. "We haven't seen or heard from her since. She was excited to tell you that we were promised."

A large smile came on Theba's face. She reached out to Christopher and gave him another hug. "I'm so happy for the two of you."

"Where's my mother?" Eck asked impatiently.

"She's at your house. My guard walked her over there several days ago. Your mother was supposed to come back here as soon as she found Abbey, but they never came. I assumed they just had a lot of catching up to do and would come when they could."

"My mother's not at the house. We were just there."

"So, Abbey is missing and so is your mother," the josser said with concern in his voice.

"I know where my mother is," Eck said. A huge smile came on his face as he explained the uneaten piece of toast and the safe room. "My mother is hiding in that room. I'm sure of it."

"Why would she be hiding?" the josser asked Eck.

"She just got out of prison," Theba answered for him. "She's scared to death. All this activity. Guards coming and going. She's afraid of being arrested again. I feel so bad for her. I should have never let her go to the house alone."

No one said anything for a few seconds. There was a lot of information to process.

"What about Abbey? Where is she," Theba asked looking at the josser.

He shrugged his shoulders.

A look of panic came over Theba's face.

"Could Abbey be one of the girls in the king's harem?" Theba asked the josser.

"What!" Christopher said loudly. "The king's harem?"

"I'll be right back," the josser said as he walked rapidly out the door.

Christopher started pacing as Theba explained to them about the harem, the virgins. They would become the king's concubines, one maybe the queen.

"This can't be happening," Christopher said as Eck and Theba tried to comfort him.

"Let's wait and see what the josser finds out," Eck said. "We don't even know that's where she is."

Theba led them into a room off of her chamber where they could sit down and have something to drink. Christopher wouldn't sit. He just kept muttering to himself.

"Good news," the josser said walking into the room, not waiting for the notifier to announce him. "She's not on the list."

"You're sure," Christopher asked.

"I have the list right here. These are the names of all the girls who were chosen to be part of the harem. Morti is overseeing the girls," the josser said directly to Theba. "Abbey's name is not on the list."

Theba let out a sigh of relief.

"Where is she then?" Christopher asked.

"Let's go back to the house and talk to my mother. See if she knows anything."

Eck stood to leave. "Thank you, Theba," Eck said, giving her a hug.

The josser gave Eck a stern look and then reminded Eck that he was in the presence of the queen and certain formalities should be kept. Theba ignored the josser and just shooed them away.

"Please let me know when you find Abbey," Theba said as they were leaving. "You can come back here if you want. I want to see her and your mother."

"We will," Eck said, not looking back.

＊

Eck and Christopher sprinted to Abbey's house. Eck unlocked the door and bolted inside and headed straight for the bedroom. He grabbed the side of the bookcase and opened it. In the far corner, laying on the floor shaking and sobbing, was his mother.

"Eck," she cried out upon seeing her son. She reached her hands out in his direction.

"Mother, you're alive," he said as he rushed to her side getting on one knee and taking her in his arms. Their tears mixed as they both ignored them. Eck led his mother out of the safe room and into the bedroom where they both sat on the edge of the bed.

"Who are you?" Elizabeth said looking at Christopher.

"You don't have to be afraid, mom," Eck said reassuringly. "This is Christopher. He's promised to Abbey. She's going to be his wife."

Christopher took Elizabeth by the hand and knelt beside her and said, "I'm so glad you're here. Abbey has said so much about you. I love your daughter very much."

A smile came across Liz's face as Eck could see the tension slowly leaving her. "You're very handsome," Liz said.

Instantly, a look of concern flashed across her face. "Where's Abbey? I want to see her." Liz said meekly, still obviously weak from her traumatic ordeal in prison.

"I don't know, mom," Eck said, not sure exactly what to say. "I was hoping you knew."

＊

Theba instructed the josser to check all the prisons and medical clinics. The josser had suggested he check with the morgue as well. Theba had shuddered at the suggestion. She couldn't blame the josser for making it. He was the cooler head who would leave no stone unturned until he found out what had happened to Abbey. His search hadn't turned up anything. They were in Theba's bedchamber discussing other possibilities.

"She's definitely not at the harem," the josser said. "This is the final list of girls." He showed Theba the piece of paper filled with the names. "Let's hope she's at the house."

Theba already knew that Abbey wasn't at the house. She could feel it. Something was wrong. Why would she be hiding in the safe room with her mother? It made sense that Liz would hide. No reason for Abbey to.

Somehow the king was behind Abbey's disappearance. She just didn't know how. As far as she knew, he knew nothing about Abbey. Or did he? Did he know they were friends? Had he seen them together? Did he know Abbey knew about the rape, that she was carrying his child?

Theba gasped. *He knows.*

The notifier interrupted her thoughts as he announced that Elizabeth, Eck, and Christopher were there to see her. Theba listened intently for Abbey's name but it never came. At least they found Liz.

A concerned look on all of their faces confirmed to Theba that Abbey wasn't there. She already knew she wouldn't be.

The king took her.

Theba put on her most reassuring face. "I have the josser, his staff, my guards, everyone looking for her." Theba said it as she took Elizabeth's hand and squeezed it.

Her thoughts were elsewhere.

The king knows. That scoundrel! Rage rose inside of her.

What did he do to Abbey? Would he kill her? Make her disappear. Of course, he would. The only logical explanation. One she would keep to herself. For now.

Theba looked at Eck, Christopher, and Liz. Telling them might put them in danger as well.

I have to find Abbey.

If he's harmed one hair on her head...

"We just have to make sure he's not alive," the josser's words played over and over again in Theba's mind.

The king must pay. For Abbey... For Jeriah.

22

Three months later

Morti had grown to love Abbey deeply. Of all the girls who'd been put in his charge, and there had been many, Abbey was head and shoulders above the rest. Not just her outer beauty was unmatched, but her inner beauty as well. A grin crossed his face as he remembered fondly their last three months together.

Abbey had been right about the food. Ten days after eating only vegetables, the transformation in her body compared to the other girls was noticeable and dramatic. She'd smugly said to Morti, "I told you so." A phrase he had never heard before. She'd made him admit out loud that she was right, and he was wrong. Even persisted until he did. A good laugh had come from it.

Those were the characteristics that endeared her to him. Abbey was funny but obstinate. Loyal but determined. Committed to right wrongs as she came across them. A fighter but the kindest heart he'd ever met. Intelligent. Only one woman compared. Queen Theba. Morti had seen those same qualities in her.

Beauty, determination, hearts of gold.

Under any other circumstances, Abbey would've made just as good a queen as Theba. If chosen by the king, Abbey would take a special role as a handmaiden. The unchosen girls would become concubines. None could become the queen. There could only be one queen at a time.

Abbey was not deserving of such a fate. A mere handmaiden. An outcome Morti was resolved to prevent if at all possible.

Not just for Abbey. But Christopher as well. The two of them loved each other and Morti was determined that they should end up together. He would never say the words out loud, but the king was not deserving of someone as wonderful as Abbey.

The day had arrived, and the girls were gathered in a room in the palace. Morti was in the josser's office awaiting his arrival to discuss the procedures for their presentation to the king.

The josser was late and seemed harried when he finally arrived. "There's been a change of plans." He opened a notebook and started poring over his notes as he continued.

"The king has decided to throw a banquet for all the high members of his counsel and his military commanders. The girls will dance before the king at the banquet, and he'll make his decision before the guests."

In the past, the girls danced privately for the king in his chamber. This was a significant change.

"Will they still dance one at a time?" Morti asked curiously.

Morti's plan was to have Abbey dance last. Hopefully, the king would choose one of the other girls. Technically, Abbey was not on the list since she was chosen by Morti after the other girls were chosen, and her name was not on the list given to the josser. If she wasn't chosen, Morti could slip her out of the palace undetected and back to her old life, and no one would ever know, except him.

If they all danced together, his plan would be ruined. The king would pick Abbey out of the crowd for sure.

"They will dance one at a time," the josser answered. "The king wants it to be entertaining for his guests. All men, by the way."

Morti breathed a sigh of relief.

"I have to tell you that the king is not in a good mood," the josser said.

"Why? What's wrong with the king?"

"The king ordered Queen Theba to attend the banquet and wear her royal crown in order to display her beauty to the people and nobles. You know how lovely she is to look at." The josser said it with a faraway look on his face.

Morti nodded. He knew all too well how beautiful Theba was. He'd overseen her transformation. He also knew all too well how obstinate she could be. Just like Abbey.

"What's the problem?" Morti asked.

"When the attendants delivered the king's command, Queen Theba refused to come. She didn't want to watch the girls paraded before her. Can't really blame her. The king became furious and burned with anger. He might have removed her as queen if she wasn't carrying his child. I think he's hoping you have a girl in your group who might replace Theba." The josser had made the statement almost like a question. Fishing for information.

"The king wants one of these girls to be the queen?" Morti asked.

The king would probably not choose any of the other girls to be the queen. Abbey was the only one who had the beauty and qualities of a queen. Morti's plan was disintegrating, and there was nothing he could do about it.

"I have appeased him for now," the josser said. "Between you and me, I don't want the queen replaced."

Thoughts rushed through Morti's mind as he tried to process all the information. Hopefully, the king would get bored after watching fifteen girls dance and just decide, before he ever got to Abbey.

The josser's words still resonated. There was a hidden message in them. Morti was trying to figure out what it was.

* * *

Abbey was, surprisingly, not nervous. Embarrassed more than anything. They had her wearing a skimpy outfit. But besides that, she was at peace and resigned to whatever happened. She kept repeating in her mind the verse Christopher had taught her, "God causes all things to work together for good." What good could come from this, she hadn't a clue, but she was trusting God, nonetheless.

The last girl had just left the room to dance. All the other girls had already danced before the king. Apparently, he'd not yet chosen anyone.

Morti entered the room a few minutes later with a look of resignation on his face. He approached Abbey as she stood to her feet. His hands were on her shoulders, as he looked her directly in the eye.

"It's your turn. The other girls have already danced, and the king hasn't chosen anyone. I have to warn you, the king and his guests have had a lot to drink. They're acting pretty rowdy. I'm sorry you have to go through this. If there was anything I could do to stop it, I would. You can handle it though. I'm so proud of you."

"I understand," Abbey said. "You've been so good to me. I'll never forget you. Either way."

"Just implement the plan like we discussed."

"I can't do that," Abbey said. "I want you to know that I'm going to do the best I can to be chosen."

"You don't have to do that," Morti said with tears starting to fill his eyes.

The plan was that if Abbey did have to dance, she would try to dance awkwardly and unenthusiastically. Maybe the king wouldn't choose her. Problem was that if she wasn't chosen, then Morti would have failed the king, since she was the last girl. The king often reacted harshly to those who failed him.

"Don't worry about me," he said. "The king won't do anything to me. He needs me."

"I can't take that chance. I owe it to you. The king might throw you in prison. Or worse. I'll do the best I can. Whatever happens, happens. I don't want anything to happen to you."

Abbey took a deep breath. Her hands were shaking. Suddenly, she was nervous.

* * *

The josser sat next to the king who was noticeably drunk. The notifier announced the last woman to dance.

"I present to you, My King, Abigail Whyburgh," the notifier said in a loud voice as the guests erupted in cheers.

The josser almost stood to his feet when he heard the name of the girl who had occupied so much of his time over the last three months while he had desperately searched for her.

He turned to his assistant and said, "Go quickly. Get Queen Theba. Tell her to come here at once. I insist. Then go to this address." He wrote on a piece of paper and handed it to him. "At the address, you'll find a woman named Elizabeth. Bring her here at once. Tell her I found her daughter."

The king sat up in his chair as soon as Abbey entered the room. A collective gasp went through the crowd.

"Why did Morti save the best girl for last? She shoulda been first..." The king slurred his words somewhat.

Abbey danced as the crowd watched in stunned silence. The music started slowly. She danced to the beat. Rhythmic. A combination of power and grace. Elegance and beauty. Modest but inviting.

The silence turned to loud cheers as she began dancing faster. The music and the beat matching her intensity. Abbey danced with all her might. Better than anyone before her. The others were not even comparable.

The king couldn't take his eyes off her. Neither could the josser or anyone else really. Everyone was mesmerized. Abbey seemed oblivious to the crowd. As if she were the only one in the room. Dancing for someone other than the king as she never looked his way.

Theba arrived but stood at the side of the room outside the view of the guests. The josser saw her enter and motioned with his eyes to the girl dancing on the floor. Theba's mouth gaped open in recognition.

The music increased to a rapid pace. Abbey kept the beat perfectly, showing tremendous stamina as she had been dancing for several minutes seemingly not tired at all. The music came to a resounding crescendo, and Abbey collapsed to the floor in a low bow as the music abruptly stopped.

Breathing heavily, she stood to her feet and curtsied to the king, never making eye contact. The josser saw Abbey and Theba's eyes meet and a smile form on both of their faces as they nodded to each other.

The crowd stood applauding enthusiastically.

"Bravo! Magnificent!" The king shouted over the din.

When the applause and shouting ended the king said to Abbey, "Ask me for whatever you wish, and I will give it to you."

Abbey didn't answer right away.

The king said again, "Whatever you ask me, I will give you, up to half of my kingdom."

Abbey didn't hesitate. "Will you swear to it?"

"I swear," the king said immediately.

A gasp went through the crowd.

"Then I will take half of your kingdom," Abbey said with resolve.

The king turned to the josser and whispered, "I may have spoken rashly."

The josser saw an opportunity.

"You've already said it. If you take it back now, you'll lose all credibility with the people who heard it. Your counsel and military advisers are all here. You need them to think you are a man of your word."

"I want her as my queen. How can I have her without giving up half of my kingdom?"

"You can only have one queen at a time," the josser said. "And Theba is carrying your child. She may give you a son. You need to wait and see what happens."

"I must have this girl. She must be my queen."

"There is a way you can have both of them as your queen."

"How?" the king asked.

"Give her half of your kingdom. Make her the Queen and ruler over the other half. Because it's a separate kingdom, you can have a queen over that kingdom. She'll be the ruler, but she'll also be your queen."

The king seemed confused. That was what the josser was hoping. He was manipulating the king and taking advantage of his drunkenness. And his lust. This was a way to wrest half of his kingdom and power away from him. He could separate Mars into two kingdoms and have two queens. The josser wanted the king to give up authority over the other half of the kingdom. The king might just do it.

The king stood to his feet. No more convincing was necessary.

"Agreed," the king said to the cheers of the crowd.

The josser stood and quieted the crowd.

"This is the royal decree of our king. His kingdom will be divided exactly in half. An eastern territory and a western territory. Half of his kingdom—the eastern territory—will be given to Abigail Whyburgh. The king will take the western half which will include Boulder Bay and all of the royal palaces. By the king's own command, she will be made the Queen and ruler over the eastern kingdom."

The josser continued. "I now present to you, Her Highness, Queen Abigail, Ruler of the Eastern Territory of Mars!"

The king had both an excited and confused look on his face. The people stood and bowed before the Queen and then erupted in applause and cheers as she left the room waving to them.

* * *

Abbey exited the room and walked toward Theba to the cheers of the crowd. Her face not giving away at all how she was feeling.

She took Theba's hand and they walked to her bedchamber not saying a word.

When they entered the room, Abbey collapsed into Theba's arms sobbing.

They were the only two in the room. Theba had motioned for everyone else to leave and the doors to be closed.

"Why did you do that? You could've asked for anything. You could've asked for your freedom."

"I know." Abbey said as she struggled to compose herself.

"But I thought about all the people. Half of the kingdom. The Cabenites. You know, the people Jeriah saved."

Theba nodded as if starting to understand.

"How could I put my happiness over theirs? This was a chance for me to free half of the people from the king's rule. The religious remissions. The wars. The oppression. As their queen and ruler, I can stop all that. There's so much good I can do."

"You know what will be expected of you. You will be the king's wife."

"I know." Abbey's voice quivered and her hands shook.

"For whatever reason, God has chosen me for this time. It's my destiny. Just like it's yours. We can do so much good together, Theba. You as the queen of the western territory, me as the queen and ruler of the eastern."

Abbey's resolve had returned.

"Your son will become the king, someday," Abbey continued. He won't be anything like Henry. I know you. You're going to be an amazing mother. Raise him with your qualities. He will become the king, and together we can change Mars forever. Maybe, I'll have a son as well. They can rule together."

At that moment, Abbey's mother burst through the door and ran straight for her. The josser was right behind her. Their embrace lasted for more than a minute.

"I'm the queen, Mom." Abbey finally said, wiping the tears away from both of their eyes. "Can you believe it? Your daughter is the queen of Mars."

Elizabeth didn't seem to understand.

"You're going to marry the king?" she asked.

Abbey nodded.

"What about Christopher?"

Abbey's shoulders sagged and tears began to form in her eyes again and escape down her cheeks.

"I know, Mom. It's something I had to do. I can't marry him now. I don't expect him to understand."

Abbey took off the promise ring that was on her index finger. She placed it in her mom's hand and closed her fingers around it.

"Give this back to Christopher. Tell him I'm so sorry. I hope he can forgive me..." Abbey was shaking. Her voice cracking. Unable to say anything else.

Abbey walked over to the desk, took a piece of paper, and quickly wrote a note.

"Give this to Christopher. Please. Help him to understand."

The josser said, "Abbey, you need to say your goodbyes. The king is waiting in his chamber."

Abbey embraced and kissed Theba. Then her mom.

She turned and faced the josser. Took a deep breath. Wiped away all of the tears. Resolved. Determination building inside of her.

"I'm ready," she said.

Abbey walked out the door as the huge doors closed behind her.

23

Satan was furious.

God had called together a great feast in heaven. Satan had interrupted it and demanded to be heard.

"You have ruined everything on Mars," Satan had said with a grating whine. "Abigail can't be queen over Mars. I won't allow it. Do you really think I'm going to allow two women to rule all of Mars?"

"It's already done," God stated. "Abigail and Theba have found favor with me. I have many plans for them, plans to prosper them and give them a future and a hope."

"I have my own plans," Satan retorted. "The king is going to right this wrong. He is plotting to kill them both right now. We will not stand for this."

"Get behind me Satan and look over my shoulder and tell me what you see."

Satan flew behind God and was looking the same direction he was looking. Standing at the entrance of heaven was King Henry.

"What?" Satan screamed. "This can't be. The king is dead? How did it happen? Did Theba have him poisoned?"

"He died of natural causes," God retorted. "He is dead of a heart attack. Ate and drank too much. His life was required of him this very night."

Satan was distraught, flitting to and fro, back and forth in a frenzy.

The king shouted out from a distance, "You're having a feast with food and wine. Beseech me to enter and eat and drink with you."

"The feast is ready," God said, "but you are not wearing a garment for the feast. How came you here without a garment?"

The king looked at the clothes he was wearing and was speechless.

"You are not worthy to enter the feast of the Lamb. You are not clothed in the righteousness of My Son. Bind him hand and foot," God bellowed.

Suddenly the king's hands and feet were bound.

"Take him away. Cast him into outer darkness. There, he shall find weeping and gnashing of teeth. He feasted and drank wine while he was on earth. He has had his reward."

"No!" Satan shrieked, letting out a loud eerie scream. "You can't do this."

"Begone Satan," the Son of Righteousness commanded him. "Leave our presence."

As quickly as he came, Satan was gone. God sent angels to the entrance with instructions that he was not to be allowed back in while they were feasting.

The guests of the feast ate and were merry until all were full, constantly giving thanks and praise to God and the Son of Righteousness. The twelve disciples were sitting in a place of honor. After they were finished feasting, God spoke from his throne, the Son of Man sat at his right hand. He addressed the twelve disciples and a multitude of angels who dined with them and a number of souls who had been redeemed from Mars.

God spoke. "The time has come for the Dark Ages on Mars to end. On my servants and on my handmaidens, I will pour out my Spirit and they shall prophesy. And I will show wonders in heaven above, and signs in the mars beneath. Whosoever shall call on the name of the Lord shall be saved."

Everyone listened intently to every word.

I will unleash my favor on Mars. Bring to them all of the gifts I have stored for them. Every good and perfect gift comes from me.

The words resonated through the heavenlies. Renaissance is coming to Mars. Pour out the gift of music and arts. Raise up composers, artists, painters, musicians.

Give them innovation. Bring them knowledge. Colleges and Universities. School for all ages. Books to learn from. Give me architects, scientists, engineers, professionals of all kinds, workers of all trades and crafts. Industry. Factories. Machines.

Give them combustion. Power. Cars, planes, trains, computers, phones, space travel. Do not hold anything back from them. Bring it to them quickly. Faster than you have brought it to other planets. The time is short on mars. The Dark Ages have gone on too long.

I'm going to thicken the atmosphere of Mars so that the planet warms. The northern ice caps will melt. There they will find minerals, oil, and resources to power their innovations. With the warming will come an abundance of food, animals, wildlife, flowers, trees, and water throughout all the planet. Give me farmers, harvesters, food processors, refrigerators, ovens, microwaves, grocery stores, world-wide distribution.

Churches will thrive. Raise up preachers throughout all of mars to preach my word. Mars will not end until my word has been preached throughout the planet and everyone has heard the message. Airbox, radio, newspaper, internet, satellites. I want my word to be able to go out to all of the planet.

Give them doctors. Cures for diseases. Medicines. Pharmacists. Technology to diagnose and treat diseases. The power to lay hands on the sick so they will recover. The enemy will no doubt put new diseases on them. Give them researchers. Help them find cures.

Inspire a new form of governing. Gather a group of men and women together in Boulder Bay and let them work together to bring equality to all men and women. To everyone on mars.

Everyone was talking among themselves, excited about these new developments. They would all have a part in bringing the glory of heaven to the mars. Many had experienced this outpouring in other planets. It was an exciting time. Busy, but exciting.

"I appeared to Queen Abigail in a dream," God said. "I said to her, 'Ask what I shall give thee.'"

"She said, 'You have shown me great mercy. Given me a chance to sit on the throne and rule over half of the people on mars. But I am but a child. I have no idea what to do. Give me wisdom. And an understanding heart to judge your people, that I may discern between good and bad. The task is too great for me without your wisdom.'"

"I said to her, 'You have asked wisely. I will give you wisdom as has not been seen ever in mars. And because you have not asked for riches, or a long life, I will give you those as well. I will lengthen your days and pour out my blessings upon you so that they will overtake you.'"

She has my favor. I will put a hedge of protection around her. Send angels to watch over her and Theba.

God continued speaking in a steady but firm voice.

You all know what to do. You also know that our battle is not with flesh and blood, but with powers, and principalities and the forces of darkness on mars. The enemy will fight you with everything he's got. He will persecute my preachers. He will create division and disunity in the churches. Divide them into denominations over silly theological disagreements.

There will be wars, rumors of wars. As men and women gain knowledge, they will think that the power is in themselves and not in me.

As innovations in technology come upon the planet, the enemy will use those to further his evil. Lust and evil desire will run rampant throughout mars. You must raise up those who will restrain evil until the last day when my son will come again to mars.

The evil one will bring earthquakes, tornados, and storms of every kind. Many will die. Tell the people to not lose heart in doing good. Bring me their prayers. I will hear them and answer them. Satan will try to keep you from getting the answers to them. Be strong and courageous. Overcome evil with good.

"Those are your instructions."

A cheer went up among the throng as they praised God for his words.

They all left the feast and went to work.

PART THREE

"Every generation needs a Reformation."
Martin Luther

24

One hundred thirty-three years later

"You're obsessed," my boyfriend had said two weeks ago when he broke up with me.

I was obsessed. I admitted it. If only to myself. Wouldn't give him the satisfaction. He doesn't get me. If he did, he'd understand.

He had a point when he said, "It's too dangerous," as evidenced by the more than a dozen death threats, I'd received over the last month. I looked out the window, confirming the security detail was still there. Not necessary. Around the clock protection was already reserved for several months. Protection that would follow me to the courthouse where I would testify in a few hours.

Who would've known my book would create an intercontinental incident.

A simple title. *The Reformation of Mars*. Subtitled, *Martian Luther and The Two Queens Who Changed the World*.

The culmination of my ten-year obsession.

Controversy was expected. The two primary religious factions of Mars had been fighting over the same issue for more than a hundred years. One of the two was inevitably going to be unhappy with my conclusions. Turns out both were.

The phone rang, disrupting my thoughts. My publisher was calling. The phone transmitted the identity of the caller directly to my mind. With my thought, I answered the phone while also telling it with my thoughts to lower the volume. The new phone took some getting used to. I often had more than one thought at a time. It kept getting confused. As did I when the phone rang when I was deep in thought, which it did constantly since my newfound fame.

"Zoe, your books are flying off the shelf," Anne Bright said enthusiastically. "I have a dozen shows wanting you to do interviews. The court case was a stroke of genius. Your testimony will be telecast live all over Mars."

"Well, I just hope we win. You never know what the judge is going to do. I need it to prove one of the theories in my book."

"You'll win. Put your hair down. Don't wear it in a bun. You'll look more sympathetic. Wear a dress, not a pantsuit. A little above your knees. Show them some leg."

"I want them to take me seriously," I objected.

"Honey, you have two doctorates and are the President of Queens College. Everyone knows your credentials. They need to see that you're more than an academic. You are a woman of the people. Like Abbey and Theba. They weren't afraid to use their beauty to their advantage as you well know. Use yours."

Queens College was named for them. My muses. My inspirations. Had been since I wrote my doctrinal thesis on the two and developed the theory of who I believe was Martian Luther. The thesis was expanded on and became a book after I became President of the college and had access to Queen Abigail's writings which were housed in the vault of the school. Writings very few people had ever seen. Works that didn't prove my theory beyond a shadow of a doubt but added significant weight to it. Hopefully, proof enough to win the lawsuit.

"Have to go. Going to be late. Love you," I said, as an alarm started beeping in my head reminding me of the court date circled on my calendar.

"Phone, hang up!" I said aloud even though it wasn't necessary.

It rang again.

I added a thought, *Hold my calls.*

* * *

Queens College was in Borea Basin in the eastern territory. The court hearing was more than two hundred miles away in Boulder Bay. Two hours by car on the international highway. Only a ten-minute flight in my aero car. Assuming no traffic. Accidents weren't an issue. The common practice when there was one was to move out of the way and to the ground until authorities could arrive. If they weren't already knocked to the ground from the accident. If there was a wreck, gawkers were an issue at a lower altitude. We would be flying at five thousand feet. In a lane reserved for VIPs, which I was even before the book.

As expected, I arrived in virtually no time at all.

The throng of reporters were visible from the air. Fortunately, we landed on the roof, and I would enter the building from there, away from the throng. With their high-powered cameras and lenses, they would get close-up pictures but would be unable to ask questions. That was a welcomed reprieve. They followed me everywhere I went. Today, I wanted to focus on my testimony.

The skyline of Boulder Bay was breathtaking with the view of the bay behind it. The red mountains with a slight amount of snow on the top reminded me of a red-haired man wearing a white cap. A slight smile formed. The first smile since I couldn't remember when.

Winter had come to Mars, but it was hardly cold. I didn't even need a jacket. Looking out at the view settled my nerves.

More than a dozen skyscrapers—all at least a hundred stories each, with various unique and creative architecture—dominated the view to my left. The old town and its historic buildings were to my right. A striking contrast between the old and the new. Ironic in a way. Similar to what would be on display in the courthouse. The new confronting the old. Who would win out?

Goosebumps came over me as I stood and stared to the right at the royal palace where Queen Theba reigned for twenty-three years after the death of Henry X. A reign that started with so much promise and ended with such tragedy. My grandmother had told me the story many times of how her mother-in-law, the Queen, had served Mars faithfully until the wrong that wrested power away from her.

A wrong that I intended to correct, beginning today.

* * *

The greatest enemy of the truth is very often not the lie but the deliberate, contrived, dishonest, and persistent myth that comes from decades of acceptance of the lie as truth.

That was the first line of my book, and I wrote it on the notepad on the table as I sat waiting for the judge to enter the courtroom. A reminder that truth was on my side. No matter the outcome. Sitting next to me was Catherine Baxter, my attorney. "Cat" as she preferred to be called. A champion on Mars for women and women's rights.

Across from us were six lawyers sitting at the table representing King Jon III and the Universal Church of the Red Planet. Another five lawyers sat behind them on the first row. Eleven lawyers to my one. That's the visual we wanted. The little guy fighting the huge establishment.

The lead lawyer, Jack Maxwell, one of the best known and ruthless lawyers on Mars, sat in the lead chair closest to us. My hand shook as he warmly greeted us and reached out to shake it. Tall. Good looking. Expensive suit and tie. Immaculately dressed for success. A fierce, cross-examiner. Hired strictly to tear me apart on the stand. Which he would no doubt try to do with all of his considerable skill.

The room was smaller than I expected. Modern, with a touch of the traditional. The original wood from the first courtroom on Mars was used to construct the judge's bench, the box where the witness sits to testify, and the back wall with the huge seal of Mars affixed.

A large screen attached to a computer for the presentation of exhibits was to my left, the judge's right. A stenographer still recorded all the proceedings by hand. A computer with voice recognition software could have recorded it all. Some traditions still persisted, unwilling to be overtaken by technology.

The jury box with nine seats was to my right. Ours was a bench trial so no jury would be seated. One airbox camera in the back of the room would send a feed to all of the networks. The gallery was packed with reporters and dignitaries who secured their seats for the spectacle through a lottery system. I noticed a sketch artist on the front row busily drawing. Probably a sketch of me, since she kept looking my direction, drawing, and then looking up at me again. At that moment, I wished I'd worn a dress and kept my hair down.

The honorable Q. Lyn Pruitt, a woman, was late. Cat said we'd gotten lucky on the assignment of the judge. Judge Pruit was tough but fair. Many of the judges in Boulder Bay were closely aligned to the king and to the church. Any break we got to level the playing field was welcomed. The battle was uphill enough as it was.

"All rise," the notifier said, signifying the entrance of the judge.

A small woman, barely five feet tall, brown hair, short and smartly cut, wore a red robe and entered carrying a bunch of papers. She was not beautiful but not homely. Professional. Successful looking. An air of confidence and authority surrounded her like a cloud. The only woman judge in Boulder Bay, I admired her rise to success in what was still mostly a man's world in the western territory where the Universal Church still dominated Mars and women on that side of the planet.

"You may be seated," she said in a strong voice not quite representative of her small frame.

Several formalities were dispensed with as I took a deep breath, knowing I would be called to the stand soon.

I was the only witness.

"Your cause of action," the judge said directly to my lawyer after the formalities. "Call your first witness."

"Thank you, Your Honor. We call Zoe Parks."

I stood and walked to the witness box, trying to match the judge's air of confidence. I barely remember being sworn in with my hand on the Bible. I remember saying, "I do." Everything else to that point was a blur. The challenge was to stay calm. Slow everything down. My breathing. Heart rate. Thoughts.

"Mr. Maxwell," the judge said, "Do you wish to question the witness, or do you defer?"

Maxwell was notorious for almost always going first. He wanted to rip the heart out of his opponent's case and witness before they ever got a chance to get their footing. Control the proceedings from the first moment on.

"We will question the witness first," he said as expected.

I was ready.

A few more formalities. Name. Occupation. Age, which got a laugh from the gallery when he apologized for asking.

He was good. Silky smooth. Personable. Charming.

Cat had warned me. He'd try to charm me. Make me feel at ease. Then attack. When I least expected it. She was wrong. He attacked immediately.

"You want to be queen, don't you?" he asked in an accusing tone.

"I think I should be queen." I'd prepared for that question and gave the perfect response in just the right tone.

"You think King Jon is an illegitimate king, don't you?"

"I wouldn't use that term. This is not the king's fault. This injustice occurred long before he was born."

"What injustice? Your great grandmother, Queen Theba was convicted of a crime in a court of law, wasn't she?"

"Yes."

"A jury of her peers, right?"

"Yes."

"Nine jurors sat in a box just like the one right there," he said, pointing. "They heard the evidence. Listened to the witnesses. Deliberated. And determined Queen Theba was guilty of the crime for which she was charged."

I didn't respond. No question was asked. He was basically testifying. A common tactic by a good lawyer.

"Miss Parks. May I call you Zoe?"

"No. I prefer Dr. Parks," I said curtly.

Don't do that! You're playing into his hands. You have to be likeable. He's the one who has to come off like a jerk.

"Please put Exhibit One on the screen," he said with a sly grin.

"Dr. Parks," he said sarcastically, making sure everyone in the audience, including the judge, caught my pettiness. "I want to draw your attention to the exhibit on the screen. What does it say?"

I recognized it as an article from the *Proclamation of Dependence*. Shortly after King Henry X died, Theba and Abbey called together fifty-six people from across Mars. Common men and women who came together to form a new government. The result was brilliant. Four co-equal branches of government of which, the Ruling Branch, the courts, were established. The rules were established for how Mars was to be governed by that document. Exhibit one displayed the rule for ascension to the throne for the Traditional Branch—the kings and queens.

Called the *Proclamation of Dependence* to acknowledge our dependency on God and each other.

"If a king or queen is convicted of a high crime or felony by a jury of her peers, he or she is to be immediately removed from office," I read aloud, matter-of-factly.

"What crime was your great grandmother convicted of?"

"The murder of King Henry X."

"By poisoning, correct?"

"Yes."

"What was her sentence?"

"She was sentenced to death."

All of this was common knowledge. He was only bringing it up for dramatic effect. It was working. Seemingly, he was the only one scoring points with the judge and the masses watching on airbox.

"So... she was lawfully removed in accordance to our Founder's articles which your great grandmother authorized and confirmed," Maxwell said slowly for effect. "Queen Theba signed the Proclamation of Dependence, did she not?"

"Yes, she did."

"In the event that a king or queen is removed, who ascends to the throne?"

"Whoever is the Josser at the time."

"And who was the Josser?"

"Jon the first," I stated.

No reason to be defensive. Acknowledge what was the truth. My opportunity would come. Maxwell just had to ask the right question. He eventually would.

"So, you've come to this court, asking this honorable judge to overturn more than a hundred years of rule by King Jon the first and his successors. On what basis?"

Now we were getting somewhere. The trial just started in earnest.

"The Queen was falsely accused. She didn't kill the king."

Ask me for my proof.

Maxwell didn't know what I knew. If he's a smart lawyer, he won't ask for my proof. *Never ask a question in the courtroom you don't know the answer to.*

"You have a book you've written," he said, changing the subject but staying on the attack. Maxwell was a good lawyer. "You're going to make a lot of marrii on that book, aren't you?"

These were obvious questions for him to ask. I was well prepared with my answers. "All of the proceeds of the book are being donated to charity," I said succinctly.

"But you agree that this trial and all of the publicity helps you sell more copies. You've become quite famous, haven't you? You'll have other books. Isn't the reason you brought this frivolous action is to increase your fame and make more marrii from future book sales?"

"I want to clear my family's name. The name of my great grand-mother, Queen Theba." A tear formed as I said it. I wasn't prepared for the emotion to come that quickly. I'd searched my heart for my own motive. Was I doing this for the publicity? I knew at that moment the answer. I was doing it for Theba. For my grandfather, Jerry. He should have been king. My mother. For them. Not me.

Maxwell must have sensed he lost that moment because he changed the subject again.

"Queen Theba became queen after her husband died in battle, correct?"

"Yes."

"Put Exhibit two on the screen."

A short pause then a page from a textbook appeared on the screen. The judge adjusted her position in the chair. I took the opportunity to do the same thing. Cat caught my eye with a reassuring smile. I was doing okay.

"This is a fourth-grade history book. Does that look familiar to you, Dr. Parks?"

"It's been awhile since I've been in fourth grade, but it looks familiar." The gallery laughed. Good answer. I was becoming likable again.

I knew where he was going with this line of questioning. He read a section from the page aloud. Theba's husband died in battle... The king felt bad for her... He married her... Made her Queen... She became pregnant... The king died... Poisoned... By the woman he tried to help. A story familiar to everyone on Mars.

I wanted to shout at the top of my lungs that's not what happened.

Patience. We'll get to that.

"Put up Exhibit three," Maxwell said.

The judge yawned.

Don't fall asleep, judge. *The fireworks are coming.*

"This is a royal decree. Please read it aloud, Dr. Parks."

"Upon the death or permanent incapacity of the king, the oldest living son will ascend to the throne. In the event that the king has no living son, the oldest living daughter will ascend to the throne. If there are no living heirs, the reigning queen will ascend to the throne."

"This was signed by the king after Theba became queen, is that correct?"

"Yes."

"The Josser Jon testified in court that Theba tricked the king into signing this decree. She got him drunk. Put the decree in front of him. He signed it. Theba was never supposed to ascend to the throne, was she?"

"That's not how it happened."

Ask me for my proof!

Maxwell did not let up. "Theba tricked the king into signing the document. Then killed him. Ascended to Queen. Abigail tricked the king as well. Into giving him half of his kingdom. That's for another day."

I was surprised he mentioned Abigail. She was beloved by the people. Disparaging her would not help his case. Theba was the villain. The most despised woman in the western territory of Mars. The more he focused on her, the better it was for him. A Separatists, a sect in the Universal Church who believed in the superiority of men, Maxwell probably couldn't resist the dig.

He had totally ignored my response and didn't take the bait. "That's not how it happened," I said again more forcefully. "Queen Theba didn't know how to read," I explained. "How could she have created a royal decree for the king to sign?"

"Objection!" Maxwell quickly blurted out. "I'll ask the witness the questions," he said, clearly annoyed. That was a good thing. Now Maxwell was the one coming off as defensive and petty. The question also caused Maxwell to pause for a moment. Apparently, he was not sure how to respond.

The judge instructed me to answer, not to ask the questions, then wrote something down. Points for me.

The trial was about to change direction. I could feel it. Excitement welled up inside me. Maxwell was about to walk into my trap. I knew where he was going with his line of questioning. He wouldn't be able to help himself. He had no idea what I was about to say if he opened the door.

"Theba was nothing but a peasant girl," Maxwell said with disdain. "A soldier's wife. What right did she have to become Queen?"

And there it was! The question I'd been waiting for. The trap.

"King Henry X raped Theba!" I said without hesitation. "Before she was queen. While she was still married to her husband, Jeriah.

She became pregnant with his child. The king had her husband killed. He made her queen to cover it up."

A collective gasp went through the entire room. Reporters rustled papers as they scrambled to write down what I had just said. The judge dropped her pen and stared at me with her mouth agape. I looked at the judge, catching her eye. She had to know my resolve. She had to believe I was serious.

I looked at Cat. Then Maxwell. My eyes narrowed as I glared at him.

Ask me for my proof!

25

"Order in the court! Order in the court!" Judge Pruitt yelled at the top of her lungs while banging a large gavel, trying to regain control.

I'd dropped a bombshell. No doubt about it. All of Mars would be shocked by the revelation. The rehabilitation of Queen Theba had begun. The victim was Theba. Not the king. I'd only gotten started—more was to come.

Several reporters scurried out the back. Others were on their phones, which were prohibited per the instructions of the bailiff before the start of the hearing. Exasperated, the judge finally called for a fifteen-minute break and then stormed out of the room. Clearly upset by the loss of decorum in front of a worldwide audience.

Cat ushered me to a conference room through a side door, away from the reporters. Ecstatic. "Couldn't have gone better," she said. A serious look came on her face as her eyes narrowed and the smile left her face.

"We haven't won yet," she warned then gave me more instructions.

Don't get overconfident. Short answers. Be likable. You *are* likable. Be the perfect balance between competent, intellectual, knowledgeable but humble.

"You're doing great," Cat said. "Expect the unexpected. Don't let your guard down. He's going to come back with guns blazing. You're smart. Trust your instincts."

"Will he ask for my proof?"

It was not easy not being in control of the questions. As president of the college, most people answered to me. I was at the top of the chain of command. Here, in court, I felt like the lowest in the chain. The vulnerability challenged my nerves. My every word was no doubt being analyzed on world-wide airboxes by "so-called" experts that very minute. One on each side. Arguing for me and against me.

Suddenly, I felt the tremendous pressure.

"I don't know," Cat answered. "Don't worry about it. It doesn't matter. The proof will get in no matter what. We'll introduce it when I question you. In some ways it's better. You can tell the story without introducing the writings."

Knowing the surprise we had in store for the other side, made me feel better.

"Is the motion ready?" I asked.

"It's ready. I have it right here." Cat pulled out a lengthy copy of a motion prepared for the court. Another bombshell would shake the foundation of the church and the king.

"I'll introduce it at just the right time," Cat said confidently.

A court assistant knocked on the door and told us the break was over in five minutes. I needed the restroom. There, I looked in the mirror and told myself I was ready. After straightening my jacket and hair, I took several deep breaths.

"You can do this." I said to myself, believing it was true as I walked back into the courtroom.

* * *

After the judge scolded the gallery reminiscent of elementary school, Maxwell stood at the podium ready to continue his questioning. I detected a sly grin as our eyes met. Was he trying to intimidate me? Did he have something he thought was going to shake me? Or was I imagining things?

I would know fairly quickly.

"Quite a little tale you told there at the end of the last session," he said smugly. "Very interesting. You seem to know a lot about your great grandmother that the rest of us don't know." He said the two sentences in a slow deliberate tone for emphasis.

Sarcasm. His new approach. That wasn't going to rattle me.

Cat rose to object anyway, "Does counsel have a question for the witness?"

She didn't object much in the first session on purpose. Didn't want to seem combative or defensive like we had something to hide. Cat expected the gloves were going to come off in the second session. She wasn't going to give him an inch of legal leeway.

"I do. I'm getting to it," he said dismissively.

"Then get to it quickly," Judge Pruitt interjected. Clearly, the judge was not going to give an inch of legal leeway either. The courtroom was to be run with a much firmer hand the second time around.

"Do you know a lot about Queen Abigail?" he asked.

"I do."

"You're the foremost expert on the Queen, are you not?"

"That's exceedingly kind of you to say. I think I am. I'm the President of the college named after her. I've read all of her writings. I know more about her than any other living person. I would say so. Yes."

Ask me questions about those writings.

"Are you aware that Queen Abigail had a stepfather?"

Not those questions.

"Yes."

"What was his name?"

"Zwilling."

"Do you know how he died?"

"He died of natural causes."

Maxwell put his hand on his chin, appearing to be deep in thought. I wasn't sure how much he knew... if anything at all.

"His body was never found, was it?"

For the first time I was defensive. Unsure how to answer. Off balance. Cat saved me.

"Objection. Relevance, Your Honor," Cat said. "I don't see what this line of questioning has to do with what Dr. Parks has testified to at this point."

Maxwell countered. "It has everything to do with it, Your Honor. As you will soon see."

The short respite allowed me time to regain my composure.

"Overruled," the judge said. "You can answer the question, Dr. Parks."

I squirmed a little in my seat. I hoped it wasn't noticeable.

"To my knowledge, his body was never found."

"Do you know what happened to it?"

"Not definitely. No."

"What do you think happened to it?"

"Objection, calls for speculation."

"Sustained."

"Let me rephrase the question and ask it more directly."

"The Queens, Theba and Abigail, disposed of the body, didn't they?"

Another gasp went through the courtroom.

The truth and nothing but the truth, so help you God.

"They weren't the queens at the time, but yes, they were involved in disposing of his body."

How did he know? I knew because Abbey wrote about it in her writings. Painful memories. Honest confessions.

"Theba told the Josser the whole story," Maxwell stated. "Are you aware of that fact?"

That's how they know. Josser recorded it somewhere. Maybe to use later against the Queen. It hadn't come up in Theba's trial.

"I have no knowledge about what the queen might have told the josser or if he related that to anyone else accurately. All I can testify to is what I know from Queen Abigail's writings."

Call her Abbey. Keep her personable. Maxwell kept calling them by their formal names for the opposite reason.

"Why would Theba and Abigail hide the body if Zwilling died of natural causes? Why not just let the coroner come in and take the body?"

"Objection. Calls for speculation."

"Sustained."

"Do you know if Abigail and Theba killed Zwilling?" Maxwell said, his tone becoming accusatory. "Did they dispose of the body to cover it up?"

"Objection. Speculation."

"If she knows, Your Honor," Maxwell retorted. "I don't want her to speculate. Perhaps Abigail confessed to Zwilling's murder in her writings."

Cat jumped up again. "Objection to referring to Zwilling's death as a murder. No evidence has been introduced to prove that fact."

"Overruled as to the first objection. She can answer if she knows. Sustained on the second objection. No evidence has been presented that Zwilling was murdered."

"Not yet," Maxwell said. "But we do have evidence that the king was murdered by Theba. I'm trying to establish a pattern of behavior for the Queen. We know that she murdered the king. Now we've learned she committed another crime before she was queen by hiding a body and covering up his death. Possibly his murder."

Maxwell didn't have any evidence that Zwilling was murdered. He was playing to public opinion. The jury. The ones watching on airbox.

"Would you like for me to repeat the question, Dr. Parks?"

"No," I said. "I know what happened with Zwilling. Queen Abigail wrote extensively about it in her Canticles."

Abbey wrote more than a hundred and fifty canticles, pouring out her heart and life story. Every emotion was laid bare. She called them her version of the Psalms in the Bible.

"Zwilling attacked her one Sunday morning," I explained not waiting for Maxwell's permission. "Zwilling was going to kill her. He'd beaten her many times. He was a monster. Those were Abbey's words. She tried to run away, but he grabbed her hair. He'd been sick. While he was beating her, he fell over clutching his chest. Probably died of a heart attack. Theba wasn't even there. Abbey didn't want to be taken away to the king's harem, so she asked Theba to help her with the body. You're mistaken, Mr. Maxwell. Abbey and Theba did not dispose of the body. Her brother, Eck did. With another friend."

"So, according to you, Zwilling died of natural causes. You also claim the king died of natural causes. Theba was involved in both deaths. Doesn't that seem suspicious to you, doctor?"

"No. That's what happened. People die of natural causes every day."

"Quite a coincidence, don't you think?"

"Abbey would have no reason to lie in her private writings."

"You'd agree that Abbey had motive to kill Zwilling. Zwilling was a rich man, wasn't he?"

"Yes. He was a rich man. No, Abbey didn't kill Zwilling, whether she had a motive or not. Abbey didn't care about money. While queen she had more money than anyone on Mars and yet she lived a very modest life."

"What did Abigail do with all Zwilling's money?" Maxwell asked, ignoring my commentary.

"I don't know."

The truth. Abigail never said in her writings.

"You told us an outrageous story about the king raping Theba. Then quite an outrageous tale about the King killing her husband, then making her queen because she was pregnant with his child." Maxwell paused for effect to let those words sink in. "Do you have some special gift, a code, that lets you read between the lines of the history books and come up with a story like that?"

"No. It's written in Abigail's canticles."

Cat stood to speak.

"Your Honor, we were prepared to introduce the canticles in our case in chief. They will prove the facts that Dr. Parks is testifying to. The defense chose to go first. Consequently, the documents have not been introduced. Therefore, we have to rely on Dr. Park's testimony as to what's in the writings. We'll introduce those writings at the appropriate time. If the defense wishes to defer, we can introduce them now."

"I move that all of the writings be excluded from admission as evidence." Maxwell stated, not waiting on the judge's response.

"On what grounds?" Cat asked in an elevated tone.

"They're secondhand information. Abigail wasn't present for the alleged rape. She has no firsthand knowledge of it. There are a dozen different objections to the writings. They need to be examined for authenticity."

"We've already done that," Cat interrupted. "A handwriting expert has verified they are in Abigail's hand."

"Nevertheless, they are still second-hand hearsay. Abigail is not here today to be cross examined. Fairness dictates that you get to face your accusers. Dr. Parks is accusing the king and the church on behalf of someone who is dead. I can't even ask how Abigail came to have this knowledge. We have no way of knowing if it's reliable or not. Further, we're getting third hand testimony from a witness who is more than a hundred years removed from the events to which she is testifying. Dr. Parks wasn't even alive when these events occurred. How would she know what happened with certainty?"

"He has a point," Judge Pruitt said. "Why should she be allowed to testify about something she has no firsthand knowledge of?"

"Dr. Parks is the foremost expert in the history of Abigail and Theba's reigns. Mr. Maxwell even offered that fact himself. Remember?" Cat looked at Maxwell with disdain.

Maxwell didn't look at Cat, rather kept his eyes firmly on the judge.

Don't say anything when you are winning the argument. Zoe watched a lot of courtroom dramas on airbox. Amazing what one can learn.

Cat continued. "She's also a family member. She wears two hats in her testimony. Dr. Parks wasn't alive at the time, but her grandmother was. Dr. Parks had many conversations with her grandmother about these events. The Sovereign Court of Mars has ruled that family lore can be admissible in a court of law. The judge and jury—the judge in this case—should be instructed to not give it the full weight of eyewitness testimony. However, the court can assess the witness and determine for herself if the testimony is valid."

Cat continued with an effective argument. "Dr. Parks is right here in front of you, Your Honor. You can read the canticles yourself and assess Dr. Parks' expert opinion on them. You are the finder of fact. You can determine for yourself if what she says is credible."

I stared at Cat with admiration. Going toe to toe in battle with the best lawyer on Mars. And she was holding her own. Win or lose, I was proud to be on her side.

"I still object, Your Honor," Maxwell said. "Although my colleague has artfully stated her position, she has misrepresented the law."

"I haven't misrepresented anything," Cat said angrily, glaring at Maxwell.

"The objection is premature," the judge interrupted. "There's not even a canticle that has been presented as evidence. I'll rule when one is put in front of me."

"But she's testifying to them," Maxwell stated. "She's telling the court what is in the writings."

"You asked her about them," the judge shot back. "You had a whole line of questioning about Zwilling and disposing of the body. She has no firsthand knowledge of that. I'm assuming her testimony was based on what she read in the writings. Didn't bother you then, when you were making your points. You can't have it both ways. You don't mind her testimony when the writings help you. Do you want me to exclude all testimony, even what helps you?"

"I think all testimony related to the writings should be impermissible, and the court should ignore all past writings."

Our worst fear.

Cat had anticipated that Maxwell would try and get the writings excluded. Without the writings, our case was much more difficult to prove. We'd be left with the motion that Cat would probably spring on them later today. Still, we needed the writings. An important argument Cat needed to win.

"I was inclined to agree with you, Mr. Maxwell," the judge said.

Her heart sank as she heard what the judge said.

"My initial reaction was the writings should be limited to what Abigail knew firsthand, and the others should be excluded. Now I'm reconsidering."

My spirits were buoyed as hope returned.

"I haven't made a final ruling. As I said, I'll take it under advisement and rule when a canticle is put before me. Continue the questioning of the witness."

I had to refocus quickly. My mind raced as I thought about the canticles and their admissibility.

"Thank you, Your Honor." Maxwell scanned his notes. His short delay gave me a moment to compose myself.

"The point is that Theba had a motive to kill the king, would you agree?"

Thankfully, Cat stood again before I would have to say yes. "Your Honor, I hate to keep objecting. Dr. Parks is not a criminologist. She's not an expert in law enforcement. How can she testify to motive?"

"Sustained."

"Dr. Parks. Rape is a traumatic event in a woman's life, is it not?"

"Yes, it is."

"If what you say is true about what happened to Theba, she was probably angry, resentful. Her husband was killed. That would create a lot of feelings in her. Anger could be a motivation to seek revenge. Would you agree?"

"Objection, Your Honor. Dr. Parks is not a psychologist. She can't possibly testify as to Theba's feelings."

"Mr. Maxwell, limit your questions to what Dr. Parks would know based on the writings." Judge Pruitt appeared to be getting annoyed.

"Let me ask the question this way. When Henry X died, Theba became Queen and sole ruler over the western territory. Is that correct?"

"Yes."

"So, she gained something of benefit when the King died."

"Just as the Josser benefitted when the Queen was convicted. He ascended to the throne, just like Theba did," I replied matter-of-factly.

Cat looked at me with a look of satisfaction as she nodded her head in approval.

"That's an excellent point, Dr. Parks. You really don't know what happened with certainty, do you? Maybe the josser killed the king to ascend to the throne. Maybe Theba killed him for revenge or to become sole ruler. Maybe they conspired together. All those are possibilities, are they not?"

"I suppose. But I believe Queen Abigail's account."

"Of course, you would. That's the account you want to believe. Someone else might look at the same set of facts and come to a different conclusion. Isn't that possible? Are you the only one who's right? Maybe Abigail wanted to preserve her own narrative to cover up the truth."

I shook my head no.

"I've read the writings," I answered. "Anyone who read them would know they are a raw and heart-wrenching account of a woman who suffered greatly at the hands of many men in her life. No one could read them and see her brutal honesty and come away not believing what she said was the truth. Abigail wrote the good and the bad. Her sins and her successes. Most people wouldn't want their innermost, darkest secrets revealed to the world."

"They weren't revealed to the world. They were hidden away. No one has seen them but you, apparently."

"I think Abbey believed they would eventually be public. That's why they were preserved. The writings are very compelling."

"That's fine. I'm sure it's good reading. So is a novel. But this is a court of law. Facts rule. You can't really expect this court to rule that Queen Theba was innocent of killing Henry X, just because Queen Abigail wrote it in some writings, years after the fact. Can you?"

"I think I can. We can prove that Theba didn't kill the king."

"You can prove it?" Maxwell said incredulously.

Ask me how?

"How can you prove it?"

A basic mistake of law. Don't ask a question, you don't know the answer to. Rookie mistake.

"We exhume Henry X's body," I stated empirically. "Perform a test. If he was poisoned, it'll still be in his remains. If no poison is found, that proves Theba is innocent, and the josser was the one lying."

Cat stood as the entire courtroom was in shocked silence. "Your Honor, I have a motion I would like to enter into the record. A request to have the body of Henry X, who is buried in Vandenberg Church less than a mile from here, exhumed. A test performed to determine his cause of death."

"I object," Maxwell shouted. "I strenuously object!

26

The judge ordered the lawyers back the next morning to argue the merits of our motion to have the body of Henry X exhumed. Both parties had agreed my testimony was irrelevant at this point. If the judge ruled in favor of our motion, the exhumation would prove our case one way or the other. If poison was found, our case was over. While the josser may have been the one to administer the poison, we had no facts to prove it. If poison wasn't found, then Theba was wrongly accused, and the judge would have to determine what remedy, if any, she would order to fix the travesty.

Cat told me I didn't have to be there. Mostly a lot of boring legal arguments, she warned. Fine by me. I had other plans. I wanted to take advantage of being in Boulder Bay to do more research on Martian Luther. As far as the press was concerned, I had left to go back home in my aero car the night before in a carefully staged exit. I hoped to sneak out of the hotel and to the library unnoticed. At least those were my plans.

Plans that were abruptly interrupted by the most surprising of phone calls.

I almost didn't answer the call on the hotel phone.

"Marsi," I said. The formal greeting in Mars. It could be used to say in place of both hello and goodbye.

"Dr. Parks," a voice I thought sounded familiar said.

"This is Dr. Parks," I replied.

"Good morning."

The caller sounded nervous.

"This is Jon calling. The king."

Must be a prank.

Obviously a radio station trying to prank me on air or a reporter. Could be anyone.

"Right! And I'm Opa," I fired back. "Would you like to be a guest on my airbox show? I would love to interview the king."

Opa was the most popular celebrity on Mars. Number one on the list of the twenty most influential women. I was number twenty. I considered it an honor to even be on the list.

I hung up without waiting for a response and continued getting ready.

Ten minutes later, a knock on the hotel room door interrupted my putting the finishing touches on my meticulous morning routine —the same in the hotel as it was at home.

Standing at the door was the manager of the hotel. Not a manager. *The* manager. Over the most prestigious hotel on Mars. He held a phone in his hand.

Must be an important call.

"Ms. Parks, King Jon is on the line and would like to speak with you," the manager stated nervously.

What does the king want?

An emotion flowed through me that I was not able to quickly identify. Fear? Panic? Embarrassment? Not sure and with no time to sort it out.

I hung up on the king. I winced at the thought.

I was suing him. Now I'd rudely hung up on him. Regardless of what happened in court, he was still the king of Mars. Now, he was calling me. Few people ever have the honor of a phone call from the king of the entire planet. In Henry's day, I would be thrown in jail for such disrespect.

I held the phone away from my ear as I wasn't sure what to say. What was the appropriate way to answer? Dr. Parks, Ms. Parks, Zoe?

I somehow found my composure enough to sound businesslike and professional as I took the phone from the manager and said, "This is Zoe."

"Please don't hang up on me again," King Jon implored with a chuckle. I realized at that moment why the voice on the first call sounded familiar. Even more so the second time around.

"Your Highness, I'm so sorry. I thought it was a prank call."

"It's my fault. Calling you out of the blue with no warning was rude. I can understand why you might think it was a prank. Can we start all over?"

I wasn't sure what he meant.

He lowered his voice to a deep bass and said in a serious tone, "Dr. Parks, this is Jon the third, King of Mars. I'm requesting your presence at the royal palace in one hour. Can you accommodate the request?"

Is he joking?

He laughed and then I knew he was letting out a sigh of relief. What about the invite? Was he serious about that? I decided to play along.

"Let me check my calendar," I said in my best fake accent. "My butler says that I have a previous commitment, but my maid says that it could be changed."

I was joking with the king. Are you allowed to do that?

I felt better when he laughed at my feeble attempt at a joke.

What was this about anyway? It's like we're in middle school.

"In all seriousness," Jon said in his normal voice, "I'd like to see you in one hour if it's not an inconvenience to your schedule," he said in a warm tone.

"Of course, I can be there," I said.

When the king of Mars summons you to his presence, you go. I wasn't sure if legally I even had a choice. Nevertheless, I needed to address the obvious.

In my most professional voice I said, "Is that a good idea? I'm suing you... Is it appropriate for us to meet?" I asked hesitantly.

"I won't mention the lawsuit at all," he said in a friendly manner. "Strictly personal, not business."

Personal. Why would he want to see me personally? Was it a trick? Was he trying to get me to let my guard down. Maybe talk me out of exhuming the king's body.

"We have some of your great grandmother's things here at the palace. I wanted to show them to you. I know how much you love her. I thought you'd like to see them." He answered my questions as if he was reading my mind.

Yes! I wanted to shout into the phone, barely able to contain my excitement. "That would be amazing. Thank you so much. I'd love to meet with you and see her things."

"There's going to be a nice man, who'll come to your hotel room. Ral is his name. He's my personal assistant. He'll bring you here in one of my cars. I'm so glad you said yes. I'm looking forward to meeting you."

"Me too," I said as I hung up the phone slowly. My mouth was still wide open. I couldn't believe the call was real.

I guess I'll find out.

* * *

Ral led me into the private office of King Jon. It all seemed like a dream, but was very real. My security detail had insisted on traveling with me but were forced to wait outside the room.

The king entered shortly after my arrival and walked straight to me with his hand extended as I curtsied before him. After the handshake, he kissed me on both of my cheeks, sending a chill down my spine.

"You're so tall," I said.

"So are you," he replied. He was easily six-foot-six and towering over me, which was unusual, since I was five-foot-ten and a half.

He seemed nervous. Shy even.

Why would he be nervous around me? He's the king. The leader of the entire world.

"I did have an ulterior motive for asking you here today," he admitted.

I thought so. Here we go.

He invited me to sit down, and then sat on the edge of his desk, leaning against it.

I'd tried to call Cat to make sure my visit was okay with her, but her phone was off. I expected it since the hearing had already started.

I didn't respond. A coldness came over my demeanor as I folded my arms and crossed my legs in a defensive posture.

"I wanted to meet you. I watched your testimony on the airbox."

"You did?" I said, relaxing a little but not uncrossing my arms.

"Well, not all of it. I watched between meetings. I had to greet some dignitaries."

"What did you think?" I asked.

"I was mesmerized. I couldn't take my eyes off of you."

Mesmerized. Did he like me? Is it wrong that I feel flattered? My face felt flushed.

"You know, my great grandfather, Jon was in love with your great grandmother, Queen Theba."

"I didn't know that."

"I've read some of the letters he wrote to her expressing his undying love."

"He sure had a weird way of showing it. Lying about her in court." I said coldly, bristling at what I was beginning to believe was his way of manipulating me. Making me feel sorry for the josser. It wouldn't work.

"He didn't know he was lying. He thought Theba did poison the king. We still don't know if he was lying. Truthfully, I would like to know the truth. I hope you win your motion."

I didn't know what to say, so I didn't say anything. The josser did lie in court about Theba tricking the king into signing the new ascension decree. Abbey said it was the josser. I assumed Abbey was telling the truth. Unless Theba lied to Abbey which I would never believe.

"Queen Theba rejected his advances," Jon continued. "She never got over Jeriah. Still, our great grandparents did so much good for Mars over the years. Theba and Abigail led Mars through the most prosperous period of time in our history. You may not believe this, but my great-grandfather was very much a part of that. They worked very closely together. Theba and Jon were a good team."

His voice cracked as he said the words. Seemed like he really meant them.

"While it lasted," I said as I maintained my cold demeanor. The king waved his hand dismissively. I didn't think he was dismissing what I had said. Rather, it seemed like he really didn't want the conversation to go that direction. The king was clearly trying to be friendly. My anger for his great grandfather was clouding my judgment about him and coming across in my attitude toward him.

"You said something about my great-grandmother's things. You wanted to show them to me," I said, changing the subject and bringing my tone back to a more friendly manner.

If the king was offended that I was noticeably cold before, he didn't acknowledge it. Perhaps he expected it. He should have. He stood and motioned for me to follow him.

A private elevator in his office took us three floors down. The door opened into a large room. A basement. Storage area mainly.

Meticulously organized. Not a speck of dust. Unusual for a storage area but expected considering we were in the royal palace where the king had all the hired help he needed or wanted.

He took my hand and said "Watch your step" as he guided me to the back corner of the room.

"This is the room where they kept the royal treasury back in the day of Henry X and Queen Theba. Do you remember the story of the josser who forged the copy of Genesis three and tried to pawn it off on the scholars as real?"

I nodded yes.

"This was the room where the document was forged," the king explained.

At that moment, all my walls and inhibitions left me. History was my passion. I had a doctorate in Martian History. It felt like it did when I first saw Abigail's writings. Tremendous excitement and anticipation. The king used the word mesmerized earlier. I was totally mesmerized and enthralled being in the room with so much history surrounding me.

The first thing I noticed was a portrait of Theba wrapped in see-through plastic. Undoubtedly, the one that hung in the royal palace, taken down when she was removed as Queen.

"Beautiful," Jon said. "I see a lot of her in you."

"She was gorgeous," I said in slightly above a whisper. Theba was sitting on a chair, facing to her right, with her head tilted back to the left. Her hands were on her lap. A sad look was in her eyes. Far away. Distant. Clearly unhappy. I couldn't quit staring at her.

Jon opened a metal compartment marked *Queen Theba's Personal Items*. He invited me to look through it.

"These were her personal items she had before she was queen."

I touched them carefully. Tears formed in my eyes as I held up a set of rings and stared at them.

"These must have been her wedding rings, Jeriah..." My hands shook as I held them.

"I think you should have them," Jon said. "These are your family heirlooms."

"Are you serious?"

"Of course." I threw my arms around his neck before I had a chance to even think about it.

He hesitated, keeping his hands off me until finally embracing me back at the moment I started to pull away.

"I'm sorry," I said, dabbing at my eyes. "I'm so emotional. I can't tell you how much this means to me."

"Come this way," he said, taking my hand. "There's more I want to show you."

I placed the rings back in the compartment.

He led me to a large wooden dresser. A piece of furniture that was old but in almost perfect condition. About seven feet tall. Inside were dresses. Beautiful gowns. Perfectly preserved.

"Were these..." I stammered. "Theba's dresses?"

"Yes," the king said. "These were all of her royal gowns."

I looked at each one, my mouth was opened wide in amazement, not believing I was actually touching my great-grandmother's clothes. Her royal gowns.

I didn't notice Jon had left my side until he touched my shoulder from behind, drawing my attention away from the dresses.

"Look at this," he said.

Theba's crown.

Sparkling. Elegant. A dozen or more sparkling diamonds adorned the base.

"You can hold it. It's okay," he said, placing it in my hands.

I didn't know what to say or do. My hands were under the crown frozen in place. Not moving. Holding my breath. Speechless.

Jon took the crown and placed it on my head.

I was wearing Theba's crown.

In that moment, I could feel her presence. Like I was her. My smile was so wide my cheeks hurt.

"You look like a queen," Jon said.

Yeah... Well... I wanted to say.

Stop it. He's being nice.

"I have a business proposition for you," he said.

"What's that?" I replied, trying to establish my business demeanor but unable to. Emotions were still cascading through me like a raging river.

"I'd like to donate these things to Queens College. All of Queen Theba's things. They shouldn't be in a basement. The college is named after her. They should be there."

"Really..." I said, not really believing what I was hearing.

"It would have to go through the proper channels, but I can make it happen. I am the king after all. These things belong to me, and I want you to have them."

"I don't know what to say. How could I ever repay you?"

"You can repay me by having dinner with me tonight."

Excitement and nervousness competed for dominance in me.

Is he asking me on a date? Of course not. It's just business for him.

"I didn't bring anything to wear to a royal dinner."

"No problem. Come casual. Nothing fancy. Do you like pizza pie?"

"Of course! Who doesn't?"

"Okay. It's a date then."

That confirms it.

It is a date!

27

Tonight would be my first and last date with the king of Mars. Admittedly, the time spent with him that morning had been amazing. The five hours since then had allowed my analytical, cynical, and suspicious mind to scramble it into one giant jumbled mess of conspiracy and mistrust.

The king was simply too good to be true. I wasn't buying it. He seemed sincere, but he had to have ulterior motives. Did he think I was going to melt in his hands like all the other girls? Like a silly schoolgirl. I'm a thirty-nine-year old grown woman. President of Queens College. A doctor. I've been around the block with guys a time or two.

Jon wanted me to drop the lawsuit. I was sure of it. I know what he wants. What men always want. Control and... *That too!* My mouth gaped open in disgust. He won't get that either.

Just because he's charming. Good looking. Nice. The king.

I'm not falling for it.

Theba's things were a nice gesture, but an obvious attempt to buy me off. "I'll keep the date," I said mumbling to myself. Even be nice.

I really want Theba's things.

Who's manipulating who now?

The thought gave me some satisfaction.

My phone rang as I walked down a long hallway toward the king's office. King Jon emerged from the room and walked toward me, a huge grin on his face. Obviously coming to greet me.

The phone flashed the name of the caller in my mind. *Cat.* I hadn't talked to her all day. I was dying to tell her about my date. She must be calling about the hearing which had become an afterthought.

I waved my phone at the king and said, "I need to take this call."

He stopped in his tracks, and I turned down a hallway to get far enough away so he couldn't hear me.

I can't believe I just did that. I'm so rude. Making the king of Mars wait while I take a phone call.

Why do I feel happy about that? This was the third time today I'd been rude to him.

"You're not going to believe where I am right now," I said barely above a whisper.

"Why are you whispering?" Cat said.

"So, he doesn't hear me." I said.

"Who doesn't hear you?"

"The king. I have a date with the king tonight," I said with a slight squeal.

"What?" Cat said with obvious shock in her voice. I could picture her face and the look of surprise. "When did this happen? How did you get a date with the king? Do you know what you're doing?" Cat was talking so fast I could barely understand her.

"I don't have time to explain. He's waiting for me. How did things go today?"

"Good. The judge is going to make her decision tomorrow morning. I can't believe you're on a date with the king. Be careful. They offered us a settlement. That's why I'm so late calling you. I've been at Maxwell's office meeting with him. Discussing the terms of the settlement. It's a really good offer."

The king stuck his head around the corner. "I'll just be another minute," I said as I turned my back to him.

"A settlement. What kind of settlement?"

"Marri. They offered you a lot of Marri if you will drop the lawsuit and go away."

"Of all the nerve!" I said, raising my voice. "They think..." I realized I needed to lower it. The king was still at the end of the hall. Looking away from me but within ear shot if I spoke too loudly.

Lowering my voice, I said, "They think they can buy me with marri. No wonder the king invited me here." My free hand balled into a fist. "He thinks he can charm me into taking it. It's all part of Maxwell's and the king's plan. How much marri did they offer?"

"Five million."

I almost dropped the phone.

"Are you serious?" I was shocked beyond belief. That was more marri than I would ever see in two lifetimes.

Then I was mad again. I glared at the king who was looking the other way, clearly trying to give me some privacy, but also letting me know he was getting impatient. I could imagine that he was probably not used to people keeping him waiting.

"I've got to go," I said to Cat. "I'll talk to you later. The king thinks he can buy me off. I'll show him. I'll call you later."

I hung up the phone and walked back toward the king. Each step intensified my anger.

I don't care if he is the king. This is going to be the worst date of his life.

* * *

The king greeted me warmly and I played along.

"You look lovely tonight," he said.

"I thought you said dress casual."

The king was dressed in a blue blazer with the king's insignia on the lapel. Blue striped collared shirt, tan dress pants, beige loafers. As if my anger couldn't get any greater. I was underdressed compared to him. Black pants, green silk blouse, accented with a small cross necklace. Open-toed black shoes, low heels. A black sweater over my arm in case I got cold.

The king chuckled. "I'm still getting used to the dress code myself. If it were up to me, I'd wear denim and a tee shirt. You look great. Perfect. Come with me."

He reached for my hand, but my arms were folded. I pretended not to notice his gesture.

You're not going to touch me!

We walked into a private sitting area off of what appeared to be the royal suite. I could see a bed through the double doors on the other side of the room.

You'll not get me in there, buddy! Don't even think about it.

The room was ornate and gaudy. A plush red velvet couch was against the wall, thickly padded, guarded by two red, high-back chairs. The room was adorned with murals, statues, antiques, and historical artifacts. My senses were overwhelmed. The sheer magnificence of this place and my love for history made me forget my hatred for the other person in the room, if only for a moment.

A vase in a glass lighted display case caught my eye, and I wandered over to look at it.

Jon followed me and said, "That was my mother's. It's not anything expensive or old. She just liked it. I miss her. She died a couple years ago."

"I know. I'm sorry," I said sincerely. No reason to be mean.

A new and rare disease was sweeping Mars. Growths of tumors from abnormal cells were attacking healthy cells. The Queen was one of the first to succumb to the disease. My mom and dad died from a car accident many years ago. Before there were aero cars. Between us, all of our parents were dead. Amazing, considering how young we were.

"When my father died," Jon said in a somber tone, "I was only fourteen. Imagine becoming king of Mars at fourteen years old."

A huge grin came on his face as he obviously wanted to lighten the mood. "Right before my coronation... Most people don't know this. I'm kind of embarrassed to tell you. I got this huge blemish on my face. Probably from the nerves."

He started laughing. I couldn't help but join him.

"I was panicked. Here I was on national airbox. Scared out of my mind. A huge monstrosity on my face." Jon made a gesture, exaggerating with his hands how big it was. We both couldn't stop laughing. The tension was easing slightly as he related the rest of the story.

I told him about giving a speech and how the same thing happened to me. I tried to cover it with face color but didn't have much success.

And so, the battle inside me began in earnest. Half of me really liked him. There was attraction. Warmth. Appreciation. He was giving me Theba's things. The gift to the college. He didn't have to do that. The invitation to dinner seemed sincere. The better half of me wanted to believe him. Believe the feelings were real.

The other half was angry and mistrustful. Questioning. Reading into every gesture. The witty comments. Cute grin. Dimples. Endearing smile. Those were probably fake even though they didn't seem like it. He wanted me to think they were sincere remembrances. Maybe they were real. Probably. At least the family tragedies. His family had more than most. Some say they were cursed. I'd felt sorry for him at the time. Sympathetic even. I'd never had ill feelings for him before. Truthfully, it was hard for me not to like him.

Now, every one of his actions filtered through the channels of attraction and mistrust.

Was I being fair? So, what if it's not real? Have fun. At least be nice.

Be the better person. I'm smart enough to not let my feelings control my decisions.

"What did you do this afternoon?" I asked as I sat down in the chair rather than the couch so he couldn't sit next to me.

"I was in your area today. Borea Basin. I spent the afternoon at the orphanage. You're familiar with the home, I'm sure. There are more than a hundred kids there now. Kids who were abandoned or whose parents died live there. I read to the kids. We took them some toys and then played with them. I love going, but I'm always sad when I leave. You know what I mean?"

I nodded in understanding. For a moment, I allowed myself to admire the benevolent work before the skepticism returned. It didn't take long for it to return with a vengeance.

Come on! Is this guy for real? He seems so sincere. Is he the kind and gentle king who visits kids in orphanages? Or the conniving, ruthless, manipulator who offered me a lot of money to drop my case?

I had to know which was real. So, I just asked. "Why are you doing this?" I blurted out.

He seemed surprised by the question. "Doing what?" he asked sincerely.

"Why did you ask me here, on this date? I'm ten years older than you."

"Nine years. I just turned thirty last week."

"Congratulations," I said somewhat smugly, somewhat sincerely. The battle was still raging. Then I realized he knew exactly how old I was. That threw me off for a moment. How did he know my age? I quickly realized that it wasn't that hard to find out for the ruler of the world. But it would take some effort. Was he that interested in me or had he just done his homework? Maybe he just read the briefing material from his staff.

"I don't know,' he said, looking down. "I like you. Seems like we have a lot in common. We both have royal blood in our veins. Both of our parents died. I want to get to know you better."

"You could have any girl you want. Why would you pursue me? Does it have to do with the lawsuit?" I asked curtly.

I immediately regretted my tone. There was no way he's not offended. A look of recognition came over his face as if he finally understood why I might be skeptical.

"Do you think I have ulterior motives in asking you on a date?" he said sharply. First time I'd seen anything other than gentleness and kindness from him.

"The thought crossed my mind. Why else would you be interested in me?"

"You obviously don't think as much of yourself as I do. Clearly, you don't think much of me." He paused, seemingly wanting to say his words carefully. "If you think that's the kind of person I am. I didn't ask you here because of the lawsuit. I wouldn't do that."

He turned his head away from me like he was hiding his emotions. I could still see his face. He wasn't hiding anger. The look was hurt. Written all over his face. His eyebrows had narrowed. He bit his lower lip as his face tightened and he suddenly became downcast.

He should be hurt. He hurt me when he offered me marri.

"What about the marri?" I asked rudely.

"What marri?"

"The settlement marri. The five million marri. Do you think you can just buy me off? Make me go away. Do you think I'm doing this for marri?"

"I don't know what you're talking about."

He's good. I didn't believe him.

"That was my lawyer on the phone. She said your lawyers offered me five million marri to drop the lawsuit. She warned me you would try to wine and dine me to try and get me to take the settlement marri."

He laughed.

"Is this funny to you?"

"First of all, I'm not wining and dining you. I don't drink, and we're having pizza. That's hardly wining and dining." He said it with a huge grin on his face. "Second. I don't know anything about the marri," he said more seriously. "The lawyers are handling the lawsuit. Believe it or not, they rarely talk to me about it. I don't care. I just go about trying to do good for the people of Mars. The rest of it will sort itself out. I've left it in God's hands."

"You really don't know about the marri?"

"I really don't."

I think I believe him.

"As to your age," he continued, "you don't look thirty-nine. Not that it matters to me. I admire you. I've heard about the work you've done at that same orphanage and for women who've been abused and abandoned. And had children out of wedlock. You have a huge heart, Zoe. I love that about you."

My heart seemed to explode when he mentioned my name.

Suddenly, I felt ashamed. Embarrassed. *He should throw me out.*

Thankfully, the door opened, and the notifier announced dinner. A man in a formal red valet suit brought a tray of food and sat it on a round table that seated six comfortably. The king dismissed him. We both stood and walked over to the table, almost bumping into each other. Things were awkward.

I lifted the fancy cover. A slice of pizza pie was sitting on a paper plate. I laughed.

"The paper plate was my idea. I told them to make it casual," the king said, laughing.

The visual was striking. A slice of pizza on a paper plate with fancy silverware, a silk napkin, and crystal flute filled with water next to it. I picked up the silverware laughing as I cut into the slice of pizza pie.

"The silverware is two hundred year's old," the king said. "Our great grandparents probably used them."

That caused me to pause as I contemplated that possibility. I'd never felt so close to Theba and Abbey as I did that day. I was also warming to the king.

If he was angry with me, he didn't show it. If he was manipulating me, he could. I was falling for him. Hard.

* * *

After dinner, Jon invited me to go for a walk through the palace. All tension and pretense was gone. Evaporated like a puff of smoke. I was no longer being careful. My heart was fully unguarded. Cat's warning was put out of my mind. I'd always felt like I was a good judge of character. Our relationship was complicated, for sure. What relationship wasn't?

We stopped in front of the portrait of Queen Abigail. Both of us stood staring at her.

"She was so beautiful," I said, breaking the silence. I hadn't noticed that my hand was in his. It felt that comfortable.

The Queen was dressed in an off-white colored gown. Lace ran along the sleeves and off the shoulders. Sitting on the throne, her shoulders were back. Her head held high. Not in arrogance. In royalty. Yet her eyes projected humility. Her lips were closed. A slight smile slipped out of the side of her mouth.

"You remind me of her," Jon said.

"I do?" I said shyly.

"You have her same heart. And her beauty. But mostly her desire to do good. Abigail was always trying to help people. I've always admired that in her."

"She was the most amazing queen Mars has ever had," I said. "No offense to your mom and grandmother."

Jon nodded and said, "No offense taken. I know what you mean. I want to be like her. Change the world like she did. Mars could be so great. Theba and Abigail were amazing leaders. They brought out the best in people. Encouraged innovation and progress. It's amazing what they did. The two of them ended all wars. They brought the eastern and the western territories together. Made men and women equal. Freed all the slaves. They brought freedom of religion to Mars. I'm in awe. It was so amazing."

"I think you're going to be an amazing king." The lawsuit flashed through my mind as I said it. I'd forgotten for a moment I was trying to take the throne away from him.

Guilt flooded my soul. I felt the urge to apologize.

Before I could even say anything, Jon's hands were on my shoulders pulling me toward him. My lips were suddenly on his. Gently at first then more passionately. The room was spinning as my knees buckled slightly.

My eyes were closed as I took in the moment that was mesmerizing.

A flash. In my mind. Something about the picture. Abbey...

I bolted out of his arms. Then pulled abruptly away from him.

"I'm sorry," he said. "I was out of line. Kissing you."

He misunderstood.

I walked away from him toward the painting of Abigail, ignoring his words. I motioned for him to follow me. "Do you see that?"

"What? I don't know what you mean."

"The ring on Abbey's finger." I moved closer to get a better look. A large black ring was on Abbey's middle finger of her left hand. I'd never noticed it before.

"What about it? It's trylicite."

Excitement raged inside me as I was trying to sort this out in my mind.

"That's a wedding ring," I said.

"Abbey wasn't married. I mean after King Henry died. She never remarried."

"I know. That's what I mean. This portrait was painted when Abbey was older. After Henry died. That's not a royal ring. That's a ring a commoner would buy. And wear."

"The ring is on her middle finger."

"Right. Now we wear our wedding rings on our index finger. Back then, they wore them on their middle fingers." I was speaking fast. Barely able to contain my excitement.

"Why would she wear a wedding ring if she wasn't married?"

"Because she *was* married," I said, putting both hands on my cheeks in amazement.

"Who was she married to?" Jon asked.

"I don't know. And why did she keep it a secret?"

28

Something was bugging me.

A memory. Perhaps triggered by my first appearance in the courtroom since my testimony. My mind rapidly scrolled through my memories trying to put a finger on the elusive thought. The nagging feeling had come upon me almost from the moment I stepped into the courtroom.

I hate when that happens. I want to remember something, but I can't. Usually, it's nothing important. This time I had a feeling it might be.

A lot of things were on my mind. The king's kiss... Abbey's ring... The judge's ruling, she would give momentarily. The other kiss as I was leaving.

Nervous wasn't a strong enough word to describe how I felt. Somewhere between anxious and panicked. A word didn't come to mind. Normally I was calm, cool and collected under pressure, and nothing rattled me. Not today. Everything in my life was being shaken to the fiber of my being, and I wasn't handling it well.

I told my foot to quit tapping incessantly. After it did, Cat put her hand on mine to stop me from drumming the pencil on the table nonstop. I pulled the edge of my skirt down several times even though the hem was well below my knees. Grabbed my teal-colored blouse right at the neckline again and again and nervously pulled it up even though only slightly and modestly below my neckline.

"Breathe," I told myself as I poured some water into a glass. I tried to put everything else out of my mind and focus on the hearing. The ruling was important. Every time I made progress in that endeavor—I'd see Maxwell sitting at the defense table. The nagging feeling returned when I heard his voice or saw his face. Something related to my testimony was bothering me, and I couldn't figure out what.

"All rise," the bailiff said as the judge entered the room.

I heard the words, but it didn't register to stand up until Cat nudged me. I scrambled to my feet almost knocking my water over.

Focus, Zoe.

The judge had a profoundly serious look on her face. Good or bad for us, I wasn't sure. I saw Cat's hand shaking as she clasped them together to make it less noticeable. One of the most important rulings of her career was about to transpire.

Definitely related to my testimony. What was it?

I couldn't stop my mind from wandering.

"Disinterment is an extraordinary remedy for a court to order." The judge began reading from her order.

All of Mars was riveted by what was now called "The Trial of The Century" and by what would be the most important judicial ruling on Mars in modern memory. The most important of Judge's Pruitt's career.

The courtroom was full. Millions were watching anxiously in front of airboxes all across Mars. Experts were locked and loaded, ready to espouse their opinions on the judge's ruling.

"The deceased has the right to rest in peace undisturbed," Judge Pruitt continued slowly and cautiously, careful to enunciate every word. "The quiet of the grave, the repose of the dead, are not lightly to be disturbed. Good and substantial reasons must be shown before disinterment is to be sanctioned."

"We're going to lose," I wrote on my notepad.

Was it something Maxwell asked or something I answered? My mind was still going between the words of the judge and my search for the memory.

"The stated purpose of the exhumation is to determine if Queen Theba was wrongly accused of poisoning King Henry X. The court is sympathetic to the arguments of Dr. Parks and the obvious consequences related to the events that happened years ago. Her family has been greatly affected by those events."

Maybe we haven't lost.

Something Maxwell asked me for sure...

"Case law in Mars allows disinterment in criminal cases where the cause of death is the primary issue before the court."

Maybe we're going to win.

"However, this case is extraordinary in that the criminal case was adjudicated more than a hundred years ago. There has never been a case before a court related to an exhumation where the sole purpose is to exonerate a person who is already dead. No criminal prosecution could come from this case because the perpetrators of the crime are no longer living. No person is in jail, having been wrongfully accused. No remedy could fully correct the injustice even if the exhumation proved instructive. Further, the law states that the medical examiner only has jurisdiction over a body for seventy-five years. After seventy-five years, the government archeologist has authority over the body. This court does not even have the authority to order an exhumation based on a criminal theory."

Maybe not.

My emotions kept going up and down like a roller coaster ride at the Mars World Fair.

"Therefore, this must be decided as a civil case. The plaintiffs have not shown that the interest of their family outweighs the right of the deceased. The only evidence presented are the writings of Queen Abigail which are a second-hand account of what presumably Theba told her. Those generally would not even be admissible in court. Therefore, the court finds that the plaintiffs have not met the threshold necessary to prevail as a civil matter."

A murmur went through the crowd. I wasn't as disappointed as I thought I would be. My judgement was clouded by my feelings for the king.

Maxwell was grinning.

Cat's lips were pursed in obvious disappointment.

The judge gaveled order back to the court as many of the reporters wrote feverishly.

Maxwell asked me a question about Abbey's writings. Something about a... What was it?

"Dr. Parks," the judge said, shocking me back into reality upon hearing my name. "You probably don't know this, but I wrote a paper on Queen Theba and Queen Abigail when I was in college."

I nodded and smiled.

"It occurred to me that I would not even be a judge today had it not been for those two women. In their day, women were not even allowed to read or enter business establishments. We owe a huge debt of gratitude to your great grandmother and Queen Abigail. I see a lot of their same qualities in you."

I was touched by the gesture of the judge. Making me feel better while she ruled against me.

It did make me feel better.

It's on the tip of my tongue. What did Maxwell ask me?

"You may not want to leave just yet," the judge said addressing the reporters who were walking out of the room. "I haven't finished my ruling."

The judge took a noticeable deep breath.

"While the family of Dr. Parks has no compelling reason to exhume the body of King Henry X, the people of Mars do. The integrity of our government is at stake. Public trust in the branches of our government are paramount to the successful future of our republic. The ascension of the monarchs is of tremendous public interest in that they are a part of our Proclamation of Dependency which acts as our constitution."

What was the judge saying? Several reporters were coming back into the room.

"A conspiracy to alter the future of the monarchy through a criminal act is of deep interest to the people who ultimately govern our great planet. The right to know if Queen Theba was removed from her rightful position as queen unlawfully trumps the right of the deceased to be interred in peace."

The smile had gone from Maxwell's face.

Cat sat up in her chair. Her eyes widened in anticipation.

"Therefore, this court orders the immediate exhumation of King Henry X!"

A loud cheer went up in the gallery. It took several seconds for the judge to restore order.

"The state archeologist will oversee the exhumation and the testing of the body," she continued. "The findings are to be reported back to this court. It is so ordered."

The judge stood and walked out of the courtroom to a round of applause from the reporters and members of the gallery. Cat hugged me as she said enthusiastically, "We won!"

Maxwell sat in his chair with his head down. Apparently, not sure how to act when he lost, which he rarely did.

Do you have some kind of special gift, a code...?

That's it!

Maxwell asked me if I had some kind of special code that allowed me to read between the lines to know what Abigail was saying.

My mind was in overdrive. The ruling. A code.

Did Abbey leave us a code in her writings? I remembered a set of numbers in her writings. I never knew what they were. Are they the key to breaking the code?

An air message was on my phone.

"Congratulations," the king said.

"Can I come over?" I messaged back.

* * *

The Archives Room in the royal palace was not opened to the public. Generally, scholars, government legislators, and members of the king's private staff were the only ones allowed in. I had my own connections now.

The king and I sat at a table with papers spread across it.

"What are we looking for?" he asked.

"I'm not sure. But I'll know it when I see it."

"Can you give me some clue?" he asked.

"I think Martian Luther was Abigail."

The king had been leaning over the table mostly looking at me. He sat straight up in his chair. "What? The real Martian Luther recanted," Jon said.

"That's been the controversy for over a hundred years. Your great grandfather captured who he thought was Martian Luther. They had a trial and offered him the opportunity to recant. He did so. He was beaten and then thrown in jail, but his life was spared because he recanted."

The king nodded and looked at me with an admiring gaze. His eyes glossed over, and his hand rested on his cheek. A slight adoring smile dominated his face.

As a member of the Universal Church of the Red Planet, the king would be familiar with that account. The church used the recantation to revert back to some of the traditional teachings. As far as they were concerned, the issue of Martian Luther was resolved.

The followers of Martian Luther didn't believe that the person captured was the real Martian Luther. So, the church split into two factions. The new faction became known as the Mars Church. The church of the people of Mars. The two factions had been warring theologically for more than a hundred years.

"I've always had my suspicions that Abbey was Martian Luther," I said. "Abbey's dad invented the printing press. All of Luther's theses were printed by a printing press."

"Abbey couldn't read," the king retorted. "How did she write the thesis? Maybe her dad wrote them. Maybe he's Martian Luther."

"Her dad was dead. He died a year before from the Black Plague. Abbey could read. She learned it from working at her dad's business."

"Women weren't allowed to work."

"I know. Her dad snuck her in the back door. She wrote about it in her canticles. She knew everything about the business."

"That doesn't prove she wrote the theses," Jon said.

I glared at him.

"We need more proof," he quickly added, apparently realizing he needed to be more supportive.

"There's also similarities in Abbey's Canticles and the theses. Use of the same words. Same syntax. The arrangement of the words was similar. Writing styles were strangely alike. Like they were written by the same person."

Excitement welled up inside of me even as I was describing it. The arguments were coalescing in my mind.

"We still need more proof," Jon said as I frowned at him. "Of which I want to help you find," he quickly added. "How do we prove something that happened more than a hundred years ago?"

"Your lawyer, Maxwell, said something to me on the stand. He asked me if I had some kind of code. What if Abbey put a code in her writings? A hidden message."

"That seems like a stretch, doesn't it?"

He was right, so I didn't glare at him. "That's what I thought too. But look at this."

I showed the king a piece of paper found with Abbey's writings. The page had a list of seven-digit numbers.

"I've never been able to figure out what these numbers meant," I said.

The king was suddenly genuinely interested, apparent as his demeanor changed. Before, he seemed to be humoring me. Now he was studying the numbers intensely.

"Math is my thing," he said. "I love numbers."

Jon picked up one of Abbey's canticles which we had printed off from files stored on my phone.

"The Canticles are numbered," he said almost to himself. "What if..."

It was my turn to admire him working. To look at him adoringly.

He started writing feverishly on a notepad. Various numbers. Combinations.

"Find canticle number twenty," he said.

I thumbed through the papers until I found it. A canticle about Martian Luther. Supporting his views.

Interesting. Why did the king single out that canticle?

"The seven-digit number I have focused on is 2030427."

"Why that number?"

"See the writing. It's different from the others. Darker. The numbers shaped differently. It stands out."

"Oh..." I said, not fully understanding the significance.

"The first two numbers could be the number of the canticle," Jon said while still deep in thought.

"Number twenty. That canticle is about Martian Luther," I said.

"That may be significant. It might be a coincidence, but I don't think so."

My heart was racing. Not sure if from the research or from Jon. Probably both.

"How many pages are in that canticle?"

"Seven."

"Look at page three. That might be the second number. Canticle twenty, page three. 203."

"What would 04 be?"

"The paragraph number maybe?"

"Could be anything?" I said.

"Not anything. These numbers are a code. I'm sure of it," Jon said. "What else could they be? It's something. We have to find out what that something is."

Jon stood up for a minute and stretched. He was pacing the room. 'I think better when I'm standing up."

"I think better sitting down."

We both chuckled. "That makes us opposites," I said.

"I've heard that opposites attract. Like magnets."

I hope so.

"I think you're right," Jon said. "Focus on paragraph four."

Abbey wrote in clear, legible, and perfect handwriting, making it easier to read even years later. However, the ink had faded slightly and blotted in a few places, making it slightly harder to decipher.

"I read in college where someone developed a code," Jon explained. "The letters were spaced, based on the code. Does that make sense?"

Not really, but I nodded anyway. I wanted to show him the same support I appreciated.

"The last two numbers are twenty-seven. What if the code is every twenty-seventh letter?"

"Which letter of paragraph four do we start with?"

"Try the twenty-seventh."

I counted the letters. The twenty-seventh letter is an I.

"That can't be a coincidence," Jon said excitedly.

"I'll count the letters. You write them down. Are you ready?"

"I is the first. The second letter is an A."

Jon wrote them down as I called them out.

"I ... A ... M ... M ... A ... R ... T ... I ... A ... N ... L ... U ... T ... H ... E ... R ..."

"Stop!" Jon said.

He tore the page he was writing on out of the notepad. He held it up and turned it slowly toward me and said, "What does that read?"

"I am Martian Luther," I read aloud with my eyes widened in astonishment, my heart pounding inside my chest. "I knew it!" I cried out.

"Abbey was Martian Luther."

29

Three weeks later

I sat on a couch in the king's office awaiting the results of the autopsy of King Henry X, which was about to be announced on the airbox. The most important and anticipated press conference in the modern history of Mars since the advent of the airbox was about to begin. Jon sat next to me. Tension filled the room as neither of us had any clue as to what the results might be nor the ramifications of them after they were announced.

A sense of foreboding came over me. Whatever the results, either way, our relationship would probably change forever. After the judge ruled in our favor on the exhumation, a noticeable distance came into our relationship. I went back to my duties at the college, and the king immersed himself in his duties as well. We'd seen each other a few times since, but things were not the same as before the ruling. I had a dreaded feeling they were about to change even more.

The king squeezed my hand as the State Archeologist stepped to the podium and started speaking. The king had a press conference scheduled immediately after the results were announced in the State Room outside the door of his office and down the hall, where a throng of reporters and dignitaries were waiting. He'd spent most of the last few minutes putting the finishing touches on his remarks, mostly ignoring me, which was fine since things were awkward anyway.

The king turned up the volume through a voice-activated feature on the airbox. The archeologist was a thin, wiry man, wearing a white shirt with his sleeves rolled up and denim slacks. A sharp contrast to most state officials who wore suits and ties. He'd been in the job for many years and was very widely respected.

"My name is Xavier Morrilton. I am the Chief Archeologist for Mars."

My heart was beating so hard I could feel it banging against my chest.

"Three weeks ago, we exhumed the body of King Henry X per a court order issued by the Honorable Judge Q. Lyn Pruitt. My team was tasked with the responsibility of performing an autopsy on the remains to determine the cause of death. The remains were well preserved and consistent with the length of time they had been interred."

The king didn't try to hold my hand, which was a good thing since they were sweating. I wiped them on the couch cushions and then folded my arms across my chest, squeezing myself almost in a hug. It had seemed like a good idea when the king asked me to watch the results with him. Now I was certain it wasn't a good idea at all. I should've watched them with Cat.

The speaker continued. "Several tests were performed and the results conclusive."

Conclusive. We will have an answer.

What were the conclusive results? I wanted to shout the question through the airbox to urge him to get on with it.

"We extracted cells from the bones of the deceased and were able to get sufficient samples to conduct our tests."

He's trying to torture me.

"Based on the results of the tests, the certainty of the results is close to a hundred percent. The odds of the results being inaccurate are one in a billion."

Here we go.

"King Henry X died of natural causes," he said with an air of certainty.

The gallery watching the press conference erupted in applause and cheers. A crowd had gathered outside the royal palace. Cheers could be heard from them as well.

I burst into tears. A sense of relief flooded my soul, and all of the months of tension all flowed out of me through the tears. The king handed me more tissues as mine began to disintegrate from the flood of emotion.

"No poison was found. A protein was found in his bones consistent with what would be found in a person who died of a heart attack."

The king turned down the volume.

"Congratulations," he said soberly.

A sudden sinking feeling...

A victory and a loss. At the same time.

Before I could say anything, our phones rang at the exact same time. Cat was calling me. I assumed his attorney was calling him. We both stood and went to opposite corners of the room. Like boxers going to their own corners after a boxing match.

"Congratulations, Zoe!" Cat said. "You did it. You took on the world and you won. I'm so proud of you."

"Thank you," was all I could muster.

How come it didn't feel like I won? Cat's mood certainly didn't match mine. I should have watched it with her. We could've celebrated together. I was happy for her. She worked hard, and it was a great victory for us. Improbable. Bittersweet.

"You always believed Theba was innocent, and you were right. Based on the judge's ruling, I think we have a good shot at winning the next round. Don't get your hopes up yet, but you may be the next queen."

I looked over at the king. He was deep in conversation. Same demeanor as before. Somber but not downcast.

"Wait a minute," Cat said. "I just got an order from the judge. Let me read it." I could hear her reading it to herself.

"The judge is ordering us to meet tomorrow morning for a settlement conference. Maxwell's office. Be there at nine. She's telling us that we need to try and settle this."

I hadn't thought any more about a settlement after we rejected the first offer. How was a settlement possible? They'd offer me more marri. I'd never take it. They'd never give up the throne voluntarily. Things were about to get really ugly between us.

The king hung up his phone and motioned he needed to leave for his press conference.

"I got to go," I said to Cat. "I'll see you in the morning."

I walked toward Jon, but he walked to the door and away from me. As he was leaving, he said, "I'm glad you got what you wanted. I really am."

At that moment, I knew our relationship was over. No way we could survive this. I wanted to bolt out of the room, run out of the palace, and away from him forever.

How could I have been so stupid? Getting involved with the king. I should've known how this would end. Win or lose, our relationship was doomed for failure. How could I sue him and win and take his crown and somehow have a future with him? He'll never forgive me.

So why did it hurt? We hadn't known each other that long. He was hurt too. I could tell.

Nevertheless, the judge was right. The results were important to Mars. The king's ancestors stole the crown away from my family. Theba died because of his great grandfather's lies. They may have not been his fault, but his family did it to us. They deserve to lose the crown. It never should have been theirs anyway.

I'd come so far. Justice demanded I keep going. Too late for Theba but not too late for my ancestors. My son or daughter will be king or queen. They deserve it. My feelings for the king will go away.

I noticed the king come onto the airbox screen. I turned up the volume. His press conference was starting. The people in the room had no idea I was in his office watching. Would've been a bigger story than what they were covering.

The king's demeanor and posture were regal and commanding. I'm sure it was the look they wanted to portray. He's the king. I'm trying to steal his throne from him. Public opinion was split. Some called it a crisis of the monarchy if the exhumation went in my favor. There were so many things to think about.

"I want to thank the State Archeologist for his work and for bringing clarity to what has been a difficult time for everyone. I accept the findings and have instructed my attorneys not to challenge the results."

Jon was being gracious in defeat as I thought he might. Not that he was defeated. I'd just won the first round. The fight would go on. All the way to the Sovereign Court most likely.

"We will continue to vigorously fight the attempt to take the crown from our family. We have served the people of Mars faithfully for more than a hundred years and will continue to do so for as long you will allow me to."

The battle lines were drawn. The fight would go on. The settlement conference tomorrow would be remarkably interesting.

King Jon continued. "Queen Theba was an important figure in the history of Mars."

He called her queen. The title had been taken from her at the sentencing.

Interesting.

"She was a part of one of the most important eras in Mars history. A champion for women's rights. For freedom of expression. Theba was a Queen of the people. She ruled Mars with dignity and integrity. I am immediately restoring the title of Queen to Theba. Her portrait will be hung in the walls of the royal palace. She will have the place of prominence in the royal history that she deserves."

I can't leave. I needed to stay and thank him for the gesture even though it's the right thing for him to do. It'd be cruel to leave. He's being magnanimous. I should too.

A long noticeable pause came from the king as he appeared to momentarily lose his composure.

"On behalf of my family..." the king was fighting back tears. "On behalf of my family, I want to apologize to Dr. Zoe Parks and her family for the role my ancestors played in causing them this considerable pain. I can't go back and change history. If I could, I would. I'm pleased the truth is out. Jesus always said the truth will set you free. I hope Dr. Parks and her family find some comfort in this ruling and some freedom in its meaning. I do hope now we can put this tragic time in our history behind us and all come together for the common good of Mars. Thank you and God Bless Mars."

A stirring ending to what turned into a powerful speech. A round of applause followed him out of the room.

Within a couple of minutes, Jon walked through the doors. The tears were wiped from my eyes along with any evidence I'd been crying. I was standing. My shoulders were back. My head held high. Resolved.

"I guess we need to talk," Jon said.

"I guess we do," I answered as I sat back down on the couch.

* * *

The law offices of Jack Maxwell were on the top floor of the tallest building in Mars with the best view of the mountains and

Boulder Bay. Actually, the top three floors all belonged to him and housed more than five hundred paralegals, assistants, secretaries, and staff lawyers. A fact he made sure everyone in the room knew.

The room held a large conference table made from red cedar wood. More than a dozen high back chairs surrounded the table. Refreshments were laid out on a credenza along the wall with a large mural of Boulder Bay above it.

Seated at the table were six lawyers on one side and Cat on the other. The time for pleasantries had long passed, and there were long periods of silence as Cat kept checking her watch, wondering where her client was.

"I'm sorry. I don't know where Dr. Parks is or why she's late. It's not like her. She said she'd be here. I tried calling her but there was no answer."

"Don't worry about it," Maxwell said dismissively. "We have all the time in the world."

"I bet you do," Cat said. "You're billing all six of these lawyers by the hour. You don't mind how late Zoe is." They all laughed dutifully. Maxwell didn't seem to find it funny as evidenced by the narrowed eyebrows and the only slight chuckle.

"After this is over, you should come work for me," Maxwell said with a grin. "You argued the motion for exhumation very skillfully."

No chance of that ever happening.

Cat was impressed with the offices but had her own private practice with two other lawyers and wanted to keep it that way. The thought of working for Maxwell made an eerie feeling run down her arms.

At that moment, the doors of the conference room burst open. Thankfully, saving Cat from having to answer Maxwell.

Zoe and King Jon III walked in. That was the last thing Cat expected to see.

Everyone immediately stood once they recognized the unexpected entrance of the king.

"Keep your seat," Jon said. "I'm glad you're all here."

"We didn't expect you, Your Highness," Maxwell said. "We would have made the proper arrangements for your arrival."

"Don't worry about it. I came here to tell you that Zoe... Dr. Parks and I have reached a settlement agreement."

"What?" Maxwell said. "How come I know nothing about this?"

"Is this true, Zoe?" Cat asked.

Zoe nodded her head yes with a huge smile on her face.

"What are the terms of the settlement?" Maxwell said.

"I asked her to marry me, and she said yes!" Jon said enthusiastically.

Zoe grabbed the king's arm and held it close.

"You're promised?" Cat said.

Zoe held her left hand out in front of her and showed it to everyone. On it was a large promise ring.

"Zoe deserves to be queen, and she will be," Jon said. "We've decided to reign together. We'll share power equally. As husband and wife. And as king and queen."

"I'm happy for you," Maxwell said, "but you should have discussed this with us first. I didn't even know the two of you knew each other. Are you sure you know what you're doing?"

"I'm positive," Jon said, looking at Zoe with deep love in his eyes. "I've never been surer about anything in my life."

"Me either," Zoe said.

"We'll leave it to you capable attorneys to work out all the details. If you'll excuse us, we have a wedding to plan."

Zoe and the king abruptly walked out of the room with everyone sitting in stunned amazement at the turn of events.

For the first time in memory, Cat noticed Maxwell was speechless.

30

Ten months later

The most anticipated wedding in Mars history became the most watched airbox event in modern history as millions watched King Jon and me become husband and wife. Hundreds of thousands of Martians lined the streets to watch my specially designed aero car, with a see-through, bullet-proof bubble roof, take me from the royal palace to the Vandenberg Church for the ceremony.

Several death and bomb threats were the reason for the added security. That was the only thing that brought any damper to the festivities. My second book *The Martian Codes* had created quite a stir in religious circles. Abbey indeed was Martian Luther. Proven beyond a shadow of a doubt in my book. Even the Universal Church admitted the evidence was overwhelming. The church officials acknowledged publicly the one who recanted was a fraud.

More than a dozen of Abbey's canticles contained secret words encoded in them. Not all of the key—the seven numbers—had been deciphered. The greatest mathematical minds and scholars of Mars were hard at work on them. The canticles were now on display at the royal palace. The public was able to view them daily. Scholars studied them at night.

Having a member of the Mars Church as queen, and a king from The Universal Church already improved relations between the two. The acceptance of the identity of Martian Luther and our resolve to reign together in unity had opened dialogue and cooperation for the first time in decades. The king and I had great plans and hope for the future. Our reigns would be modeled after Abigail and Theba.

Abigail once said in her writings that every generation needs a reformation. We intend to bring a new reformation to Mars. A new age of technology. Discovery. Peace. Prosperity. Unity.

Jon had a vision to perfect space travel so we could colonize other planets. He believed life existed elsewhere. Planet Earth was the closest and would be our first attempt at space exploration. If intelligent life was there, Jon wanted to find it and bring the gospel of Jesus Christ and a Mars-style reformation to it.

Plenty of time to consider those things.

I'm getting married!

I stood at the altar of the Vandenberg Church almost in tears. The bride had the choice of walking the aisle first or after the groom. I chose to go first. King Jon would soon make his entrance and walk down the aisle to stand next to me. A boys' choir sang. A harp played. Music filled the room. There were an abundance of flowers. Royal banners hung from the ceiling.

I wanted to stand at the front of the church alone and take everything in. It was fitting our wedding would be in this church. So much history had happened here. A few minutes before, I'd walked through the same doors Abbey had nailed her theses to. Just a few steps from me, was the resting place of King Henry X. Where he was reinterred. The pulpit where Jon's great grandfather preached many sermons stood on the podium right behind me.

The balcony. That was where Abbey and Theba sat years before. I pictured them looking down on me. I wondered... Were they looking down at me from heaven?

* * *

Theba and Abbey stood together in heaven looking through a portal down to Mars. A cold, rushing wind suddenly engulfed them as Christopher and Jeriah flew by, circling until finally landing next to them. The four embraced enthusiastically.

"What are you doing?" Christopher asked. "We've been looking for you."

Abbey pointed to the portal.

"We're watching the kids get married," Theba said.

"A wedding," Jeriah said. "On Mars. How exciting."

There is no marriage in heaven. None of us had seen a wedding since we left Mars and came to heaven. Theba's heart warmed that God had allowed her to watch this.

"That's my great granddaughter, Zoe" Theba said with great satisfaction. "She's Jerry's granddaughter. Your namesake," she said to Jeriah. "She's the queen of Mars. Or will be in just a few minutes."

Jeriah nodded in understanding while putting his arm around Theba, squeezing her tightly. Christopher and Abbey, arm and arm were next to them. Permanent smiles filled their faces.

"Look at the necklace Zoe is wearing," Theba said. They all gathered closer to the portal and gazed in.

"Those are the rings I gave you," Jeriah said with joy.

"They are. Those are my wedding rings. She put them on a necklace and is wearing them around her neck."

Christopher started jumping up and down. "Look Abbey! She's wearing the ring I gave you. Our promise ring."

Abbey kissed Christopher on the cheek and said, "You remembered! That makes me so happy."

"The wedding is starting!" Theba proclaimed excitedly.

The four watched in silence as the two said vows, exchanged rings, and were pronounced husband and wife.

The portal window suddenly closed.

"Thank you, God, for letting us see the wedding," Theba said, lifting her hands in praise.

"What should we do now?" Jeriah asked.

"I don't care," Abbey said, "as long as we're all together."

"I'm so happy I get to spend an eternity with all of you," Theba said, as they all flew away hand in hand.

* * *

"I'm the queen of Mars!" I shouted as we exited the church and walked to the aero car, waving to the throng of people gathered outside the church beyond the barricades.

"I'm married to the best man in all of Mars," I added, the wide grin seemingly permanently affixed to my face. "This must be what heaven is like," I said. "Only heaven will be better, I'm sure."

The aero car took us along the parade route back to the royal palace and the wedding reception.

"I can't believe it. I'm your wife. I'm the queen," I said, waving to the cheering crowd.

"The most beautiful queen Mars has ever seen," the king said sweetly.

"You've made me the happiest woman in the world."

"I noticed you're wearing Abbey's ring. The trylicite ring." King Jon took my hand in his and touched the black trylicite ring Abbey had worn in the portrait.

"I wanted a part of her with me at the ceremony."

"Did you ever find out who she was married to?" King Jon asked.

"No," I said looking up to heaven.

"I guess there are some secrets the past generations just don't want us to know."

THE EDEN STORIES

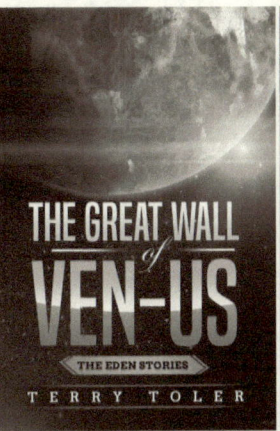

THE LONGEST DAY

WINNER 2020 BEST BOOK AWARD FOR RELIGIOUS FICTION

About the Author

TERRY TOLER is the author of *The Eden Stories* series, along with the Alex Halee and Jamie Austen book series. He is a minister, public speaker, counselor, and retired entrepreneur. Impacting the lives of people worldwide through storytelling has become one of his passions in life. He can be followed at terrytoler.com.

www.ingramcontent.com/pod-product-compliance
Lightning Source LLC
Chambersburg PA
CBHW020231260626
47156CB00002B/623